I0646548

THE PRYCE OF GREED

KARI BOVÉE

VINCI
BOOKS

By Kari Bovée

The Pryce of Murder

The Pryce of Conceit
The Pryce of Deceit
The Pryce of Greed
The Pryce of Ambition
The Pryce of Pride

Vinci Books

vinci-books.com

Published by Vinci Books Ltd in 2025

1

A CIP catalogue record for this book is available from the British Library.

Paperback ISBN: 9781036706432

Chapter One

TUESDAY, DECEMBER 5, 1885

The Bella Saloon hummed and buzzed with music, dancing, and laughter. It was one of our busier nights as Mr. Archibald Archer was hosting a party. Among the many guests were his sister, Bertha Stewart; her son, Ralph Stewart; and his wife, Mrs. Mary Alice Edwards-Stewart. They had come from California for their yearly visit earlier in the fall.

"My dear Mrs. Pryce, I understand you are responsible for running this year's annual Winter Festival," Mrs. Edwards-Stewart said. An elegant woman, she was striking with golden hair and an intense emerald gaze. Her well-defined cheekbones added a certain grace to her appearance, creating a look that was both striking and refined. Her taste in clothing was on par with mine, and her mink-collared coat and cuffs were of the highest fashion.

I nodded. "Yes. Apparently, the honor of planning the

festival has always fallen on the manager of the Arabella Hotel, and as I have no manager at present, that is me."

"The little children of St. Anne's Orphanage so look forward to the occasion," she said with a demure smile. "It is the bright spot in their year. We are not at all religious, but the family likes to support charitable causes."

I forced a smile. "I have a wonderful committee this year, so we will do our very best for the children." A knot formed in my stomach as I said the words. As an acclaimed actress, I was good at displaying confidence and assurance with my expressions and gestures, even if there was a host of anxious feelings brewing inside me. Focus was required to deliver my gift to others. And, if I do say so myself, I excelled at my art.

"You will do a marvelous job!" Mr. Archer, also known by the rather gauche moniker of Boss, exclaimed. "And you will make Archer & Archer Mining Company proud. Our little Winter Festival is one of the hallmarks of La Plata Springs."

Mr. Archer was a formidable presence in the room and about town. He was the founder and acting Mayor of La Plata Springs and owned of many of the nearby mines. He also owned nearly all the businesses in our bustling community and had a reputation for wanting every last one of them in his control . . . the Arabella included.

He had approached me on numerous occasions about buying the Arabella, and I had been sorely tempted to sell, as there had been, and still were, many problems with the hotel. But my late husband, who had bequeathed it to me, made it very clear that I was to run the hotel for an entire year in order to gain my full inheritance, which was a vast sum. He also expressly demanded I not sell to Mr. Archer. Apparently, they had not got on well. I didn't know the reasons behind the animosity, and I didn't care to. It was true Mr. Archer was ruthless in business, but so far, in the five months I had been in town, I had found him charming and supportive.

Mrs. Stewart, who had an even more daunting air about her than her brother, looked at me with a distinct coolness. I hadn't been acquainted with her for more than a few days, yet it seemed she consistently wore an uncompromising expression on her pale face, her lips tense and thin and her jaw rigid. If she'd let her features relax, she might be attractive. She had a glorious head of light-brown hair highlighted throughout with silver streaks, which she wore in a loose top knot.

The man standing next to her, a Dr. Cornelius S. Briggs, remained quiet but seemed attentive to the conversation. I wondered at his relationship with Mrs. Stewart. Was he a paramour or merely her doctor who traveled with her? No one had offered up the information, and it would be rude to ask.

"It's important that La Plata Springs be seen as a town that is inviting to tourists," she said. "Along with the railroad and the mines, not to mention the neighboring Indian communities, the township must convey to the public at large that this is a fashionable place to visit."

The blood drained from my head as I read into her words the prospect of failure in my duties as the organizer of the Winter Festival. Failure was something I could not endure. I always had, and would now, do everything in my power to succeed.

"Oh, Mother." Ralph Stewart chuckled. "You are putting too much pressure on this lovely woman. Everyone always has a good time at the festival, especially the children."

Just then, Bijou, my little Havanese dog, scampered up to us and danced on her hind legs, begging for attention. Her paws and long ears were sodden from the snow outside.

Mr. Stewart bent down to tousle Bijou's head, which she delighted in. He was a devastatingly handsome man in his early thirties, whose looks rivaled that of a Greek Adonis. He had a head of thick brown curls, dreamy dark eyes, and full sensual lips. Not that I took particular notice, of course, I told myself as my pulse quickened at the tenderness he showed Bijou.

"I'm so sorry," I said. "Bijou, sit!"

With a pitiful look in her little button eyes, she obeyed, embarrassed to be scolded in front of the guests.

"There you are!" Cordelia, my assistant, companion, and best friend, rushed up to us and picked up the dog. "Bijou would not be deterred from joining the party," she said, quite breathless from her sojourn outside. Her complexion was rosy from the cold and her sable eyelashes wet with moisture. Droplets of melted snow shimmered on the coil of thick, reddish-blond braid at the crown of her head. The shoulders of her dress were damp, too.

For such an intelligent woman, I wondered at the fact she had not worn a coat to take the dog outside, but she could, at times, get a bit lost in her own musings and did not often think outside of them. She did, however, have the wherewithal to bring a towel for Bijou, and she wrapped her up in it.

"I took her outside to do her business," she explained. "I had hoped the fresh air would distract her from the party but to no avail. She wants to be with the guests. Besides, it was just too wet for her to be out there for long."

I glanced at the large windows near the street entrance

of the saloon. The snow was now coming down in sheets, blanketing the ground.

"Very well, Cordelia. I'll take her."

"All right," she said with a shiver and handed the dog over to me. "I'll be right back. I'd like to change my dress."

"Yes, please do. We can't have you catching cold." I turned to the group. "Again, I apologize for the dog. She can be a little overenthusiastic at times."

Mr. Stewart reached out to pat Bijou's head again. "She is no bother, Mrs. Pryce. She is as charming as you are."

"Don't be such a sycophant, Ralph," his mother chided.

He dropped his gaze away from mine and pulled his hand back, giving me a slight bow. My eyes traveled to his wife, who regarded me with a prim smile.

Breaking the odd tension, Mr. Archer clapped his hands. "I must thank you again for tonight's party," he said. "You have once more organized a lovely gala. I knew I could count on you."

By "once more," he was referring to a wedding reception I had hosted a few months ago. Unfortunately, however, the groom was unable to attend as he had been murdered that very day.

Mr. Archer turned his attention to the group. "Did you know that in addition to Mrs. Pryce's beauty, and her accomplishments on the stage, and her social grace"—I balked at the word *grace* as, in truth, I had a tendency toward clumsiness. Some might even say I was accident prone, as the handsome sheriff in town, Mr. Clayton Marshall, had noted on several occasions—"that Mrs. Pryce is quite the detective? She has solved several mysteries since her arrival. We are so lucky to have her here."

I smiled at the praise of my sleuthing skills, though it

was a bit thick. From the sternness of her countenance, Mrs. Stewart seemed to agree.

I had only been prompted to solve said mysteries to either save my own neck or to support a friend. I had no wish to solve another murder—should another befall us, God forbid—ever again.

"Oh." I batted a dismissive hand in the air. "You are too kind, Mr. Archer. I am no detective. Just a concerned citizen," I demurred.

As to his other compliments, I will admit that in addition to my panache on the stage, I did excel at entertaining. One did not spend a good deal of one's life in New York society without mastering such skills. The city's elite clamored to be invited to one of my parties at our Fifth Avenue mansion.

How I longed to get back to that life, but I was here, fulfilling my duties at the hotel. So, I would make the best of it, despite the somewhat crude amenities of the limited kitchen and lack of an accomplished chef. But Lottie, our new cook, did have her own set of skills, and they were improving by the week.

Though flattered by his words and the confidence he'd placed in me for the welcome reception for his sister, I was a bit surprised Mr. Archer insisted his family stay at the Arabella and not his hotel, the General, just three doors down, for the weekend of the festival. He was determined to make his hotel a rival to mine.

"If you don't mind my saying," I said to the group, "and don't get me wrong, I certainly appreciate the business, but I had assumed you all would have stayed at Mr. Archer's hotel this weekend or continued to stay on at his ranch."

"Well," Mr. Archer said, tilting his head toward the window, "we decided to leave the ranch for a few days as we were concerned the weather might prevent us from attending the party, and—"

"I prefer staying in town, anyway," Mrs. Stewart cut in.

Mr. Stewart chuckled at his mother. "Mother is a city dweller through and through, and she does love her creature comforts," he explained. "We have been at Uncle Archibald's house for several weeks now, and we felt we were wearing out our welcome."

"Bah!" Mr. Archer said. "Nonsense. You are always welcome. But as I was saying, Mrs. Pryce, we were concerned the weather might impinge on our attending the festival. As to the General—"

"It is substandard in amenities," Mrs. Stewart said, interrupting him once again. She glared at him with such fierceness it made me flinch. Mr. Archer cleared his throat, obviously uncomfortable with his sister's blunt assessment of his hotel.

In that instant I felt sorry for the man, though I had to agree. However, I never would have said as much to Mr. Archer's face. The General was nothing compared to the Arabella. Mine was the best hotel for miles, and it rivaled any luxury accommodation in Denver. Mr. Archer's hotel was simple in its offerings, with rudimentary furnishings and without food service or the niceties of a fine hotel. It served primarily as a rooming house for the miners in Mr. Archer's employ.

Mr. Archer cleared his throat again and then addressed me with a restrained smile. "The Arabella is a much more suitable lodging," he finished. "And I figured you could use the business."

I blinked at the tone of condescension in his voice and bit back a retort. He wasn't wrong about my needing the business, but how rude to say so in front of everyone!

Mrs. Stewart scoffed. Perhaps she, too, thought his comment uncalled for.

Uncomfortable with the tension in the air, I was about to change the subject but was diverted when a sudden wave of icy coolness permeated the room and the distinct smell of pipe tobacco tickled my nose. A zing of anxiety coursed through my body that the others might sense the presence of yet one more guest, uninvited as he was: Mr. Percival Blank, the Arabella's resident ghost.

Chapter Two

Much to my annoyance, which also verged on fear, Percival stood between Mr. Archer and Mrs. Stewart with his hands behind his back and a ridiculous smile on his transparent face. Bijou, who sometimes read my emotions better than even I did, barked. She usually barked or growled when he appeared, and I often wondered whether she could see him or merely sensed his presence.

"Hush, girl," I said, lowering her to the floor.

"So, Mrs. Pryce," Dr. Briggs resumed the conversation, obviously just as uncomfortable as I was with the strain between Mr. Archer and his sister, for which I was grateful. However, at the moment, I found myself tongue-tied at Percival's sudden appearance. "Tell me about this detective business," he continued. "I find it quite fascinating."

Snapping out of my paralysis, I shook my head and looked at him. He was every bit the distinguished gentleman, with an intelligent demeanor and inquisitive gray eyes. "As I said, I'm no detective. I just lend a hand when necessary."

9

I glanced at Percival who raised his eyebrows at me. My involvement in the investigation of La Plata Springs' most recent murder had been vexing to Sheriff Marshall. He claimed he was concerned for my safety, which I don't doubt, but I had believed I'd had good reason to pursue such a task, as I was helping a friend. But that was finished, and now I could concentrate on matters of the hotel.

Mrs. Stewart crossed her arms, clutching them to her sides. "My goodness, I suddenly feel quite a draft in here," she said with a shiver and a look of utter distaste.

"Do you?" I asked, giving her a smile. "I'm quite warm."

Despite the chill that always accompanied Percival, I was overcome with heat. This particular ability to see spiritual entities had caused me a good deal of trouble, and I daresay trauma, as a child. It had instilled in me the perpetual fear that should someone learn of my abilities or witness me interacting with a person who was not visible to anyone else, I would succumb to the fate of some of my distant relatives who had been accused of witchcraft, or insanity, and had ended up in an asylum because of it.

I knew not everyone had the potential to see Percival, only those who shared my sensitivities, and so far, no one in the town seemed to do so. Should he choose to, my ghostly friend could still make himself visible, but it required a good deal of effort on his part. Especially if the viewer had a natural resistance to that phenomenon. However, there were other ways he could make himself known, as he was doing now with the frigidity of the air.

"It *is* a bit cold in here," Mrs. Edwards-Stewart concurred with her mother-in-law.

"Very well." I nodded toward the fireplace on the south wall of the saloon. "I will have Clarence stoke the fire. I'll go fetch him." I glared at Percival and gave a discreet tilt of my head toward the door that led to the hotel lobby. "The drafts in here can be quite bothersome!" I added.

With Bijou on my heels, I pushed my way through the lead and glass door and entered the lobby. A wave of cool air followed, sending a shiver up my spine. I hustled my way to another door, which was positioned behind the reception area, and entered into a narrow hallway that led to the hotel's annex.

Once through it, I whirled around to find Percival standing there with that pensive and Byronic expression he often wore on his translucent face. Bijou barked again, and I shushed her.

"What are you doing, Percival?" I asked in a loud whisper.

He lifted a shoulder in a shrug. "I don't know why you worry so. I mean no harm."

"Yes, I know you mean no harm, but—"

"I just wanted to join the party. It's been some time since I've seen the Stewarts. I see young Ralph has finally settled with a wife. He's always been quite the ladies' man."

"I don't have time to talk with you, Percival. I must get back to my guests."

"Very well." He sighed with a forlorn expression on his face. "Are you banishing me to our rooms?"

I rolled my eyes at him. "They are *my* rooms, and of course not. Do as you wish. Just stay away . . . please?"

"If you insist," he said reluctantly.

When I entered the Bella once again, I was affronted with loud, arguing voices. Bijou scuttled over to Kitty Carlisle, the manager of the Bella, who shared a glance with me at the commotion. One of the saloon girls picked up the little dog and held her protectively to her chest.

A man with his back to me was confronting Ralph Stewart. "I know you did it!" the man said, his voice thick with a Mexican accent. The room had gone silent and all eyes were on the small group.

"Here now, Mr. Valdez," Mr. Archer said, stepping in.

The man rounded on him. "You are the cause of it all!"

I rushed over to them. "Excuse me, is there a problem here?"

The man straightened his coat. He had a proud face, with deep-set coal eyes, heavy brows, and an equally heavy, if not impressive, mustache that trailed to his chin. He wore a thick gold chain with a pendant around his neck. It looked to be a religious medal of some sort.

"This man"—he pointed a finger at Mr. Stewart—"killed my brother!"

Mrs. Edwards-Stewart narrowed her eyes at him. "How dare you—"

The elder Mrs. Stewart remained silent, but her expression was hard as granite.

"Now, now, Valdez." Mr. Archer laid a hand on his shoulder. "Let's finish this business at another time, shall we? We are upsetting the guests."

The man shook off his hand. "This isn't over, *señor!*"

He gave me a quick nod and then stormed over to the bar.

"My goodness." I glanced over at Mr. Stewart, whose eyes, glinting with rage, followed him.

Killed his brother?

There had been an Enrique Valdez who had been a guest of the hotel a year ago and was found dead in his room. Could it be the same man this Mr. Valdez had been referring to? I had not yet arrived in La Plata Springs at the time of Enrique Valdez's death, but from what I had learned, there had been no visible evidence of murder, and according to Mr. Archer, there had been no doctor to examine the body. It was assumed he'd died from drink or natural causes.

Mr. Archer let out an uncomfortable chuckle. "It's of no issue, Mrs. Pryce. A minor . . . family matter."

I glanced over at the bar. Mr. Valdez had ordered a beer and sat perched on one of the barstools, his gazed fixed on Ralph Stewart.

Ignoring him, Mr. Stewart's features rearranged themselves to reassume his charming countenance. He graced me with that dazzling smile of his as his startling and powerful gaze settled upon mine. "A trifle, Mrs. Pryce. Do not worry yourself over it. Though, I must say, you are quite captivating with the glow of concern on your adorable face."

"Oh— I" Despite my shock and utter confusion at Mr. Valdez's accusation of murder, I found myself blushing at Mr. Stewart's boldness, especially since his wife was standing right next to him. "I-I'm fine," I said. "As long as everything is all right here."

"Your solicitude is admirable," he said, his voice like butter and his eyes holding me hostage.

"Ralph." A stern voice echoed behind me, shattering the tension in the air. Sheriff Clayton Marshall strode up to us. His stormy blue eyes settled on me, and a hint of a smile turned up his lips. It vanished as fast as it had appeared when he refocused his attention on Mr. Stewart.

"Sheriff Marshall," Mr. Stewart said with a distinct coolness. He gave the sheriff a stiff nod of greeting.

"You are here for the Winter Festival or some other business?" the sheriff asked.

Mr. Archer cut in. "Clay, you know the family is always together for the Festival."

Just then, Andrew Archer, another of Mr. Archer's nephews, appeared. He was a permanent resident of La Plata Springs and had been raised by Mr. Archer after the death of his parents. At the sight of him, Mr. Stewart's face lit up. The two embraced, as familiar as brothers, and immediately launched into a private conversation, wandering away from the group, their attention solely on each other.

"There will be no separating those two while Ralph's here," Mr. Archer said with a wide grin. "Thick as thieves since they were kids."

"How lovely," I said, touched at their boyish enthusiasm for each other.

"Yes . . . lovely," Mrs. Edwards-Stewart drew out with a roll of her eyes. She then excused herself and departed from the group. A couple of gentlemen took her place to greet Mr. Archer, his mother, and Dr. Briggs.

Clayton took me by the elbow and led me over to the fireplace, away from the other guests. "Was that Cristoforo Valdez I just saw leaving?" he asked.

I glanced over at the bar and Mr. Valdez was gone. "I don't know his first name, but I suppose so. He accused Ralph Stewart of killing his brother. I assume he meant Enrique Valdez?"

He nodded. "Yes. There has been tension between the two families over the past few years."

"Oh, what kind of tension?"

"I'm not sure, exactly. Valdez invested in one of Archer's companies several years ago, in some mines north of here in La Linda, before Archer set up camp here in La Plata Springs. One of the mines collapsed, and some of the miners were killed. It was a terrible accident. Valdez pulled out of the company. I thought that was the end of it, so I was surprised to see Cristoforo here."

"But why would he accuse Mr. Stewart of killing Enrique?"

"I don't know. There was no evidence of foul play, and we didn't yet have a doctor in town to examine the body. From my limited experience in pathology, I would guess he had a heart attack. Enrique Valdez lived hard and fast."

The sound of laughter pulled my gaze toward Mr. Stewart and Andrew who were sharing some kind of humorous exchange. Some of Kitty's girls were circling the two dashing men, but they were focused on each other and a young woman who had joined them. She was small in stature yet voluptuous, with delicate features. Mr. Stewart had his arm wrapped around her shoulders, and she looked up at him adoringly.

I glanced over at Mrs. Edwards-Stewart, who was now seated with a pretty red head in one of the booths at the back of the saloon. Her eyes were riveted on the merry trio, and her countenance had clouded over with wrath. The ginger haired woman tried to engage her in conversation, but Mary Alice stood up and left the room.

"Who is that young woman?" Clayton had settled his gaze on Mrs. Edwards-Stewart's companion. He'd asked the question with a good deal of interest, and my stomach folded in on itself. I hated to admit that my feelings for the sheriff and his stormy blue eyes were hard to ignore. While there was a definite chemistry between us, nothing had come of it—thus far—which was decidedly for the best, as I could not afford any romantic entanglements at the moment. Still, it bothered me that it bothered me to see him so curious about such a beautiful young woman. Looking around the room, it was clear he was not the only man with an eye for her.

"I haven't the slightest," I said with a lift of my chin.

"Well, I'm going to go find out. Excuse me." He walked away, leaving me feeling quite annoyingly bereft.

A cool waft of air settled above my head and drifted down my shoulders. I looked up to see Percival perched on the fireplace mantel next to a decorative porcelain urn, his legs casually crossed at the knees, his pipe set between his teeth as he puffed away on it. I glared at him, and my jaw clenched so hard my teeth hurt. Hadn't he agreed to stay away? He shook his head in admonishment, pulled the pipe from his lips, and gave me a teasing little pout.

"Don't start," I whispered and then quickly glanced around to make sure no one had seen me speaking to the urn. "What are you doing back here?"

He sighed. "Cordelia was changing her attire. I thought it would be ungentlemanly to stay."

Though I wished he had not come back, I couldn't argue his point. Even though he could be terribly vexing, he was indeed a gentleman.

"I must say—" he glanced over at the sheriff who was speaking to the beautiful young woman "—do I detect a sparkle of jealousy in your lovely eyes?"

"Oh, do be quiet—"

A blood-curdling shriek came from behind me, and the sound of glass shattering sent my heart into spasms. I whirled around to see Miss Constance Chatterley, owner and editor of the *La Plata Springs Herald,* pointing at Percival, her glass of wine a broken, puddled mess at her feet. All eyes turned to her, and my knees went weak.

My worst fear had come to light. Someone had seen me conversing with a ghost.

Chapter Three

Having caused quite the commotion, Percival vanished.

Constance's eyes rolled back in her head, and she sank to the floor. I quickly gathered my wits about me and rushed to her aid. Several of the guests surrounded us.

"Get her some water please!" I said to no one in particular.

Bijou had wriggled her way through the mass of legs and immediately starting licking Constance's face.

"No, Bijou," I whispered and scooted her away. The little dog let out a pitiful whine. Cordelia, who had returned from changing her dress, picked her up and stood back, giving us some room.

In moments, Kitty Carlisle pushed her way through. Clayton knelt down beside me and lifted Constance's shoulders to help her sit with some effort, as she was a woman who liked her pastries and sweets.

Always flamboyantly attired, Constance was no less colorful than usual in a crimson-and-violet patterned silk jacket and skirt, black ruffles flaring at the throat, on the sleeves and down the bodice. Her matching hat, adorned with purple ostrich feathers, had been knocked askew on her head. Her small eyes fluttered, but she could not seem to fully open them.

"What happened?" Kitty asked, handing me the glass of water. A stately woman with raven hair and keen dark eyes, Kitty had a stern schoolmarm air about her, but the woman's heart was good as gold.

"I-I'm not sure," I stammered. I gently tapped Constance's cheek.

Her eyes blinked open.

"Drink this." I held the glass to her lips, and she took a sip. She looked at the crowd that had gathered around us and then her attention settled on me.

"There was— I . . . I saw—" she croaked.

"Let's get her to a chair," I said to Clayton. He gently helped her to her feet and walked her over to a vacant table near the window. I pulled out the chair and set the glass of water in front of her.

Dr. Briggs was suddenly at my side. "May I be of assistance?"

"She fainted," I said.

The doctor approached Constance, who seemed to have gone mute with shock. "May I take a look at you?"

She gave a brief nod. Dr. Briggs proceeded to check her pupils and take her pulse. He examined the back of her head and ran his hands down her arms. "I think you'll be fine. Must be the excitement of the party." He gave her a sympathetic smile. "You need to rest." He then turned to me. "Someone should probably be with her, to check on her from time to time."

"She lives alone," Cordelia said.

"She can stay here at the hotel," I said. "I'll keep an eye on her."

Though concerned for her well-being, I also wanted to assure her what she saw was merely a figment of her imagination. I offered her the water again, and she sipped, this time eagerly. The color was coming back to her cheeks, but I could feel the blood draining from mine.

The terror of my "gift" being found out oozed over my body like black ink, making my pulse race. Of all the people to experience Percival, I could think of no one worse than Constance Chatterley, who had a voracious penchant for gossip. There had already been rumors of the hotel being haunted, and this would only add fuel to the fire, which would be bad for business and terrible for me. How could I sell a hotel reputed to be haunted?

"I believe room twelve is vacant," Cordelia added. "I'll get the key."

"Thank you," I said to her and then returned my attention to Constance. "Do you think you could walk, Constance?"

"Yes . . . yes, I think so." She turned her gaze to Clayton and gave him a coy smile, batting her eyelashes at him. "With some help."

"Come on, everyone," Kitty said to the onlookers. "She's all right. Go on and enjoy the party. Who needs another drink?"

A resounding murmur filled the room, and in seconds, the commotion with Constance was forgotten as the crowd went back to their merrymaking.

Clayton took her by the arm and helped her to her feet again. I picked up the unfinished glass of water and followed them. Once we were out in the lobby, Cordelia met me with the key to room twelve. Bijou danced at my feet, wanting my attention.

"Shall I come with you?" Cordelia asked.

I shook my head. "No, the sheriff and I have got this in hand. But, if you would, please go back to the party and help Kitty."

"Absolutely," she said.

"This way," I said to Clayton. His charge leaned heavily against him, her face flushed and a faint smile on her lips. She was loving the attention of the gallant sheriff.

I led them down the hallway adjacent to the lobby to room twelve. I opened the door, and we stepped inside.

"I've got it from here, Clayton," I said, taking hold of Constance's other arm.

"I'll leave you to it, then," he said, tipping his hat.

"Must you go, Sheriff? I'm terribly frightened," she said with a waver in her voice and a pitiful look on her face. "I saw— I think I saw—"

"Come, Constance." I tilted my head toward the bed, diverting her from continuing. "You need to rest. The sheriff will be in the Bella. You have nothing to fear. I'll sit with you."

"I'll be around for a while," he said and then quietly left the room.

I walked her over to the bed and encouraged her to sit down. I took off her shoes and helped her get settled. Once she was prone, I placed the throw at the foot of the bed over her.

"I must be losing my mind," she said and then hiccupped. Her eyes were glassy, and the flush of alcohol consumption had returned to her face.

"Don't be silly. Your mind is perfectly fit, Constance. You just have a very active imagination. That's what makes you such a good writer." I hoped the flattery would assure her.

"But I didn't imagine it. He was sitting right there on the mantel."

I blinked, feigning ignorance. "Who?"

"A man. He was wearing a paisley smoking jacket . . . and he was smoking a pipe."

I let out a nervous laugh. "Goodness! Paisley. How droll."

"You know this hotel is haunted," she said, her mouth turning down in a frown. "They say that the late Mr. Blank, the architect who helped your husband build the hotel, still resides here. There have been sightings."

"Really? Who has seen him?" I swallowed down the trepidation creeping up into my throat, threatening to lodge there and choke me.

Constance wrung her hands. "Well, I'm not exactly sure, but I suppose it's what people have *heard* in the hotel. Banging around, especially in the attic. Even Mr. Pettyjohn said he has heard things."

I waved a dismissive hand in the air. "Oh, well, you know Mr. Pettyjohn. He's a little, um, you know . . . how should I say, scatterbrained?"

Mr. Pettyjohn, the reception clerk, had been a permanent fixture in the hotel since the beginning. I found him to be a walking contradiction, as he was very efficient in his duties but had a tendency toward absentmindedness and was in the habit of losing things.

"Don't get me wrong," I said when she looked at me a bit affronted, "he's a valued member of my staff, and I adore him, but he can be a bit . . . dotty." I used the word that Maggie, the hotel's head maid, had used in regard to the man.

"Also," I whispered conspiratorially, "we've had a problem with vermin. They make all kinds of noise in the walls and in the attic, but please don't tell anyone. I'm sure that's what Mr. Pettyjohn, or anyone else, must have heard."

"But I saw—"

"Did you perhaps have a bit too much wine?" I asked, remembering the broken glass at her feet.

She put her palm at her temple. "I did have a couple of glasses . . . I usually don't partake, but it was such a festive occasion. Mr. Stewart is such an engaging young man, and so charming. I daresay all the women in the room were quite taken with him. His wife is a little full of herself, but she comes from a good family. Bertha arranged the marriage, you know. And did you see the young woman he and Andrew were speaking with? I've heard she is an old paramour of Mr. Stewart's. I wonder what she could be doing here. She certainly didn't come by way of invitation from Bertha or Mrs. Edwards-Stewart. I suppose Mr. Stewart could have—"

From the way she was prattling on, I concluded she was feeling quite herself again.

"Well, the wine must have gone to your head," I interrupted, not wanting to engage in any further gossip. "Why don't you rest here for a while?" I handed her the glass of water. "Drink this. I'll check in on you later."

"Yes," she said, settling deeper into the pillows. "I have been having trouble sleeping lately. I think a little rest might do me good. Thank you, Arabella."

"Think nothing of it, Constance. Take all the time you need."

I walked out and shut the door behind me, heaving a sigh of relief. Hopefully, I had successfully diverted a crisis.

I made my way back to the party, my arms and legs still a little jittery at what transpired between Percival and Constance. From her reaction, it was clear she had never before experienced the soul-rattling phenomenon of seeing a ghost. I wondered if Percival intentionally appeared to her, and if so, why?

Of late, he had been after me to "introduce" him to Cordelia. He felt since we were all living together in the owner's suite of the hotel, she should be acquainted with him. But I didn't know how she would react, and I wasn't ready to find out yet. I didn't know if I'd ever be ready.

Though I didn't like it, his pleas to allow him to appear to Cordelia did make sense given we were all cohabitating. But why had Constance seen him? Perhaps she had always had the ability but was closed off to it until recently. Either way, I hoped it didn't cause problems for me or the hotel.

When I entered the Bella once again, the volume in the place had risen. The piano player Mr. Archer had hired was merrily banging away on the keyboard, and several of the patrons were dancing and singing along.

My eyes traveled to the back booth where Clayton was sitting across from Mrs. Edward-Stewart's attractive, ginger haired friend. The young woman giggled at something the charming sheriff said, and my heart fell to the pit of my stomach. Which was silly, really. Why should I care who the sheriff charmed? It was none of my business.

My attention was drawn to the other side of the room where voices had risen and were not merry at all. Mr. Stewart and his lovely companion were in an argument. Andrew stood by, watching with a look of apprehension on his face. Dr. Briggs left Bertha's side and made his way over to the couple. A few words were exchanged, and then Mr. Stewart shoved the doctor away, nearly knocking him down.

The music and singing was so loud the guests didn't seem to notice the altercation, but the sheriff did. He left the beauty in the booth and strode over. As he passed he gave me a nod.

Suddenly, Mr. Stewart's beautiful companion threw a drink in his face. She smashed the glass on the floor and ran through the Bella and into the hotel lobby. I watched her leave, and then my gaze settled on the ginger haired young woman, who had obviously seen the disagreement because she was grinning like the Cheshire Cat.

I followed the distressed woman and found her sitting on one of the Queen Anne settees in the lobby. I approached the reception desk where Mr. Pettyjohn stood sentinel.

"Is there a problem?" he asked. His carefully manicured, upturned mustache twitched.

"Of sorts," I answered and then whispered. "Who is she? Is she a guest?"

He quickly scanned the registration book, and his thick, ebony eyebrows pressed down toward the bridge of his nose. "She is Victoria Clement. Mr. Stewart is paying for her room."

"I see. Thank you, Mr. Pettyjohn."

I went over to the woman. She was looking out the window, sniffling into a handkerchief. "Miss Clement, are you all right?"

She gave me a brief glance and then turned to the window again.

"Can I get you anything?"

She shook her head. "No. Thank you."

I held out my hand. "I'm Arabella. I own the hotel."

She reluctantly shook my hand. It seemed she did not want to be bothered, but I hated leaving her in that state.

"Are you sure you are all right?" I asked again.

She stood up and smoothed down the front of her skirt. "Yes, just tired. Good night." She gave me a tight-lipped smile and made her way to the stairs.

I went back into the noisy saloon. Cordelia was assisting Mr. Stewart with his spirit-soaked suit. He took off his coat and handed it to her. She took it to the bar, and I met her there.

"My goodness," she said, shaking her head. "I don't think I've ever seen the saloon so filled to the brim or the customers so . . . animated." She opened a bottle of soda water and poured it onto Mr. Stewart's jacket in an attempt to clean it.

"Yes," I agreed. "Mr. Archer's family has seemed to create a stir, in more ways than one." My attention was drawn to the elder Mrs. Stewart and Dr. Briggs, who were heading my way.

"Mrs. Pryce," Dr. Briggs said, "thank you for your hospitality this evening. Bertha and I are retiring to our rooms. It's not good for her to be up so late, and I'm afraid the commotion has quite upset her."

I glanced at Mrs. Stewart whose complexion looked quite blanched. Her lips were an uncomely shade of lavender, and her eyes carried the look of fatigue. She was positively undone.

"Yes, yes, of course. Do you need assistance?" I asked.

He shook his head. "No. We will be fine, thank you."

Mrs. Stewart raised her chin. "I am sorry you had to witness the spectacle of my son and his . . . friend. He really does associate himself with an undesirable element."

"Oh, not to worry, Mrs. Stewart. These things happen," I said in a weak attempt to assure her.

"Yes, and with Ralph, they happen quite often." She darted a look in his direction. He was quietly conversing with Andrew. Gone was the Peter Pan look about him. In fact, he looked quite disturbed and pensive. Andrew reached out and laid a hand on his shoulder.

"Good night," Dr. Briggs said and ushered Mrs. Stewart out of the saloon and into the lobby.

"There," Cordelia said. "Now, once it's dry, it should be good as new."

"I wonder what they were arguing about. Have you learned anything about Miss Clement?"

Cordelia shook her head. "Only that she is an artist, and Mr. Ralph Stewart is her patron. He is working to help establish her in the art world. I guess you could say he is her manager."

"I see." I wondered what he could have possibly said to have induced such a violent reaction from Miss Clement. And did their relationship extend beyond business?

Mr. Stewart suddenly appeared at my shoulder, Andrew in attendance. He gave me a polite nod.

"Good night, Mrs. Pryce. Thank you for the lovely party."

I noted a sheen of perspiration on his forehead, which I thought odd as it was comfortable, if not verging on cool, in the room. His eyes had become droopy, the pupils dilated. I put it up to exhaustion and strain from his encounter with Miss Clement.

"You are quite welcome, Mr. Stewart. Should you need anything, don't hesitate to ask."

"I will," he said.

Andrew flashed a smile. "Good night, Mrs. Pryce."

After they left, Mrs. Edwards-Stewart's lovely companion arose from the booth and was heading for the door.

"Excuse me," I said to Cordelia. I left her and approached the woman. "Hello. I don't believe we've met. I'm Arabella Pryce, owner of the establishment."

She rewarded me with a wide smile that made her sage green eyes dance. Her dress was of a modest cut and fabric, but it did nothing to dim her beauty. She really was quite enchanting. No wonder the sheriff had been interested in meeting her.

"Of course," she said. "Mary Alice told me who you were. I'm Cherrie Fontaine, secretary to Mrs. Bertha Stewart." She spoke with a hint of Southern accent.

"Ah, yes. Please let me know if there is anything you require for your stay," I continued.

"Thank you. Good night, Mrs. Pryce," she said. "By the way, I love your hotel. It has the feel of luxury, but it's very homey."

"Thank you." My heart swelled with pride, which surprised me. I'd wanted nothing but to endure my tenure here, bring the hotel to its former glory, and go back to New York, to my theater and my fans. But her words took hold of me, and I found myself beaming. "I hope you enjoy your time here."

She smiled and made her way to the door. Mr. Archer, the last of the Archer clan present, came over to me.

"Arabella, once again you've outdone yourself. I have every faith you will make this year's Winter Festival one to remember."

Heat rose to my face, and I smiled with pleasure.

"I'm sorry about my nephew, Ralph," he continued, his

countenance darkening. "He seems to find trouble wherever he goes."

He certainly did tonight, I thought, remembering his previous altercation with Mr. Valdez.

"My sister indulges him, lets him get away with far too much," he went on. "Always has. He's a spoiled, ungrateful child who, if he is not reined in, will bring this family to ruin."

Ruin? I blinked at him in surprise. Clearly, he did not think much of his nephew. I wasn't sure how to respond.

"It's nothing," I shrugged. "Everyone seemed to have a good time. Don't worry yourself over it."

"Good night, my dear," he said with a weariness in his voice. He left the saloon through the street entrance.

Cordelia approached me, hands on hips. "Mr. Archer's family has all left?"

"Yes," I said absently, watching Mr. Archer walk by the window, bundling himself against the snow and the cold. "It's gotten quite late."

She looked at the watch necklace she wore around her neck. "Oh, so it has. Everything all right?"

I nodded, but a sinking feeling weighted down my chest. "It seems not everyone finds Mr. Ralph Stewart as charming as we do."

Chapter Four

DECEMBER 6, 1885

Despite the fact I had not gotten to bed until around one o'clock in the morning, I woke early, at 6:00 a.m., my mind aflutter with the tasks I needed to accomplish that day, one of which was to read and respond to correspondence sent by Mr. Thomas Blackthorn, the man who managed my theater, the Pryce Theater, in New York City.

My heart ached with the desire to be back there again, performing onstage, going to after-parties, and living the life of a celebrated thespian. I missed that connection with my audience, and I missed my other ghostly friend, Leticia Crookshank, who took up residence at the theater. We loved to talk about theater life, and she also provided some excellent coaching, both in acting and life in general.

The loss of my former life left a hole in my heart. I knew it was temporary, but it did nothing to quell my anxieties about being forgotten by my fans. They were always present, churning in the back of my mind like the low hum of something monotonous. It ate away at my nerves.

In an attempt to remain relevant in my celebrity, I had Cordelia regularly send news of my life here in Colorado to Mr. Theodore Rankin, the editor of the *New York City Times*. He had agreed to run a series of stories about me in my absence, for which I was grateful. Other than that, there was nothing to be done but simply bide my time here in La Plata Springs until I could return to my former life.

I loosely plaited my waist-length hair, tied it with a ribbon, and put on my dressing gown. Having risen before Cordelia, which was highly unusual, I tiptoed through her bedroom and made my way to the parlor, Bijou pattering along behind me.

Our accommodation was not the most ingeniously designed—our two bedrooms were connected by a bathing room—but we had learned to manage it. I suppose I could have gone out the other door of my bedroom that led to the fourth-floor hallway, but it was terribly chilly on this winter morning, and the hallways were always frigid.

Once in the parlor, I set about making a fire in the fire-place, as it was too early even for Maggie, the head house-maid, to begin her duties. As head housemaid, she needn't do something as menial as tending to my fireplace, nor cleaning my room—she could have delegated it to one of her staff of four others—but she insisted on taking care of me, which I found endearing.

Once the blaze was going, Bijou settled herself on the floor in front of the fire between the two wing backed armchairs, and I went to the stately walnut desk to review Mr. Blackthorn's latest letter.

I sat in the chair to finish reading the letter when the sound of keys jangling outside my door startled me.

Maggie came into the room. "Oh! Mrs. Pryce, I didn't think you'd be up. I came to wake you."

"Wake me?" This was indeed unusual. She had never done so before. "Why?"

Her girlish face, which often bore a quizzical expression, paled. "I'm afraid there has been an accident."

"An accident? What sort of accident?"

"It's Mr. Ralph Stewart. He's—" She went quiet, biting her lip. "He's, well, he's dead, ma'am."

I jumped up from the desk. "What?!"

My shout startled Bijou, and she barked.

"Yes, ma'am. I'm afraid so."

"What happened?"

"I think you need to come see. The sheriff is here."

Cordelia came into the room, also in her dressing gown. "What's happened?" she asked, her voice groggy from sleep.

"I'm not sure, but Mr. Stewart is dead," I repeated, still trying to grasp the concept.

"Please come, Mrs. Pryce," Maggie said with a waver in her voice. Though completely adept at her job, and quite a good manager of the other maids, Maggie was a tender-hearted soul and was clearly upset by this turn of events.

We followed her down the stairs, Bijou at our heels. She led us down into the lobby and then to the hallway that led to the annex. Once at the end, we went through another doorway that opened to the outdoors. A blast of cold air sucked the breath from my lungs, and I wrapped my arms around me, pulling my velvet dressing gown tighter. I didn't relish being seen in such a state of undress, but it wasn't the first time I'd been roused from my bed because of a murder.

Several of the miners and their families who lived in the annex were standing on the porches of their little houses, which encircled a grassy, or rather, snowy courtyard. And some of Kitty's girls had come out of the two split-leveled houses where Kitty ran her "sporting" business. They were scantily clad and shivering in the cold.

I looked over at Clayton, who was armored against the frigid temperature in a leather duster with sheepskin lining. Pity and concern showed on his face. I followed his gaze to the unmoving body of Mr. Ralph Stewart, and my stomach caved in on itself at the sight. His legs were twisted at unnatural angles, and his lifeless, dark eyes stared at the heavens. A pool of blood surrounded his head.

"Looks like he fell out the window." Clayton pointed to an open second-story window. The curtain sheers swayed in the icy breeze.

"Poor man," Cordelia said. She had picked up Bijou and was holding her close to her chest.

"I've sent for Doc Tate," Clayton said, referring to the town's physician, and then turned to face everyone who'd come outside to see what had happened. "You all go back inside, now. Stay warm. Go about your day. There is nothing to be done here."

Slowly, the observers went back into the warmth of their houses.

"Clayton, what do you suppose happened?" I asked.

He shook his head. "I have no idea. Do you know what time he left the party?"

"I—I think it was around eleven."

"Yes, yes, it was around eleven," Cordelia confirmed. "I was cleaning his coat with soda water and just happened to look up at the clock on the mantel behind the bar."

My arms and legs were growing numb from the cold, and probably the shock as well. I shook from head to toe.

Noticing this, the sheriff pointed to the door. "You two go back on inside now. I'll wait for the doc, and then I'll come back to see if I can make sense of any of this. His family will have to be alerted. I'd like to speak with them."

"Yes, yes, of course," I said. "As soon as I get dressed."

"Right," Cordelia agreed. "As soon as we are dressed, we will gather the family."

I looked over at her, grateful for her no-nonsense approach to all things, and her continual strength and willingness to be by my side no matter what the circumstances.

Nevertheless, a sinking feeling hit my stomach. I usually didn't have a hard time speaking with anyone, but in this instance, what in the world was I going to say and how was I going to say it?

An hour later, we were all gathered in the suite of rooms Cordelia and I shared. We had come up with the idea to tell the family we were calling an emergency meeting about the festival. With the help of Clarence, the young bellman, more chairs were brought into the parlor to accommodate the group. The only family member not present was Mr. Archer, and Cordelia had already gone to the General to fetch him.

"What is this about, Mrs. Pryce?" Dr. Briggs said, a bit impatiently. "Is there some kind of problem with the festival?"

I pressed my palms together. They were damp with perspiration. I didn't want to say anything until everyone, namely the sheriff, was present.

"I'll tell you all about it when Mr. Archer gets here," I said, stalling for time.

"Where is Ralph?" Mrs. Stewart, who was sitting

between Dr. Briggs and her secretary, Cherrie Fontaine, asked her daughter-in-law.

Mrs. Edwards-Stewart pulled back her chin, looking a bit affronted. "How should I know? I'm not his keeper. Who knows where he's off to this morning? He might not have even gone to bed. When he and Andrew get together, there's no telling what they get up to."

She and her husband had reserved separate rooms. This did not seem to be a surprise among the others in the group, and I wondered if they had separate bedrooms in their home. It wasn't all that unusual. William and I had kept separate rooms, mostly on account of our opposing schedules. I often arrived home late at night, and he was an early riser.

Just then, Cordelia entered into the parlor, followed by Mr. Archer, the sheriff, and Victoria Clement. Bijou let out a little yip of joy at seeing more opportunities for attention enter the room. She ran over to the sheriff and raised herself up on her hind legs, dancing for his approval. He bent down and gave her a pat on the head.

"Good morning, all," Mr. Archer said. "What's this about the festival? I hope it's not serious. Those children are counting on it, and I have no intentions of letting them down."

Before I could open my mouth to answer, Mrs. Edwards-Stewart pointed to Victoria. "What's *she* doing here? She has nothing to do with the festival. I'm not even sure why she is in town," she finished with a glare at the pretty young woman who stared back at her. Her words carried the weight of something only the two of them knew about . . . and it wasn't friendly.

"I've asked her to join us," Clayton said. "This concerns her as well."

From the open doorway, Andrew Archer came into the room. He swiped his hat off his head and held it between his hands.

"Sorry I'm late," he said.

"Andrew, do you know where Ralph is?" Mrs. Stewart asked him.

"No, ma'am," he said. "I thought he'd be here."

I cut a glance at Cordelia, and she gave me an assuring smile.

"Everyone, please take a seat," Clayton continued.

I wasn't expecting Miss Clement or Andrew, so there weren't enough chairs. I stood up and offered Miss Clement my seat. With a gracious smile, she accepted.

I went and stood next to Andrew and Clayton.

"I'm afraid I have bad news," Clayton said. "It's about Ralph. This morning we— Well, we found him in the annex. It seems he'd fallen from the window of his room, and—"

"Oh my heavens!" Mrs. Stewart clutched at her throat. "No . . . no!"

"He's dead?" Dr. Briggs asked.

The sheriff nodded. "I'm terribly sorry for your loss."

"No!" the elder woman shouted. She grabbed hold of Dr. Briggs's arm, looking into his face. "No, it can't be! It's not true!" The doctor wrapped an arm around her shoulder. Miss Fontaine took hold of the older woman's hand.

My gaze traveled to Mrs. Edwards-Stewart. She was slowly shaking her head. Her eyes were closed, and tears seeped out from beneath her lashes.

"This can't be true," Andrew said. "I walked with him up to his room. We had planned to play cards, but he was tired. Said he was going straight to bed."

"Did you go into the room with him?" Clayton asked.

Andrew shook his head. "No. Since we weren't playing cards, I decided to look for Maggie, to tell her good night." He pressed his fist to his mouth in anguish. Andrew was often seen roaming the halls at night, looking for his sweetheart to bid her farewell for the evening.

Victoria Clement choked out a sob as if she'd been trying her best to keep it contained but just couldn't any longer.

Mr. Archer made his way over to my desk and leaned heavily against it, his knees looking as if they were about to buckle. Andrew quickly went to his aid, but Mr. Archer waved him off.

"I'm all right," he assured his nephew. "This is just . . . just so . . ." He couldn't finish.

"I've just come from his room," Clayton said. "The window looks like it was forced open. And I found this." He held up a piece of paper with writing scrawled across it.

"What is it?" I asked.

"It appears to be a suicide note."

"What?!" Dr. Briggs bellowed, startling the already stunned and sobbing Mrs. Stewart. "Suicide? That's ridiculous!"

"He wouldn't," Mrs. Edwards-Stewart said.

"Let me see it," Andrew demanded.

Clayton handed it to him. His eyes hastily scanned the paper. "I don't believe this." He shook his head in dismay and held the note out for Mrs. Stewart to read, but she denied it with a violent shake of her head. The poor woman couldn't bear to see her son's fateful words boldly scrawled in black and white.

"I'm afraid I'll need to look at this a bit more closely." Clayton held his hand out for the note. Andrew returned it, and the sheriff tucked it into his vest pocket. "Dr. Tate is now evaluating the body."

"For what reason?" Mr. Archer seemed to find his feet again. "If it's clear he fell out of the window, what will looking at it more closely do? Let us grieve in peace, man."

The sheriff pressed his lips into a thin line. "I'm going to ask all of you to stay in town until we get the matter settled."

"He wouldn't have killed himself," Andrew said, looking over at Miss Clement, who nodded in agreement. "He had everything to live for. He has—had—a charmed life. The kind of life anyone would envy."

Miss Fontaine stood up. "I don't think this is good for Mrs. Stewart. Please, let me and the doctor take her to her room to rest."

Mrs. Stewart's body had crumpled against the doctor's, as if her bones had turned to liquid. Her face was a ghastly shade of gray.

"Of course," Clayton said. "Again, I am sorry for your loss."

Mr. Archer went to Mrs. Edwards-Stewart and helped her to her feet, and Andrew crossed the room to aid Miss Clement, who didn't really seem to need it. She had gathered her composure and silently swiped the tears from her cheeks. They all filed out of our parlor and into the hallway.

Clayton stayed behind.

"Suicide?" I asked. "I never would have guessed."

"The man seemed so self-possessed . . . so . . ." Cordelia tried to find the words.

"You mean self-*obsessed*," Clayton added. "I have to concur with the group. It was completely out of character for him to have killed himself."

"But the note," I reminded him. Clayton pulled it out of

his pocket and handed it to me. I read it out loud. *"You'll be Sorry. You will all be Sorry."* I studied the words, taking note of both the *S's*, which were capitalized.

"That doesn't really sound like a suicide note, does it?" Cordelia said. "It sounds more like a threat."

"I think it could go either way." Clayton took it back and put it in his pocket again.

"Maybe it wasn't meant to be found. Maybe he was writing it to someone he intended to send it to, or take it to, or leave somewhere. Perhaps his falling out of the window was an accident," I said. "Maybe he wanted a bit of fresh air when he got to his room. You said the window looked like it had been forced. I'll admit, some of them are jammed because of a less than meticulous paint job. So he wrestled with the window, and once he got it open, he toppled out of it."

"That is a possibility, Arabella. I'll give you that. But this note, this *threat*, was really not his style. Ralph Stewart was anything but subtle. He was a man of action. If he wanted something, he got it."

"What are you saying, Clayton?" I asked.

"I'm saying there is more to this than meets the eye."

"You think he was murdered."

"I can't be sure. Hopefully, Doc Tate can give me a little more insight, but something definitely doesn't smell right."

Chapter Five

There was little activity in the hotel that day, and a pall fell over the atmosphere, which was not at all surprising. Ralph Stewart's death was a shock to us all. And to have occurred at what was to be the most festive time of the year was most sobering.

Later that afternoon, I finished my letter to Mr. Blackthorn with some difficulty. My mind whirled with Clayton's suspicion of Mr. Stewart's untimely demise being the result of murder rather than some kind of horrible accident.

I felt for his family and friends, but another worry took hold of me. This tragic situation could very well put a damper on the Winter Festival. There was a chance we might have to cancel altogether as the Archers and Stewarts were such important sponsors. And that meant disappointing a number of orphaned children, some who very well could have never experienced such a gay affair.

Sympathy stabbed at my heart. I knew what it was like to be standing on the sidelines of holiday gaiety. The holidays, Christmas in particular, had always been overlooked in my youth. My mother had kept me too busy with acting, voice, and dance lessons for us to partake. It had left a giant void in my life, and now, as an adult, I always made a big show of the holidays. I desperately wanted to do the same here.

I must admit I'd been a bit overwhelmed when I'd heard I would be responsible for planning the event. But as it was a reality, I wanted it to be magical. It was, after all, a performance of sorts on my part, and if I could bring happiness to those children, it would be worth the work. The situation played on my anxieties. I couldn't bear to disappoint anyone.

In the meantime, I would go about my business at the hotel, seeing to the comfort of the grieving guests. I also had to address the issue of the dilapidated porches in the hotel annex. It was next on my list of things to accomplish before selling the hotel.

I tidied up the desk and was about to step out the door when a distinct coolness filled the room and the smell of pipe tobacco filled the air. I looked up into the mirror and saw Percival's reflection sitting in the love seat nestled in the bay window behind me.

"Are you angry with me?" His lips were pursed in a pout, and his luminous dark eyes turned down in the corners, giving him the same regretful appearance as Bijou when she'd been naughty.

"Angry?" And then I remembered. "Oh, you mean about scaring the living daylights out of Constance Chatterley? Yes. I am decidedly angry at you. What were you thinking, Percival? You are becoming more and more reckless."

"I really had no idea that Miss Chatterbox possessed your sensitivities. I have been in her presence on many occasions and she has not seen me. In fact, she has almost as tough a veneer as your handsome sheriff. I wonder what has changed."

"He's not my handsome sheriff," I shot back quickly.

Percival gave an indifferent shrug.

In thinking about Constance, I remembered my first encounters with otherworldly spirits. They had occurred whenever I was at my most vulnerable. In my childhood, Oliver Shrewsbury had appeared to me when I was on a picnic with my mother and some of her theater friends. I had been working extremely hard, performing in two plays at the same time, and I was exhausted and depressed. I felt like I was nothing but a means to an end for my mother . . . and, in truth, I was.

When I had experienced my next encounter in adulthood with Leticia Crookshank, the ghost who occupied my theater in New York, I had just lost a valued treasure from my estranged father who had long ago abandoned my mother and me to pursue his poetry in France. The treasure had been my good-luck charm, and the loss of it had caused me to grieve my father all over again.

Had Constance been feeling vulnerable? Was she currently undergoing some kind of emotional challenge? I wished I had stayed and talked with her longer when I had taken her to her room last night.

"She really was in a terrible state," I continued. "I meant to check on her this morning, but then we received the news about Mr. Stewart, and by the time I got to her room she was gone."

"Yes, she left quite early—before sunrise."

"You saw her? She didn't see you again, did she?"

"Yes, I saw her, and no, she did not see me."

"That's good. Percival, you really should be more careful. Joining the party last night was risky."

"Agreed," he acquiesced.

"I don't suppose you know anything about Ralph Stewart, then?" If he had known about the terrible tragedy, I'm sure he would have brought it up right away, but I thought I should ask anyway.

"What about him?"

"It's terrible. Awful. He died last night. Fell from the window of his second-floor room. You haven't seen—well, his spirit, have you?"

Percival's eyes narrowed, and he raised a hand to his chin. He looked like he was about to say something but remained silent.

"Percival?"

"No. But it often takes time . . . if it happens at all. Not all who are deceased stay back. He might have gone on to the beyond. Do you know what time this happened?"

I shrugged. "It must have been sometime after eleven. Andrew said he had walked him to his room around that time. Mr. Stewart's body was found at around 5:30 or 6:00 a.m., so before that. Why do you ask?"

He pressed his lips together and folded his arms across his chest. "I saw that Valdez fellow lurking about in the middle of the night."

"Well, he is a guest at the hotel," I reminded him.

"Yes, but he has a room on the ground floor, does he not?"

"I would have to ask Mr. Pettyjohn—"

"His room is on the ground floor," he said, quite certain. "I saw him carry his bag into it early yesterday afternoon."

"Okay . . ."

"Yet, I saw him on the second floor around midnight."

"What was he doing?"

"He was coming down the stairs."

I recalled how angry he had been at Mr. Stewart during the party. Had he gone up to Mr. Stewart's room to continue their argument?

"I also saw that pretty woman, the one with the red hair."

"Miss Fontaine? The elder Mrs. Stewart's secretary?"

"Yes, her."

"Well, she and the Stewart party have rooms on the second floor, with the exception of Mrs. Stewart. She is in one of the two third-floor suites. Dr. Briggs is in the other."

"Well, it might mean nothing, but I thought you should know." He held up his palm, flipped his fingers over, and examined his nails, as if suddenly bored with the conversation.

"I should check on the Stewart party. I haven't wanted to disturb them in their grief today, but perhaps I should see if there is anything I can do to make them more comfortable."

Percival suddenly popped out of the room. The door to the parlor opened, and Bijou came in, Cordelia close behind. Bijou ran over to her water dish and then settled on her little bed under the window.

Cordelia hung the leash on the hook next to the door. "I just saw the sheriff on the second-floor landing. He said he was going to speak with Mrs. Edwards-Stewart and then go to Mrs. Stewart's room next."

"I wonder if he has news from the doctor."

"He had a pretty grave look on his face."

I stood up from the desk. "I was just going to go see both of them myself. Do you want to join me?"

Cordelia nodded.

We reached the third floor to find the sheriff at Mrs. Stewart's door.

"Hello, Dr. Briggs," he said to the open doorway.

We quietly joined him. Dr. Briggs looked at us expectantly.

Clayton's handsome face was devoid of its usual ruddy color and he hadn't shaved. "I need to speak with Mrs. Stewart, Dr. Briggs. May I come in?"

"Bertha is lying down in the bedroom. Give us a moment please." He closed the door.

"What is it, Clayton?" I asked.

He rubbed the stubble on his chin. "I've heard from the doctor."

"And?"

"This is a little more complicated than we thought."

The door opened again. "Come in," Dr. Briggs said. "I'm afraid Bertha is indisposed. I've given her a dose of laudanum to settle her. She is asleep. Is there a message I can give her?"

We filed into the suite's parlor.

"I'm afraid I have more bad news," Clayton said, taking his hat off and addressing Dr. Briggs. "Dr. Tate has examined the body. He said that due to the injuries sustained, the fall definitely could have been the cause of death, but there is something else."

"What is it?" Dr. Briggs asked.

"Based on the evidence so far, the doctor is quite certain that Ralph was poisoned."

"Poisoned?" Cordelia and I said in unison.

"I'm afraid so."

"Good god." Dr. Briggs rubbed at his forehead. "You're sure?"

The sheriff nodded. "You are welcome to visit Dr. Tate at his infirmary and speak with him."

Dr. Briggs shook his head. "No. That won't be necessary. It's just— This is going to be so hard on Bertha. She is quite ill. I've been treating her for about a year now, and I've seen some encouraging progress. I'm afraid this situation will set her back."

"Oh dear. I'm so sorry," I said.

He took in a deep breath and then let it go. "Well, it is unfortunate, but we must carry on as best we can. Did the doctor say what kind of poison?"

The sheriff shook his head. "No. He hasn't been able to ascertain that yet. The only thing we know for sure is someone wanted Ralph Stewart dead."

Chapter Six

DECEMBER 7, 1885

The following day I dashed off a handful of notes to be delivered to the Winter Festival committee, summoning them for an afternoon meeting. The committee included Cordelia, Andrew, Maggie, Kitty, Sally Dean—who was one of the barmaids at the Bella—Constance Chatterley, and Miss Cynthia Mayes, the local dressmaker and Mr. Archer and Mrs. Stewart's cousin. She had not come to the previous meeting, which, I am afraid, was on account of me.

The woman was still mad and hurt by my implication she'd had something to do with a transgression—well, a crime actually. To be clear, I all but accused her of murder. As I thought back on the whole thing, I cringed. I really did need to handle such things with a bit more care. I had been swept up in the moment trying to help a friend and I had gotten carried away. But that was all behind me now. I would stick to more domestic matters, like running my hotel and returning it to its former glory so that it would be most attractive to a buyer in the late summer, God willing.

Though, I would be lying if I said there weren't things about this town and the community that I found refreshing. I loved the way the sun rose over the mountains, casting a sparkling glow over the businesses and homes nestled in the little valley. La Plata Springs was cocooned in glorious views of majestic snowcapped peaks. I liked the way people here supported one another, offered a helping hand to those in need. Even though I still felt like an outsider for the most part, the majority of the people here had been kind to me— once I had cleared my name of murder when I'd first arrived. It also helped that I'd stopped a trio of swindlers who'd come to town intent on stealing the fortunes of rich men. But that's a story for another day.

As I was jotting off the last note, Percival appeared in the mirror. "So, poor Ralph Stewart was murdered."

I nodded. "He was, I'm afraid."

"Ugly business. Are you going to put your keen and newfound sleuthing skills to task?"

Having to support my mother and myself when I was a child was something that had made me strong and, I'll admit, a bit hard around the edges. Yet, it instilled in me a work ethic and gave me a sense of self-worth. The problem was, it also instilled a fear in me that if I didn't work in that world, the world of performing, then what was I good for? I believed my husband had known this about me, and though I had railed against the conditions of my inheritance, I was beginning to see why he had done it. While it was tempting to take on the investigation—to direct my energies into proving to myself I was worthy of the praise I had received in solving the previous crimes—I knew I shouldn't. I had to focus on the hotel. And the upcoming Winter Festival, should we continue with it, which I hoped we would.

I shook my head. "No. I think I'll leave that to Clayton. I have enough on my plate at the moment."

"You mean the festival? I thought you dreaded the prospect."

"Not exactly, Percival." I was annoyed at his assuming I dreaded my part in it. "It's true the task was one more thing put upon me, and while I normally would be indignant about the matter, instead I find myself a little intimidated . . . but challenged . . . and dare I say, excited."

"Excited?" He gave me a droll smile. "My, my."

"Don't tease me. I like the opportunity for accomplishment. It lights me up from the inside."

"Solving a murder is a substantial accomplishment," he stated matter-of-factly.

"Yes, I know. But it's really not my job. It is the sheriff's, and he doesn't like it when I— Well, anyway, I need to focus on the festival and the hotel."

"I see." His tone was still in jest, but I knew he meant no harm. He liked to banter with me.

"Besides, in its own way, the festival harkens back to my life in New York."

"Really? How so?"

"You see, because I missed out on the season's festivities every year in my childhood, I always hosted a large gala at our manse this time of year. I did it big, making up for those lost magical times. Our home was filled with everyone from business associates to theater people to families in the neighborhood. It was the most talked about party of the year."

"I have no doubt, Arabella."

"So I want to do the same here. It won't be as grand or as fancy, but I aim to make it beautiful and fun for those poor orphaned children. Solving murder is off the table for me right now."

As I said the words, I hoped Clayton would soon get to the bottom of the awful crime, as the festival was in a week's time.

Percival and I were interrupted by a knock on the door. He popped out of sight.

I opened it to see Maggie standing there. "The committee has gathered in your office in the annex, Mrs. Pryce."

"Thank you, Maggie."

I followed her downstairs. When we reached my office, all were assembled. The room was not large. Unlike the other little two-room houses in the annex and Kitty's two-storied ones, this particular unit was a single. When I'd inherited it after the death of the previous manager, I had removed the small bed and replaced it with a settee and two armchairs. I also had a couple of straight-backed chairs placed next to the small wood-burning stove. I kept the modest pine desk and chair and the oak filing cabinet. Two additional chairs had been brought in for Maggie and me.

The diminutive size of the room and the bodies occupying it greatly helped the wood-burning stove to heat the room. It was nearly stifling.

"Good morning," I said.

The mood of the group was subdued, naturally, owing to the news of poor Mr. Stewart.

"Are we going to continue with the festival?" Miss Mayes asked, her back straight and rigid as a ramrod.

I sat down. "That is what we are here to discuss." I, of course, wanted to continue, but I needed to make sure we were all on the same page.

"We must go forward with it," Andrew said. "It's what

Ralph would have wanted. He looked forward to the festival every year." His sun-kissed face was all eagerness and concern. The only male member of the committee, Andrew had taken on the role of my silent co-chair. He was in charge of the parade and the annual holiday play. He, like Mr. Stewart apparently, was passionate about the event. I was grateful for his participation and advice, as he had been a member of the festival committee for the last five years.

"And it means so much to the children," Sally Dean added. Sally, one of Kitty's former "sporting girls," had recently left that occupation when she became the sweetheart of Mr. Everett Emerson, the manager of Archer's Dry Goods. There were rumors the couple were about to become engaged.

"We mustn't disappoint the children of St. Anne's," she said. "This is the only time of year the sisters can bring them. It coincides with the annual visit of other nuns from their order in New Mexico. They have the extra help to travel with the children."

I wholeheartedly agreed we couldn't disappoint the children, but I wanted to hear from the rest of the group. "Well, then," I said. "What does everyone else think?"

"I think we should move forward. It would be good for the community," Kitty said. "It would give everyone something positive to focus on. It's awful what happened to Ralph, but why should the rest of La Plata Springs be pulled down into the mess? Isn't the season about hope, charity, and—"

"Love," Maggie interrupted. "We should honor our love for Mr. Stewart by continuing with the festival."

I smiled. Maggie was not one to assert herself so readily. She was shy and quiet but had found a new part of herself with her elevated role at the hotel. It pleased me to no end.

"Anyone else?" I asked.

No one said a word. Not even Constance Chatterley, which was highly unusual. In fact, she seemed a bit subdued, which was also not in character for her.

"All right, then. Let's put it to a vote. All in favor of marching forward with the festival?"

All hands were raised.

"Wonderful!" I said. "Now, what should we discuss first? Miss Mayes, how are things going with the other shopkeepers? Is there anything needed for the Shops' Crawl?" I asked her first because I was endeavoring to break the ice.

She opened her mouth to say something when the sheriff and Archibald Archer, both men of some size, squeezed into the room.

"Excuse the interruption." Clayton took his hat off and smoothed his hair. "But we'd like to have a word."

"Of course," I said.

"I know you've all worked hard, but I believe we should cancel the festival," Mr. Archer said. My heart sank.

Andrew jumped up from his chair. "What? But why? Ralph would have wanted us to continue."

He sighed, giving his nephew a sideways glance. "Perhaps. But Ralph is gone. It is for the sake of his mother and his wife. They are distraught."

Andrew placed his hands on his hips and let out an irritated breath. "Mary Alice has never been supportive of the festival. Or anything Ralph was passionate about."

I noticed Mr. Archer did not make eye contact with his nephew.

"I'm surprised Bertha would want to cancel," Miss Mayes said. "She was always so indulgent with her son, and she knew what this meant to him."

Mr. Archer nodded. "Understandably, she is not herself.

I'm disappointed, too. But I'm not sure it's appropriate to have a celebration when Ralph is dead and his murderer is roaming free."

"Please, Uncle," Andrew implored. "Give the sheriff a chance to find the culprit. The festival will be a meaningful homage to Ralph."

"All right," he said on a sigh. "But if the murderer is not brought to justice in the next few days, I'm afraid we will have to wait until next year for the festival. I won't bring those children here as long as there is any threat of danger."

I certainly understood the reason for this deadline, and the children's safety was paramount. I sighed with resignation. The committee had been working on the festival for some weeks now. I enjoyed our meetings. The members of the committee were getting to know me, and I them, and I relished the feeling of unity among us. It was comfortable, familiar, like I was at my theater among our band of actors. But, alas, if the murderer was not found, it looked like it was about to end.

Chapter Seven

Clayton and Mr. Archer exited the office, leaving a somber silence in their wake.

Andrew looked particularly aggrieved.

"I'm so sorry, Andrew," I said, keenly commiserating with his disappointment.

He shook his head. "This isn't right. My aunt would want us to go on. I know it. If nothing less than to promote the town for tourism. It's what Ralph wanted, and it's what my aunt and my uncle want. This is Mary Alice's doing."

"Why would she want to cancel the festival?"

"She doesn't care about La Plata Springs. She just wants to get back to her socialite life in California."

"My, that's a rather harsh statement. She's just lost her husband," Kitty said.

"She didn't care about him, either. Their marriage was arranged by their families. It was a business union. She needed his money, and my aunt needed her father's political contacts."

"Is her father a politician?" I asked.

"No. He's— Well, he's . . . he's just got connections, shall we say."

"Oh, I see." That sounded a bit ominous, but I didn't want to pry.

"But what about the orphans?" Sally asked.

At her words, Andrew gave Maggie a knowing glance, and she returned it with a sympathetic smile. I wondered at the exchange.

"Hopefully, the sheriff will find out who killed Ralph, and we can push forward," Cordelia said. "If that is what the family wants."

"Yes," I said. "But, for now, I think we need to put our planning on hold. I don't want you to take time away from your businesses if we have to cancel the festival."

"We've accomplished a great deal so far," Sally said with some eagerness. "If we don't have to cancel, it won't be too difficult to catch up."

"Quite right." I smiled, appreciating her optimism.

I then adjourned the meeting.

Kitty and Sally got up from their chairs and left the room, but Andrew, Maggie, Cordelia and Miss Mayes stayed behind. Constance, who still remained oddly quiet, was about to follow Kitty and Sally out of the room. I was a little worried about her after what she'd witnessed yesterday.

"Constance," I called after her, "can I have a word?"

She gave a nod, and I indicated with a tilt of my head for us to step outside. It had begun to snow again so we stayed under the cover of the portico.

"Are you feeling better?" I asked. "You know, after the turn you took at the party last night?"

Her smile did not reach her usually merry eyes. "Yes. Yes, I am quite restored."

"Are you sure?"

"Absolutely!"

I wondered what she was thinking about her vision of Percival. Had she put it out of her mind, or did she fear what the implications might be if she could actually see someone who'd passed on?

"But about what you said you saw——"

She laughed. "Oh, that! Too much wine, that's what that was. I must have let the rumors about the hotel being haunted get into my brain. How silly! I would have to be mad to have seen a ghost, right? And I am certainly not that!" She tapped her finger on her temple. "Solid as a rock. Just like you. I mean, you're here all the time and I'm sure you've never seen . . ." She looked eagerly into my face.

Not knowing what to say, I returned the laugh. "Goodness, silly indeed! Isn't it funny how these kinds of rumors get started? Well, I am glad you are feeling better."

Relieved I had somehow managed to avert the subject, and that she had chalked up her experience of Percival to succumbing to rumor and over imbibing, I began to relax.

"Yes. Too bad about the possibility of cancelling the festival," she continued. "Interesting what Andrew said about Mary Alice. I wouldn't be surprised if it's Bertha who wants to call the whole thing off."

"But Andrew said she was indulging Mr. Stewart's wishes."

"Yes, she might have been, but she's never been very supportive of Archie—er—I mean, Archibald and his vision for La Plata Springs."

Had she just called him Archie? I'd never heard him referred to as Archie before.

"Why not?" I asked.

"I'm not sure. But he said as much once."

"I see. Well, it's not important who wanted it or not.

The matter is now out of our hands. Hopefully, justice will prevail. And soon."

"Yes," she said. "Well, I'm off. Have a good day, Arabella."

As she left, Miss Mayes, Cordelia, and Maggie came out from the office.

"I'd better get back to work," Maggie said.

"Me too," said Cordelia.

"Yes, I believe I'll join you," I said.

Miss Mayes was about to walk past me when I stopped her. "Thank you, Miss Mayes. I appreciate you being on the committee. I hope we will be able to continue to work together, either this year or next."

Her nose haughtily in the air, she eyed me up and down. I put on my warmest smile and her countenance softened a little.

"Yes. Me too."

Well, that's something. It might take some time to mend this little fence.

I noticed Andrew had not come out of the office. I bid Miss Mayes goodbye and then stepped back into the room. "Everything all right, Andrew?"

"No!" he said, rubbing his forehead. "Things could not be more wrong."

"I'm so sorry about Mr. Stewart. It must be terrible to have lost your cousin."

He shook his head. "We were more than just cousins; we were friends. Good friends. Even though we lived in different states, we always kept in touch. Wrote letters regularly."

"You will miss him."

"More than you know."

"Was this festival truly that important to him?"

He nodded. "Yes. And we must find a way to continue with it."

I bit my lip. Andrew's grief seemed to hold him hostage to this festival.

"I'm upset about all of this too, Andrew, but for now, it's out of our hands," I said.

"It *has* to happen!" He raised his voice, making me flinch. "I'm sorry." He held up a hand in apology. "It's just — Well, there's more at stake than just the festival."

I blinked, not getting his meaning.

His gaze bored into mine. "You have to find Ralph's murderer so that we can continue with the festival."

"Me? Andrew, the sheriff—"

"Please. You're good at this. Since you've come to town, you've solved three murders. I know you can do it. You and the sheriff work well together. He as much as said so to me after you caught those swindlers."

I opened my eyes wide, taken aback by this declaration. The sheriff had wanted me nowhere near any of those cases. "He did?"

"Well, he said you were tenacious."

"Oh." I wasn't sure if that was good or bad in the eyes of the sheriff. "Andrew, what is at stake if the festival doesn't happen?"

He rubbed the stubble on his chin and then went over to one of the chairs and sat down. He placed his elbows on his knees and then his head in his hands.

"Andrew?" I sat down in the chair next to him.

He raised his head and looked me in the eye. "The welfare of a child and his mother are at stake."

"What? What child?"

"Ralph's child."

I pulled my chin back in surprise. "Mr. Stewart has a child?"

"Yes."

"I see." I wasn't sure where he was going with this or what it had to do with the festival, but I remained silent to give him room to continue if he wished.

He didn't.

"Andrew, I need to understand why you are asking me to do this."

"He's one of the orphans."

"He's an orphan? But—" Obviously, this was not Mrs. Edwards-Stewart's child.

"Ralph just recently found out about the child," he said in a whisper. "I've known for some time."

"Is the mother dead? Is that why the child is at St. Anne's?"

"No. She's alive."

I heaved a sigh. Speaking with Andrew was akin to speaking with Percival, who could be very cagey and cryptic. I decided to pursue a line of inquiry. "She's not able to care for the child?"

"Correct."

I tried to put the pieces together but still didn't have enough information.

"If Mr. Stewart didn't know about the child, how did you know about him . . . or her?"

He looked over at me. "The child's mother. She confided in me because I am—was—so close to Ralph. I really shouldn't be telling you this, but I don't know what to do. The mother and the child should be together. She wanted Ralph to meet their son, if for nothing more than to persuade him to give her some financial support so that she could have her son back."

"But now that he's gone?"

He pulled in a deep breath. "I was hoping to appeal to my aunt. She wanted Ralph to have an heir so much, to continue the family line and secure the business. If she could meet this boy—"

"Who is this woman? Is she in town?"

He sighed but hesitated in answering my question, which led me to believe she was. Had she been at the party? There were a bevy of young women surrounding Mr. Stewart that night, mostly Kitty's girls vying for his attention. Could it have been one of them?

And then I remembered the young woman who he and Andrew had been speaking with: Victoria Clement. She'd thrown a drink in his face that night. Had she told him about the child? Had he reacted poorly?

"Is it Victoria Clement?"

He sniffed. "See? You are good at this."

I shook my head. "Guessing the mother of the child is nothing like solving a murder."

"I know," he said resignedly. "But please . . . Won't you help me?"

"Why don't you just tell your aunt about the child?"

"No. She wouldn't believe me . . . and she didn't approve of Ralph's patronage of Victoria and her art. If only she could see the boy. Victoria said he looks just like Ralph. It's proof of his parentage."

"You could take your aunt to the orphanage."

"Briggs wouldn't allow it. She's too ill. The only way to get there is by coach, and the trip would be too arduous. They traveled here by private railcar. I offered to take Victoria to St. Anne's to retrieve the boy, but without significant proof that Victoria can provide for him, the nuns won't permit her to remove him from their care. The only way is for the child to come to the festival with the other children . . . who are all in need of some happiness. If just for a day. Please help me find Ralph's murderer so the festival can go on as planned."

I sighed. I felt for Andrew, and the child and his mother, but I had nearly gotten myself killed solving the previous murders. I was finally making some headway with the refurbishing of the hotel, and I now had a few months less than a year, if all went well with the repairs, before I could get back to my life in New York. And I was quite enjoying my new friendship with the sheriff. Did I really want to take the chance of ruining it?

"I'm sorry, Andrew. I just can't."

Chapter Eight

DECEMBER 8, 1885

The following afternoon, I sat at my desk trying to work, but my conscience poked at me for refusing Andrew's plea. It also pulled at my heartstrings that Mr. Stewart's son might not be able to meet his grandmother.

But what if Andrew was wrong, and instead of enfolding the child in her arms, she rejected him? I didn't know the elder Mrs. Stewart at all, but at first glance, she seemed rather cold. And what about Mrs. Edwards-Stewart? Presenting the family with her husband's illegitimate son would just be rubbing salt into a wound.

At any rate, it was none of my business. It wouldn't do to insert myself into a family scandal.

I tried my best to set aside my thoughts and deal with the issue of the hotel's bills. The corner of one was sticking out from the pile and caught my eye. It was from Billings Building and Co. Looking at it made my stomach turn. The company had filed a lien against the hotel for services not paid. Not paid by the former manager, mind you. When my dearly departed husband left me with the hotel, allowing for only a small stipend from his estate to keep it operational, he did not know about the lien. I had been able to persuade the executor of the estate, Mr. Tisdale, to allow me a little more money against my inheritance to start paying it off, but the amount was akin to a trickle, and it was going to take some time. I needed to wait until I received the full inheritance to pay everything off.

In the meantime, I would do my best to keep the building from falling into complete disrepair. The projects at hand were the porticos in the annex. Unfortunately, I might have to wait until the spring to fully replace them because we could not seem to go an entire week without snow. I should have seen to this in the fall, but truth be told, the snow had started early.

For now, we would have to continue fortifying them against the weather as best we could until it cleared. I'd had a carpenter build some T-beams to buttress them in the most damaged areas, lest anyone find themselves under a pile of rubble. It looked ghastly, but it wouldn't do to risk injury to the guests. Thankfully, Kitty's part of the annex had the least damage, so that could wait.

I spent a couple of hours going over the accounts and the bills. My eyes bleary from strain, I decided to go to the saloon to get some lunch. As I was locking the door to my office, Mr. Pettyjohn came through the door leading to the hotel.

"Mrs. Pryce, have you seen Sheriff Marshall? Mrs. Stewart is asking after him."

I set the keys in my pocket. "No. Not since the committee meeting yesterday. Have you checked his office?"

"Yes. I had Clarence go to fetch him, but the building was locked up tight."

"Oh. Well, perhaps he is about town working on the case?"

Mr. Pettyjohn sighed. "No one has seen him."

I put a hand on his shoulder. "I wouldn't worry about it. He'll turn up, I'm sure. Maybe he went to his house for something."

As I said the words I realized I did not know where Clayton lived. It had not come up in any of our conversations. I assumed he did not live in town.

"Do you know where he lives?" I asked.

He nodded. "Yes. He lives in a log cabin down by the river, just north of town. Lovely spot."

I recalled how much Clayton loved to fish. In fact, he'd been fishing when we'd first met. I chuckled remembering how he'd dragged me from the river like a drowning cat.

"Have you had Clarence check his home?"

The tips of his black, caterpillar brows pressed down toward the bridge of his nose. "Clarence is needed at the hotel. I can't have him traipsing about all day. The sheriff lives too far away."

"Well, hopefully he'll be back soon." I was about to brush past him when he reached out and touched my elbow.

"Mrs. Stewart is quite insistent upon seeing him."

"Well, she'll have to wait."

"That would not be a good idea. She is quite . . . . Well, it's prudent not to provoke her."

"Mr. Pettyjohn, I—we—are not the sheriff's keepers. I'm sure he's attending to important business."

He cleared his throat. "She could make things . . . uncomfortable for us. The hotel is already on shaky ground, and I would hate to give her any reason to be unhappy with us. She wields a lot of power in the community . . . and beyond."

"I thought this was Mr. Archer's town."

He raised his brows and then looked around conspiratorially, as if making sure he would not be heard. He leaned closer and lowered his voice. "Yes, but she has a, well, shall we say, vested interest. I should also note it is her desire to raise the status of the General. I heard her talking with Mr. Archer. Not only do they plan to refurbish the place but she wants to expand. They have plans to add on to the existing building. That will put it in direct competition with the Arabella. They want to bring more tourism into La Plata Springs. And she is adamant her son's killer is found. And soon. I'm afraid since he died at the hotel, there may be repercussions if—"

"Oh dear. Right." This would not be good at all. I was working so hard to return this hotel to her former glory, and any kind of taint would impact her future. And mine, competing hotel or not.

"Very well. I'll go find the sheriff. Please send for Mr. Ellis and the coach."

My musings about Mr. Stewart and the festival continued as the coach made its way out of town. The sun shone brightly this afternoon, and the snow-laden landscape sparkled like a jewel, but it did nothing to distract me from my thoughts.

Mr. Pettyjohn's statement in regard to Mrs. Stewart's power was surprising to me. While it made sense she was the matriarch of the family with her steely demeanor and intimidating glare, I had assumed her role in the family was merely that of a figurehead and did not extend to the business side of things. I suppose it was because of her frailty and the illness Dr. Briggs spoke of.

My impression had been that La Plata Springs was Mr. Archer's town, and he controlled nearly everything that went on here. The Arabella was one of the few businesses, if not the only business, that did not have an association with him. I suppose that put me in the minority. A lone holdout.

A shiver snaked up my spine, and it wasn't from the cold. I shook it off and turned my attention to the beautiful scenery outside the window. The town had dropped behind us, and the coach made its way along the ribbon of road that followed the river. I marveled at the stillness and silence of the landscape. Only the horse pulling the carriage made any sort of noise. His hooves thudded against the carpet of snow, and the sound of his rhythmic breath lulled me into a serenity I had never experienced before coming to Colorado. My gaze settled on the tall white stalks of the Aspens, which stood out among the pine trees. The boulders along the river's edge were covered in snow, resembling large and misshapen marshmallow confections. My mouth watered at the remembrance of the sweet treat I'd first experienced in France as a young woman.

We soon came upon a cabin nestled in a thicket of forest. It was modest in size but had a marvelous wraparound porch. In a little corral behind the house, which was attached to a small barn, the sheriff's horse, Queenie, was pacing the fence line. If Queenie was here, then surely Clayton must be here. But why was there was no smoke coming from the chimney on such a cold afternoon?

Mr. Ellis helped me down from the coach. He was a sturdy man in his fifties with a ruddy complexion, a head of thick, sandy-blond hair with gray at the temples and a sprinkling of gray in his grizzled beard.

I carefully picked my way through the snow until we reached the porch. As I stepped up, Mr. Ellis knocked on the door. I pulled my shawl tighter around my shoulders.

There was no answer.

"Must be out in the barn," Mr. Ellis said.

We stepped off the porch and headed back to the barn. Seeing us, Queenie stopped her pacing and let out a low nicker. Her eyes were wide with apprehension, which was unusual, because the mare often looked like she was about to fall asleep.

"Sheriff!" Mr. Ellis yelled.

"Here!" came a muffled response. "I'm in here!"

We hurried into the barn. Clayton was on the ground near a large pile of hay. A stout ceiling beam lay across his legs and on top of him as a gaping hole let in the cold. Small piles of snow that had fallen from the trees and littered the area. The grayness of his usually sun-kissed complexion contrasted with the garish blue of his lips.

The man was freezing to death.

"Is this really necessary?" Clayton asked Dr. Tate.

At the doctor's suggestion, Clayton had been installed in room fifteen at the Arabella. It only made sense. The poor man couldn't very well be expected to keep the fireplace going in his cabin when he could not walk outside to retrieve wood. And who would cook for him and see that he was properly taken care of? It had been the only sensible solution.

Dr. Tate cast a glance in my direction and then back at

the sheriff. "Clay, your left leg is broken and the other is severely bruised. You won't be on those legs for a while, so you can't be alone in your cabin."

"How long is 'a while'?" he asked.

The doctor lifted a shoulder. "We'll have to see how the right leg heals. You may be able to get around on crutches in a couple of days."

"It's a good thing Mrs. Pryce and Ellis found you when they did," Andrew said.

"I'm just glad you happened to be passing by the sheriff's cabin." I smiled at him. "I don't know how we would have gotten him to town without you."

"The turkey hunt can wait," Andrew said.

"Here we are!" Sally entered the room with a tray of beef stew, a large piece of crusted bread, and a mug of beer. "This will keep you satisfied. Lottie put some extra meat in this portion."

She brought the tray over to the nightstand. Maggie came in next and inspected the area around the wood-burning stove.

"We will need more wood. I will have Clarence or Mr. Johns bring some. We must keep you warm." Mr. Johns was our other bellman who also helped with other tasks around the hotel.

"I'm plenty warm," the sheriff snapped and then winced as he tried to adjust himself in bed. His color had improved at least. The grayness was gone, but a pallidity still lingered. His usually captivating indigo eyes were dulled with pain.

Maggie darted a look at me and frowned, obviously affronted by his sharp response. Sally took her hand and smiled at her.

"I'm sorry, Maggie," Clayton said. "It's just I don't want a fuss. I'm fine."

"You need to stay warm, and you need to keep up your strength," Dr. Tate admonished. "It's the best and fastest way to heal."

"You heard the doctor, Maggie," I said. "You were right. Please have one of the bellmen get some more wood."

She gave a bob of her head and then left the room.

"I'll bring your dinner this evening," Sally said. "You listen to the doctor." She shook her finger at him and followed Maggie out of the room.

"How is your pain at the moment?" the doctor asked him.

"Tolerable," he said with some effort. The man was lying through his teeth.

"Right." Dr. Tate raised his brows dubiously. He opened his medical bag, pulled out a three-inch-tall glass bottle and then addressed me. "To put the plaster cast on his leg, I gave him some morphine, but it's clearly wearing off. Here is some laudanum. Give him a few drops in some water after he eats. It will help him rest."

"I don't need it, Doc. I need to be clearheaded. What about Ralph's murder? What can you tell me about your examination of his body?"

The doctor shook his head. "Not much so far, other than he was poisoned. With what I haven't determined yet. By the time I had arrived on the scene, it was clear he'd been dead for some time based on the body temperature. I'd say five or six hours. That's all I have at the moment. So, in the meantime, you need to rest."

"But what about keeping law and order in the town?" Clayton asked. I noted a hint of helplessness in his voice.

"I'll see if Archer won't finally bring in an officer from

Denver," Dr. Tate said as he packed up his bag. "You let these fine people help you, Clay. Doctor's orders." He looked at me over his spectacles. "I'll be back later to check on the patient."

He departed, leaving only me and Andrew in the room with the sheriff.

"You need to eat something, Clay," I said.

"Fine," he grumbled and tried to push himself up to a sitting position and bit back a yelp. Andrew rushed to help him.

Once Andrew got him comfortably propped up, I set the tray on his lap. "Is this all right?" I worried about the weight on his legs, even though the injuries were farther down.

"Yes." He didn't make eye contact with me. "Thank you."

"You're welcome."

I knew it was hard for him to be in such a vulnerable position. He was in charge of keeping the town and all its inhabitants safe, and he took great pride in his job. It must have rankled to be completely helpless now.

"I'll be back in a few minutes to give you your laudanum."

I stepped out of the room and was about to close the door, but Andrew was right behind me. We stepped out together.

"This is *not* good," he said.

"I know," I agreed. "The festival is supposed to take place next week. Hopefully, your uncle will get a deputy here quickly."

He shook his head. "It won't be easy. As you know, the Denver police department is stretched. The population over there is booming. They need all the officers they can get. My grandmother is not a patient woman, Arabella. She wants the killer put to justice. And there's something else . . . something that might complicate things."

"What is it?" I asked, not liking the tone of his voice.

"She's called on an old friend of the family's—and yours—to write a story about the Winter Festival, and now that Ralph has been murdered . . ."

I sucked in a breath. "No," I said through the exhale, fearing the worst. "You don't mean—"

"I'm afraid so. She's contacted Atticus Brooks. He's currently in Arizona working on a story about the Pueblo Indians. He's due to arrive any day."

I set my hands on my hips to steady myself. Atticus Brooks was no less than my arch nemesis. He was a theater critic who was now writing stories of the American West. In the past, and possibly now, it seemed he'd made it his mission in life to ruin me. The fact that Mr. Stewart had come to his demise in *my* hotel under *my* watch would be delicious fodder for the hack writer. During his previous stay, he had delighted in the accusations of murder against me. He wrote about it and sold the story to none other than Mr. Rankin, the same editor who'd been publishing my stories of my life in Colorado. Thankfully, the smarmy Brooks had to retract his story, as it was wildly inaccurate, but I feared the damage to my carefully guarded image had been done.

I took in another deep breath and let it out. Mr. Pettyjohn was right about Mrs. Stewart possibly making things uncomfortable for us, especially now that the rat Atticus Brooks was coming to town. If the Arabella became known as a murderous hotel, then it was finished. Archer would have the leverage he needed to buy it. As much as I desired to leave the hotel and La Plata Springs, I didn't want my stay to end that way. I couldn't let that happen to

William's memory. He loved this hotel. I needed to leave it in better condition than when I arrived: proud and strong, and able to withstand any kind of competition.

"Arabella?" Andrew brought me out of my thoughts. "What do you say? Will you investigate the murder of my cousin now?"

I bit my lip, hesitating. As Andrew mentioned, it would be some time before an officer might arrive, if one arrived at all. Clayton was laid up for who knew how long, and with Atticus Brooks coming to town, the Arabella's good reputation was at stake.

I gave a firm nod. "Yes. I absolutely will. But you will need to tell me everything you know about Mr. Stewart and who might want to kill him."

Chapter Nine

Andrew and I agreed to meet upstairs in my rooms in an hour's time.

I went back to room fifteen to check on Clayton. I was glad to find he'd eaten most of the food and had drunk half of the beer. His color was still off and pain still dimmed his eyes, but at least he'd had an appetite.

"I'm glad you enjoyed the meal." I took the tray from his lap and set it on the night table. I pulled the chair from the desk up to his bedside.

"Thank you," he said. "I was hungrier than I thought." He shifted his position in the bed and winced.

"It's probably been awhile since you've eaten. How long were you stuck under those beams?"

"Overnight. I had gone out to feed Queenie and—" His eyes clouded with concern. "Queenie. Is someone taking care of her?"

I gave him an assuring smile. "Mr. Parkhurst went out to your place to get her. He'll be taking care of her at the livery until you are better."

He let out a sigh of relief. "Good. I know she is in good hands with Bob."

"You needn't worry about anything," I said. "You need all your energy to get better. Oh, I almost forgot." I pulled the bottle of laudanum from my pocket. "Time for your medicine."

He held up a hand. "It'll make me sleepy."

"That's the point," I said. "Rest will help you heal. And you look like you're in pain."

"I don't want the medicine. I can handle the pain." He shifted again and then growled, his body making a liar out of him.

"I can see that." I went to the bureau where Maggie had brought a pitcher of water and a glass. I filled the glass half full of water and administered the prescribed dose of ten drops.

I then went back to the bed and held out the glass to him. His annoyance at his helpless situation was evident from the furrowed set of his brow.

"Don't look at me that way," I teased. "Drink up." I took his hand and set it around the glass. Our eyes met, and a thread of heat passed through us. The tension in his brow relaxed, and by the way he looked at me, I could tell he'd felt it, too.

Startled, I pulled my hand away and cleared my throat. "I'm not leaving until you take this medicine," I said quietly.

He managed a small smile and held me in that captivating blue gaze. "So, if I don't take it, that means you'll stay? I guess that's not so bad. I enjoy your company."

My breath caught in my throat. Even in his pained and injured state, the man could still manage to send tingles up my spine with a touch, a few words, or a meaningful glance. In the last few weeks, we had been spending more time together—only for the sake of the riding lessons he was giving me, of course—and I, too, enjoyed his company. More than I cared to admit.

"You heard the doctor." I pointed to the glass, needing to break this thread between us in order to collect myself. I couldn't let my feelings get away with me. "Down the hatch."

With a roll of his eyes, he drank and then handed the glass back to me. I set it on the tray atop the night table. He reached back to adjust one of the pillows and grimaced.

"Here, let me." I took hold of his elbow, and he took hold of mine as I helped him sit forward so that I could adjust the pillows behind him.

"There you go. Comfortable?"

He gave a reluctant nod. "I'll need to question the guests about the night of Ralph's murder. You'll have to bring them to me."

I was not at all surprised he would want to continue the investigation. He was not a man who would be put off easily, even if he was temporarily crippled and in serious pain.

"You need to rest, Clay. You heard Dr. Tate. He's going to ask Mr. Archer to hire a deputy."

I, of course, refrained from telling him I would be investigating. It would only upset him.

He laid his head back onto the pillow and his eyes grew heavy. The laudanum was taking effect.

"I need to know what is going on concerning the case." His voice was thick, his words mashing together.

"Yes, yes." I brushed his hair from his eyes. "But for now, sleep."

His breathing deepened, and his eyes closed. In seconds, he was off in dreamland.

I stood, watching him. My heart grew light with the mere sight of his handsome face. I could have stood there for hours looking at him. I had never allowed my eyes to really linger on his strong jaw, the full kissable lips under his neatly trimmed mustache, the curve of his chiseled cheek-bones. When he set that mesmerizing blue gaze on me, it took every ounce of my resolve not to melt in his presence. I couldn't let myself go there. I would not give in to these feelings that threatened to make me weak. My stay here was only temporary. Why embark on something that would only cause sorrow later? I'd had too much pain in my life. I wouldn't risk more.

The sound of someone clearing their throat startled me. It came from near the window. Percival had appeared in the full-length oval mirror standing next to it, arms crossed over his chest and a rather annoyed expression on his face. His presence reignited old anxieties.

"A new guest," he said flatly.

"Yes," I said, looking down at Clayton once again, hoping he would not rouse and hear me, but it was evident he was completely unconscious. Still, I didn't want to take any chances. The good sheriff was indeed in a vulnerable state, and though Percival had claimed Clayton would not be receptive of the presence of a spiritual entity, I didn't want to take the chance. The fewer people who knew about Percival, the better. Especially now with the threat of Atticus Brooks coming to town.

"I don't want you in here," I said. "No funny business, Percival."

He only responded by holding up his hands in mock surrender.

"Let's go to my rooms," I suggested. I wanted to ask him about Cristoforo Valdez. Based on Mr. Valdez's accusation against Mr. Stewart and the threat he'd issued in regard to the matter not being over, it seemed he might have a motive for murder.

As I mounted the stairs leading up to my rooms, I picked up the watch pendant I wore on a long chain around my neck. Andrew was not due to arrive for another fifteen minutes.

I entered the parlor to find Cordelia at the desk working at something. Probably some of my correspondence. I couldn't speak with Percival with her present. I wished I'd thought of that before when I'd told him to meet me here.

"Is the sheriff all settled in?" she asked cheerily.

"Yes. He's asleep."

"Good for him. Sleep is the best cure for injury."

"Cordelia, I've asked Andrew to meet me up here to discuss the festival. He'll be here in fifteen minutes or so. Would you mind getting us some refreshments from the kitchen?"

She smiled. "Lottie is trying her hand at making scones. They are quite good. Would you like me to bring some?"

"Please. That sounds wonderful." That would give me enough time to speak with Percival before Andrew showed up and Cordelia returned.

She left the room, and I sat down on the love seat in front of the bay window. Bijou left her bed and joined me, crawling onto my lap.

A blanket of coolness filled the room, accompanied by the fragrant scent of pipe smoke. Percival's transparent form materialized before me. Bijou barked.

"Can she see you?" I asked. "She is always startled and barks when you're around."

"Not necessarily," he said. "She is very attuned to your emotions and physiology. I don't believe she can see me, but she definitely senses a shift in you, and perhaps in the atmosphere."

I rubbed her head and then ran a silky ear through my fingers. "It's all right my little *chouchou.*" She rested her head on my thigh.

"You wanted to see me? Away from the sleeping sheriff?" His tone was slightly sharp. He was probably upset with me for telling him to stay out of Clayton's room, but I had to take precautions.

I decided to ignore his moodiness and proceed. "What do you know about Enrique and Cristoforo Valdez?"

He moved over to the bay window and gazed outside. "I've already told you what I know. I first met Enrique at a party at Archer's ranch."

"Yes, that was the night before you died. You said something about a woman . . . ."

"Right. Having seen her again, I remember. It was Bertha Stewart. She was there. She had that charming secretary with her then, too."

"Cherrie Fontaine."

"Yes. That's it."

"Did Mrs. Stewart and her son come to La Plata Springs often?"

He turned from the window and joined me on the love seat. "No, actually. Only for the festival . . . and that one other time that I know of, that is. So, you asked what I know. Not much."

"At the party, the sheriff said something about a feud between the Stewarts and Enrique Valdez, involving another mining business in La Linda. There was some kind of accident and Enrique withdrew his investment. Do you know anything about that?"

He shook his head. "Only that there was an accident, and Boss and Ralph were partnered with Enrique in the concerns of the La Linda mines."

"Yes," I said absently. "I will have to speak with Cristoforo about the matter, I suppose, but I need to be careful how I go about it."

"Andrew will be here soon," Percival said. "He might know something. You might also inquire with Cynthia Mayes and Constance Chatterley. They have been here since La Plata Springs was founded. Miss Mayes is part of their family, and I've heard that the Chatterbox and Mr. Archer were sweethearts at the time."

"Constance and Mr. Archer? I never would have thought." It seemed an odd pairing, but who was I to judge? "How interesting."

There was a knock on the door, and Percival vanished.

It was Andrew. Behind him, stood Victoria Clement.

"Come in," I said, a little surprised she had come.

"Thanks for agreeing to do this, Mrs. Pryce. You remember Victoria."

"Yes, come in."

Cordelia came up the stairs behind them holding the tea tray and scones. "Oh, hello. I didn't know you'd be here, Miss Clement. I'll get another teacup—"

"Not necessary," Andrew said. "I appreciate the gesture, but I'm not a tea drinker. Victoria can have mine. Besides, unfortunately, I can't stay long. My uncle needs me over at the General."

"Well, you can have a scone or three. I brought plenty of them." Cordelia set the tray, complete with a heaping plate of somewhat misshapen scones, a teapot, and three teacups and saucers down on the desk. I supposed Lottie was still working on mastering the dough for the scones.

"All right, then," I said. "Let's sit down and figure out best where to begin." Andrew and Miss Clement took the love seat, and I dragged the desk chair over, leaving one of the two armchairs for Cordelia once she finished serving our tea.

"I'd like to tell you how much I appreciate you helping my boy, Charlie." A smile lifted Miss Clement's lips as she said his name. "It is my hope that Mrs. Stewart will honor Ralph's obligation to him and that we may be together."

Cordelia shot me a questioning glance. I hadn't yet had the chance to tell her about the young boy. I gave her a quick shake of my head, signaling I would tell her about it later. Without missing a beat, she seemed to understand my meaning.

"You're welcome," I said. "But I'm afraid we have a lot of work cut out for us. And I make no guarantees. I'm not a professional detective, Miss Clement."

"I understand." She gave me a tight-lipped smile and sipped at her tea. "And please, call me Victoria."

I nodded, then continued. "I thought we should start with Mr. Cristoforo Valdez because of his accusation against Mr. Stewart for playing a part in his brother's death. Do you know anything about this allegation, Andrew?"

"I know there was bad blood between Enrique Valdez and my uncle and Ralph. Before my uncle developed this town, he and Ralph had attempted to grow another mining camp in La Linda. They had partnered with Enrique."

"But there was an accident," I said.

"Right."

"What happened?"

"There was an explosion. The mine collapsed."

"That's horrible!" Cordelia exclaimed.

"How many were killed?" I asked.

"About a dozen men."

I sighed and shook my head. Horrible indeed. "What happened after that?"

He had a mouthful of scone and held up a finger while he finished chewing. "They abandoned the project. My uncle's involvement with the railroad had become more demanding, and his time was needed there. A few years later, in conjunction with the railroad, he started over again, here in La Plata Springs."

"Without Mr. Stewart?"

"Yes. Ralph had gone back to California. One of their gold mines needed managing."

"And what of Valdez?"

"He left. Went back to Mexico. That's all I know."

"I see. Then how did they get to Cristoforo accusing Mr. Stewart of killing his brother?"

He shook his head. "I honestly don't know." He brushed the crumbs of scone from his hands. "I'll do anything I can to help you, Mrs. Pryce. But, for now, I have to go to my uncle. He's in need of my artistic advice for the refurbishing plans for the General."

"Of course," I said with a smile.

"I'll walk you out," Cordelia said. "I need to go to the post office to mail some letters." She grabbed her coat, which was hanging on a coat rack near the desk, and picked up some sealed envelopes I had laid in the stationary box.

I watched them leave the room with a niggle of worry in my stomach. So, what Percival had said was true. Mr. Archer was aiming to put the General in direct competition with the Arabella. He had unlimited resources to do so, and quickly. I would never be able to catch up, and it would be difficult to find a buyer for the Arabella in its current state. I took a deep breath, trying to settle my anxieties. I needed to focus on one thing at a time, and right now, finding Ralph Stewart's murderer took precedence.

I glanced at Victoria. She had produced a handkerchief from her pocket and was wiping tears from her eyes. Bijou had jumped up onto the love seat next to her and settled herself at Victoria's hip.

"Are you all right?" I asked.

She shrugged, reaching over to stroke Bijou's head. "Yes," she said. "I'm sorry. This is just so . . . difficult."

"I'm sure," I said. And then I remembered she had thrown a drink in Mr. Stewart's face at the party. I wondered at the depth of her relationship with him. Was she crying because of his loss? Worry about her son? Worry about her own future?

She stood up to leave. "I won't keep you."

"Please stay a moment," I said. She nodded and sat back down. "I'm sorry for your loss."

She sniffed and gave me a small smile.

"Were you and Mr. Stewart . . . I mean, had you continued to . . . ."

"Yes," she said, her jaw tightening. "We continued to see each other."

"But he didn't know about your son?"

"No. Not until recently."

"Why didn't you tell him earlier? He might have helped support the child."

"Our relationship was . . . tenuous. His mother did not approve of his patronage of the arts, of me. She threatened to cut him off if he continued to support my work. She wanted him focused on the family businesses and on Mary Alice. His mother desperately wanted an heir—a legitimate heir. Ralph was able to slip me some money for my art, but it wasn't enough to support a child. I needed that money. I was afraid if I told him about Charlie, then he would panic and leave me altogether. I'd have been completely destitute."

"But you did end up telling him."

"Not exactly. He found out."

"How?"

"He saw a letter from St. Anne's. It had slipped out of my portfolio. They send me updates on Charlie. It's really so kind of them. They aren't required to . . ."

"So, he put it all together?"

"Yes."

"How did he react?"

She gave me a tentative smile. "Not well, at first. But then he said he would find a way to make it work. He said he was going to leave Mary Alice and we were going to get our son back."

I bit my lip, trying to decide how to proceed. I figured the best way to get answers was to be direct. "But you were angry with him at the party," I stated matter-of-factly. "Why?"

She sighed. "Yes. I was. I thought everything was arranged. But he told me he hadn't broken it off with her yet. The way he was talking, it seemed as if he was getting cold feet. I was scared and angry. I reacted poorly. But then he assured me he was going to do it that night after the party."

"I could see why that would be upsetting." I could also see that if he had indeed told his wife, she might have been very angry about the situation.

Perhaps angry enough to kill.

Chapter Ten

DECEMBER 9, 1885

The next morning, Cordelia and I sat in front of the fireplace, sipping our tea and nibbling on more of Lottie's scones. This particular batch was infused with lemon, and the shape was nearer to perfection.

"So," Cordelia brushed some flour from her fingertips, and then promptly took up another scone. "From what you told me last night, it seems we have a bit of a scandal on our hands with Mr. Stewart, Victoria, and their son, don't we?"

"Yes," I agreed. "Which may also mean we have an additional suspect."

"Right. The betrayed wife."

"But did Mr. Stewart really tell his wife he was leaving her after the party? She departed the party early, and Mr. Stewart and the rest of the Stewart party left quite a bit later. Would Ralph have gone to her room in the dead of night to deliver the bad news or wait 'til morning?"

Bijou leaped off the love seat and ran over to the door.

She then raised herself up on her hind legs and, with her teeth, pulled at the leash that was hanging from the hook next to the door frame, telling us she wanted to go outside.

"Mrs. Edwards-Stewart could have been waiting up for him," Cordelia suggested, taking the leash down. "And then gone to his room when she heard he had returned. Their rooms are right next to each other."

"True," I mused. "I will definitely need to speak with her. But first I want to find Mr. Valdez. He publicly threatened Mr. Stewart."

Bijou let out an impatient yip.

"Okay, girl." Cordelia bent down, rubbed Bijou's head, and then attached the leash to her collar. "Let me get my coat. It's freezing out there."

I glanced over at the window. The snow was coming down heavily. Even though it was late morning, the cloud cover made it seem like nightfall. The yellow glow of the gas streetlamps and light from the shops and businesses illuminated the snow blanketing the street. A lone horse pulling a carriage made its way slowly down the road. All was quiet in La Plata Springs, its inhabitants not yet wanting to emerge from the warmth of their houses. I hoped the weather would clear soon. Sunshine would help to lift the spirits of the bereaved, if only a little.

Cordelia emerged from her bedroom fully clad in a coat, a fur hat, gloves, and her heaviest boots. "We won't be long," she said.

"Be careful." I knelt down and took Bijou's little face in my hands. I planted a kiss on her forehead. "I'll follow you out. I'm going to have a word with Mr. Valdez."

We made our way to the lobby. Bijou, having pulled the leash out of Cordelia's hands, scampered toward the ornate, beveled glass doors at the entrance to the hotel. We both laughed, and Cordelia hurried after her.

I stopped at the front desk where Mr. Pettyjohn was standing in front of the room cubbies distributing mail. "Hello, Mr. Pettyjohn."

He slowly turned around. "Mrs. Pryce. What can I do for you?"

"What room is Mr. Cristoforo Valdez occupying?" I nodded toward the guest book sitting on the counter next to him. He brought it over and flipped through the pages.

"Room eleven, madam."

I flinched at the moniker. *Madam* was a word that brought up my ire. I was not really sure why. It was a term of respect, after all, but for some reason, it evoked the image of an elderly matron, a woman past her prime— someone like Mrs. Bertha Stewart, who was decades my senior. As someone who had always prided myself on my youthful appearance, it rankled. There was also the fact it was how one referred to a woman like Kitty, a procurer of down-on-their-luck girls who'd turned to the oldest profession in the world to survive.

Kitty, I had come to realize, was more of a mother to her girls than the stereotypical hawker of female bodies. But she was an anomaly. At least from what I knew of the trade.

"Very well. Thank you, Mr. Pettyjohn."

I was about to go up the stairs to Mr. Valdez's room when Dr. Tate appeared at the front of the hotel lobby, followed by Miss Cynthia Mayes, who carried a cake tin in her hands. They were both damp from the snow. I quickly went over to help them with their coats.

"Good day," I said to them as they approached the desk. "Miss Mayes, lovely to see you."

"Mrs. Pryce." She gave me a prim smile. She had still

not completely warmed to me, but I could feel the ice melting. "I've come to bring the sheriff some homemade fruitcake."

"How thoughtful of you."

"Would it be possible to bring him some coffee?" she asked. "It tastes best with good, strong coffee."

"She's too modest." Dr. Tate looked over at her appreciatively. "Cynthia's fruitcake needs nothing to enhance its deliciousness. I know from experience."

"I'm sure it doesn't," I said, "but since she has asked, I will see that the sheriff has his coffee."

"How is the patient faring?" Dr. Tate asked.

"He's none too happy about being confined to bed," I said. "He's worried about Mr. Stewart's murder."

The doctor shook his head in dismay. "Unfortunately, on that front, I've not got good news. I've just heard from Archibald. There was an avalanche up north, and I'm afraid it has buried the train tracks. It could be some time before a deputy arrives."

"Oh dear," I said. I worried this news would push Clayton to attempt to get up and around before his body was fully healed. If I could do the work for him, and quickly, then he would have time to recuperate. I wondered if this storm would affect the imminent arrival of Atticus Brooks, too. Though it was doubtful as Andrew said he'd be coming from the west. I frowned. Oh, would that he had been in Denver . . .

"Well, I'm sure he will be glad to see you, nonetheless. You remember, Doctor, he's in room fifteen," I said. "I'll lead the way as I'm going to see Mr. Valdez, and his room is just up the hall from the sheriff's. Miss Mayes, Mr. Pettyjohn will have someone from the kitchen bring the sheriff his coffee." I nodded to the reception clerk.

"Mr. Valdez is in the saloon," he said.

I blinked at him. "Oh. Why didn't you say so earlier?"

"You asked which room he occupied, not where he was at the moment," he said matter-of-factly, as if I should be more careful with my words.

I found Mr. Valdez sitting alone at the bar. The other few patrons were seated at tables, which was much more suitable for playing cards. Soon the place would be full to bursting, given the hour.

"Mr. Valdez?" I approached him. "I'm Arabella Pryce, the owner of the hotel."

He gave me a cursory nod.

"How are you finding the accommodations?" I wanted to blurt out my questions but decided it would be best to take it slowly. I'd never even met the man before.

"They're fine," he said. He gave me the once-over with an appreciative smile. *"Muy bonita."*

Though my Spanish was limited, I knew what he had said was "very pretty." I was fairly certain he was referring to me but proceeded as if he were speaking of the hotel. I caught the eye of Mr. Greer, the bartender. A bear of a man with a rock-solid physique, he could easily be mistaken for a lumberjack with his beefy arms and enormously broad chest. He did not look like a man who made his living standing behind a saloon bar all day.

"Mr. Greer, another for the gentleman," I said. "On the house."

The bartender retrieved an open bottle of whisky and gave him a generous pour.

"Please let me know if there is anything else you require," I said politely.

His coal-dark eyes lingered on my face. "Have a drink with me, *señora.*"

I didn't fancy drinking so early in the day, but I nodded at Mr. Greer to pour me a glass of whisky as well. I much preferred champagne but didn't want Mr. Greer to open a bottle, lest I should have to drink it all so it wouldn't go to waste. I sat down on the barstool next to Mr. Valdez and took a sip from the tumbler. I stifled a cough as the stringent liquid burned my throat.

After I'd recovered, I began my inquiry. "Mr. Valdez, I know your brother passed away in this hotel, before my time here. May I offer you my condolences?"

His glossy black mustache twitched. "You may. *Gracias, señora.*"

"I understand he died of . . . natural causes. Heart failure, was it?"

He scoffed. "So they say."

"But, you don't believe that was the case?"

"*Mi hermano* was in perfect health. *Mi familia tiene longevidad.* My mother lived 'til she was ninety, my father eighty-eight."

"I see. That is a strong line indeed."

"*Sí.* So, no. He did not die of natural causes. That bastard Stewart was responsible for his death."

"My goodness." I put a hand to my chest. He obviously did not remember I had been standing within earshot when he'd made that accusation to the man's face. He'd been in a blind rage. "How can you be certain?"

He shook his head. "If you mean do I have proof, I do not. *Porque* Enrique knew things . . . things *malas para la familia,* things they wanted kept quiet."

I leaned closer to him, keeping my eyes riveted on his. "Really? What kind of things?"

He turned his body to face me, and our knees touched. I refrained from pulling away. I wanted to keep his attention.

"Enrique invested in one of their mines up north. There was a big explosion, and the mine collapsed. Many died."

"Yes, so I've been told."

"The mine was built very quickly. It wasn't safe. They sent workers in there anyway. My brother knew this and tried to stop them. He wanted his community to be safe."

"But he wasn't able to stop them?"

He shook his head. "No. Husbands, sons, fathers died, leaving many in the community without a way to support themselves, and then the old man and Ralph closed the mine and left."

"They didn't do anything to help those left behind?"

His mouth turned downward into a bitter frown. "Nothing. My brother said he was going to investigate the collapse."

"And did he?"

He nodded. "The mine was not built properly. There was not adequate ventilation. Flammable gases build in the mountain. And with the light source—"

"The miners lamps?" I asked.

"*Sí.* It was only a matter of time before there was an explosion. Yet, they continued to send miners into the death trap."

"What happened after the investigation?"

He shrugged. "Nothing."

"What do you mean?"

He shrugged. "My brother was a broken man. They destroyed him."

"So, you came here to . . . ?"

"To make them own up to what they did and to make them—" He stopped himself, shook his head, and took a swig of his whisky.

"To make them pay for Enrique's death?" I ventured.

His jaw flexed, and the hardness in his gaze made my throat catch. I swallowed hard.

"He had a wife and many children. Their means of support died with him. I've tried to help, but I have my own *familia.*"

I lifted my tumbler to my lips. "I could see how that would make you very angry. But why confront them now? It's been well over a year since your brother died."

"*Territorio neutral.* I tried to confront them in California, but I could not get near them. I knew they would be here for the festival, and they would likely not bring their watchdogs."

The glass still raised to my mouth, I took another sip. This time it went down smoother. "I saw you speaking with Mr. Stewart at the party. Did you seek him out later that evening?"

He scoffed again. "Are you asking me if I killed him, *señora?*"

I gave a shrug but didn't answer.

His mustache twitched again, and he looked away from me. "It pains me to say that no, I did not kill him. Though, I wish I had."

I bit my lip, wondering how much I should press. "You were seen on the second-floor landing that night, and your room is on the first floor. Why were you up there?"

He stiffened, caught off guard by my question. He still would not look at me. He then nodded. "*Sí.* I did go up to the second floor."

"To his room?"

He nodded again. "But there was no answer. Someone was in the room with him. A woman. They were arguing. I left, thinking I would have my opportunity later."

"Do you know which woman?"

He turned his face to me and looked me straight in the eye. "No, *señora.*"

"I see. What do you intend to do now?" I asked.

He shrugged. "I will get what Enrique is owed. Even though Ralph is dead, my business with the *familia* is not over."

"So, you're staying?"

"*Sí.*"

"Well, I hope you get what you came for," I said.

His gaze softened and lingered on my face, his lips curving into a slow smile. He lifted his glass. "*Un otro?* I'll buy this time."

"You're too kind." I slid my unfinished glass of whisky to the side. "But I have work to do."

"Pity," he said, giving me the once-over again.

I smiled. "Please let me know if there is anything we can do to make your stay more comfortable."

He held his glass up with a questioning look in his eye. Getting his meaning, I caught the attention of Mr. Greer. "Another drink for Mr. Valdez."

Chapter Eleven

I left Mr. Valdez in the saloon, my mind racing after our conversation. He'd admitted he'd wanted to kill Ralph in revenge for his brother. The thought crossed my mind that he could definitely be lying about his visit to the second floor.

As I entered the lobby, Cynthia Mayes and the doctor were passing through again.

"How was the patient?" I asked.

The doctor pushed up his spectacles. "He claims he's not in much pain, but I find that hard to believe. He's a hard man to keep down. The injury to his good leg is not as bad as I had thought, though. The swelling has gone down, and I was able to further examine him. He might be able to walk on it in a day or so, with the aid of crutches. We'll just have to see how he does. In the meantime, plenty of rest. Don't hesitate to encourage the laudanum."

"Of course," I said. I focused my attention on Miss Mayes. "I'm sure he was delighted with the fruitcake."

She smiled broadly. "Yes. Clayton loves my fruitcake."

"I'd love to taste it sometime," I said, hoping to get into her good graces again, not only for the reason of finding out more about the Archer/Stewart family but because I couldn't stand the thought that she was displeased with me.

Her smile faded, and she lifted her chin. Had I offended her instead?

"Your coat is ready for the final fitting," she said. "Come round to my shop at your convenience. I'll save some of the fruitcake for you."

My heart lifted with surprise. "Very well. I will. Thank you."

After they left, I went to room fifteen to pay a visit to the good sheriff.

"I hear you are healing well," I said as I breezed into the room. I took the chair that had been placed next to the bed.

He was propped up on some pillows, and the sheets were tucked neatly and securely around his waist. To my delight, his face brightened at seeing me.

"Not fast enough," he said.

"You need to be patient, Clayton."

"How can I be? The doc said the deputy will be delayed. The town is left with no one to look after it, and then there's the matter of Ralph's murder. I don't know how long I can detain the family and any possible suspects when there is no active investigation."

I bit my lip. Should I tell him I was looking into the matter?

"Has Valdez left town?" he asked.

"No. No, he hasn't. I just spoke with him. I don't think he intends to leave quite yet . . . He indicated he had further business with the family."

His face took on a dubious expression. "So, he just

volunteered this information? That he had further business with the Stewarts and the Archers? Why would he do that?"

I shrugged. "I may have— Well, we had a very intense conversation."

He narrowed his eyes. "Really. You didn't happen to ask him anything about Ralph's death, did you?"

I swallowed, not sure how to reply. "We were having a drink, and he just . . . sort of opened up to me."

"I see. You. Having a drink in the middle of the day. With one of your guests. A guest you witnessed openly threatening Ralph Stewart. So, you were just passing the time?"

I sighed. "Okay. I might have asked him some questions—"

He closed his eyes and shook his head. I couldn't tell if he was mad, disappointed, disgusted or—

"Tell me about the conversation," he said.

What a surprise! It seemed he wasn't going to admonish me in some way or give me a lecture on the dangers of investigating a crime . . . yet. That might come later after I told him what I knew. At any rate, the cat was out of the bag so I divulged the information.

"So, he came to town intent on killing Ralph," he reiterated.

"Yes. He said he wished he had killed him. If he was telling the truth, someone else beat him to it."

"I'll have to find out who was arguing with Ralph in his room that night. And who might have penned that suicide note."

"Yes," I drew out skeptically, wondering how in the world he intended to do this from his sickbed. It seemed he was determined to defy the doctor's orders.

"And I'll need to search Ralph's room again," he added.

"We haven't touched it since he died, but, Clayton, how do you suppose—"

"Good. As soon as I get those crutches— Agh!" His face contorted in pain.

I leaned forward, placing my hand on his shoulder. Moist heat radiated through his shirt, and the sheen of perspiration glistened on his forehead.

"What is it? Are you all right? Do you need more laudanum?"

He pulled in a breath and shook his head. "No. It's passed."

I was about to argue with him when his features relaxed and he sank deeper into the pillows.

"According to Dr. Tate, crutches could be a few days away. You must rest, Clayton, and we don't really have time—"

"Time?"

"You heard what Mr. Archer said. If we—you—don't find the murderer before next week, we will have to cancel the festival altogether. You said you won't be able to detain the travelers much longer if there is no active investigation. What if one of them is our perpetrator?"

"Well, if I don't get on my feet soon, I'm afraid that's what will happen, Arabella."

"Unless . . ." I dipped my head and looked at him from under my lashes.

"Unless?"

"Unless you have some help. I can do the legwork, and—"

He rolled his eyes heavenward. "Not this again."

"But why not? Haven't I proved useful in these situations?"

"Yes, but—"

I reached out and took his hand. "I know. You are concerned for my safety. But you can't protect me all the time. I can look out for myself. I've been doing it since I was a child. You underestimate me."

He chuckled. "I would never make that mistake. But, Arabella—"

I squeezed his hand. "I think we'd make a really good team."

His brilliant blue gaze met mine, and his fingers tightened around my palm. An electric heat coursed through me.

"Yes. I believe we would," he said so soft and low it made my heart skip a beat. He'd taken my meaning further than I had intended, and part of me wanted to pull my hand away, but somehow I couldn't.

Suddenly, the heat I'd felt was replaced with a dense chill. I glanced over toward the mirror to find Percival's transparent form leaning against the wall next to it, his legs casually crossed at the ankles, his unlit pipe in his raised hand, and a moody scowl on his face.

I gasped and pulled my hand out of Clayton's. A look of confusion crossed over his face. I clenched my jaw, irritated that Percival had broken the spell. What was he playing at?

Thankfully, Clayton didn't seem to sense his presence or feel the icy chill in the air. As Percival had mentioned before, Clayton seemed to be closed off to otherworldly phenomena. Still, I wasn't sure of Percival's intentions at the moment.

"All right, then," Clayton said, his voice all business once again. "But only because I am laid up. And you must tell me everything you find out. If it looks like things are getting dangerous, then it's over—festival be damned. Do you understand?"

"Perfectly," I said, pulling my gaze back to him. Perhaps if I ignored Percival, he would give up and leave, but something told me he wouldn't.

I leaned back in the chair and raised my hands, then pressed them together in a steeple formation. I tapped my fingers together, deciding if I should give voice to the thought that had just crept in my head.

"What is it?" A look of caution flashed in Clayton's eyes.

"I guess this means you'll have to deputize me—temporarily, of course."

He gave me a sideways glance, and then, letting out a breath, he shook his head. "You are relentless."

I grinned at him. "Deputy Pryce. I quite like that."

He rolled his eyes. "Fine. But only until I get those crutches."

I chuckled. "Very well. Only until then. And what about a badge?" I blinked at him. "You gave Mr. Johns a badge when you deputized him. "

"Don't push it, Arabella."

I sighed. "All right. What would you like me to do first?"

"You'll have to keep an eye on Valdez. If he says he has more business with the family and he did kill Ralph, they might be in danger."

"Right. I believe we should also look at two other people who could have motive for killing Ralph: Mary Alice Stewart and Victoria Clement. It might have been one of them who was arguing with Ralph on the night he died."

"What makes you say that?"

I told him about the child and Mr. Stewart's affair with Victoria.

"You really do have your ear to the ground, don't you?"

I shrugged. "On occasion. I'd also like to speak with Cynthia Mayes."

"You think she's a suspect?"

"No. But she's part of the family. She might know something that could be helpful."

"Yes. You'll probably have to speak with Mrs. Stewart as well."

"Agreed." I stood up, ready to get started and feeling grateful that I had Clayton's blessing.

I was also eager to leave the room to give Percival a piece of my mind. He was becoming bolder by the minute.

I had tried to encourage the sheriff to take another dose of laudanum so he could get more rest, but he would not be persuaded. I left his room intent on going to see Mrs. Stewart. I came back to the lobby and rounded the corner to go up the stairs when something caught my eye down the hallway I'd just left. Dr. Briggs was standing in front of Cristoforo Valdez's room. His hand was on the doorknob as if he was going to walk in, or could he have just closed it? He then proceeded down the hallway and left the hotel through the back entrance.

I stopped at the reception desk, and Mr. Pettyjohn looked at me expectantly.

"I just saw Dr. Briggs at Mr. Valdez's door. Do you know anything about that?" I asked.

"Dr. Briggs? No. I was not aware he'd come downstairs. He's been with Mrs. Stewart for some time. He must have slipped by when I stepped out for a moment." He tugged at the tips of his vest, straightening it over his slightly protruding paunch.

"Hmm. Very well. May I please have a piece of paper and a writing instrument?"

He reached into the desk drawer and procured both. I ripped the paper in half and on one half wrote to Miss Mayes inviting her to tea and would she please bring some of her fruitcake. She had mentioned my coat was ready and waiting for a fitting, but I didn't want to take the time for that at the moment. I had too much to do here at the hotel. I also wrote to Constance inviting her as well.

"Please have Clarence deliver these." I folded both notes, addressed them, and gave them to Mr. Pettyjohn.

"Yes, madam," he said, making me flinch once again. I had all but given up on asking him to refrain from addressing me with the offensive moniker. I didn't really see how it mattered anymore anyway.

I gave him a cursory smile, turned to the staircase, and nearly jumped out of my skin to see Percival above me on the landing. I lifted my skirts and quickly made my way up to him.

"Please don't surprise me like that," I whispered. "You really must stop that awful habit. And what were you doing in the sheriff's room? Are you trying to provoke me?"

He gave me a haughty look. It seemed as though he was angry with me. "I was looking all over for you. I should have known you would be there."

"What does that mean?"

He held up his palm, curling his fingers to examine his fingernails. He did this often when he was trying to feign nonchalance, but that was not often the case.

"Do you care for him?" he asked, avoiding my eyes.

I scoffed. "Of course I care for him, but not like you think. And even if I did, what would be wrong with that?"

He put his hands behind his back and straightened his shoulders, clearly unable to answer my question.

"And I don't appreciate you putting me on the spot like

that. Appearing to me when I am in the presence of others. It's very distracting."

"Forgive me," he said, but the scowl on his face made the apology very unconvincing. "But I wanted to tell you something."

Voices below indicated someone was at the reception desk speaking with Mr. Pettyjohn.

"Not here!" I hissed. I brushed past him and made my way to the second floor. I ducked into a broom closet that was situated at the back corner of the floor.

Soon, the little room chilled into an oversized ice box. Percival appeared. The room was so small we were nearly nose to nose. I had not been this close to him before, and the sensation it provoked in me was unnerving in a way I couldn't define. His luminous eyes glowed in the dark, which seemed impossible given his transparent form, but glow they did, and I felt myself somehow being pulled into them. A shudder ran through me.

"What is it?" I choked out.

He said nothing but continued to keep me trapped in his gaze. I tried to turn my head to look away, but I couldn't move it. I then attempted to raise my hand to my mouth, but I was paralyzed. My breath froze in my lungs. The sensation sent a spike of fear through me.

"Stop it," I said.

He raised the back of his hand toward my face, and he caressed my cheek with his knuckles, sending a river of chills down my spine. He then lowered his hand. My body warmed again. He placed his hands behind his back and took a step backward. I sucked in a welcome breath.

"I saw something rather unusual the day before Ralph was murdered," he said as if nothing had just happened. "It may not have to do with his death, I just thought it odd."

Mystified by the sensations I had just experienced, I held his gaze, which felt completely different now. It was normal. Just two friends who were engaged in polite conversation. Normal, if everyone could see and converse with the dead, that was.

He raised his eyebrows at me, waiting for me to ask him what he'd seen, but I felt myself speechless.

"I saw that red haired woman, the one who was sitting with Mrs. Edwards-Stewart in one of the booths in the back of the saloon the night of the party—"

"Cherrie Fontaine," I said, finally finding my voice.

"I saw her going into the woods on the other side of the river. She kept looking over her shoulder as if she was afraid she'd be followed."

"On the other side of the river? How did she cross? Did she swim?"

He shook his head. "There is a footbridge about a quarter of a mile downriver. Lovely spot. I'd like to take you there sometime."

Our gazes locked again, but afraid I'd get stuck there once more, I blinked and averted my eyes for a moment. I looked back at him, ready to continue our conversation . . . without the strange interplay.

I then remembered I'd seen the footbridge from the window in my parlor room.

"Did you follow her into the woods?" I asked.

He lifted a shoulder. "No. I had no reason to. I thought perhaps she was meeting someone—perhaps for an assignation. I didn't want to intrude."

I sniffed. He had no problem intruding on my private conversations. I let the annoying sentiment pass.

"I agree, that is a little strange, but I'm not sure it means anything."

"I just thought you should know. Now that you are working so closely with Mr. Marshall, *Deputy Pryce*." He said the title with some disdain.

I lifted my chin. "It's only temporary. Just until he gets back on his feet."

Percival stepped closer again, his eyes boring into mine, and I could feel myself freezing up. "Be careful," he said.

I was not sure if he meant be careful as in watch out for the dangers of investigating the crime, or to be careful in regard to the sheriff.

"I must get back," I said, willing myself to look away from his gaze. "Thank you for the information."

He did not move or vanish into thin air, so I took it upon myself to walk through him. As I passed through his ethereal form, time stopped and I felt as if I were floating on a cloud. I became completely unaware of my body, and it was as if only my mind existed. Knowing this was not a natural state for me as a living, breathing woman, I pushed myself through, and my physicality returned. Warmth oozed back into my limbs, and I felt completely normal once again.

I looked back into the closet, and Percival was gone. I took in a deep breath, rattled by this new experience with him. I wasn't sure if I liked it or not.

Chapter Twelve

I sat in one of the mahogany spoon-back chairs that flanked the window in Mrs. Edwards-Stewart's room. She was opposite me in the matching chair, silently gazing out at the south end of town. From here, we had a full view of the annex, the General, the train depot, and a rise of mountain that contained a few miles of tunnels carved out of its belly to access the fine metals within. All was blanketed in snow, which sparkled like diamonds in the sun. I was glad the weather had turned for the time being.

"Your hotel is lovely," she offered out of nowhere. "I can see you've made improvements since the last time I was here."

"Thank you," I said, quite pleased. She did not seem to hold the hotel responsible in any way for her husband's death as Mr. Pettyjohn feared her mother-in-law might do.

I glanced down at some of the sagging porch rooftops in the annex, and a niggle of anxiety bloomed in my chest. I really must get someone to remove the snow or I'd have a disaster on my hands. I hoped the temporary reinforcements I'd had built would last.

"There is still much to be done, but these things often don't happen quickly."

"I daresay, I don't think Archibald's General will ever hold a candle to the Arabella, no matter how much money he puts into it. In my estimation, he'd have to level the whole thing and start over." I detected a hint of disdain in her words.

"Well, I suppose he is right in that two fine hotels in town would be good for La Plata Springs," I said. "As he is growing it and improving it to attract tourists."

She scoffed. "It's hard to imagine that anyone would want to come to this backwoods boondock. I don't see the appeal."

It wasn't that long ago I felt the same way, but to my surprise, I found myself feeling a little defensive at her remark.

"How did your husband feel about La Plata Springs?" I asked.

"He was interested in making money, and there is a lot of money to be made here."

"Ah. Yes, of course," I said. "How fortuitous that Mr. Archer has paved the way for that."

She looked over at me with a jerk of her head, and her eyes flared as if I'd said something that offended her. But then her lips turned up at the corners in an attempt to smile. "Yes," she said.

I wanted to get to the subject of Ralph's death but wasn't sure how to proceed. Condolences would be a good way to start. "Mrs. Edwards-Stewart—Mary Alice—I am so very sorry for your loss. I feel just terrible about the whole thing."

She gazed out the window but didn't respond.

"Mr. Stewart seemed like a very nice man," I continued. "Quite charming and generous. His, and the family's, inviting the orphans to town is commendable."

She cast her eyes in my direction again, the fire in them blazing once more, but she remained quiet. Did she know about the boy?

"It's hard to imagine someone would want to do such a nice man harm," I went on.

She leaned forward, her eyes still aflame. "Oh, there is someone who would."

I opened my eyes wide. "Really? Who?"

She scoffed. "That woman. Victoria Clement."

"Oh? Why her? I thought she was his patron, that they were friends."

"Friends? Oh, yes, they were friends. But she wanted more than friendship. She's made a complete nuisance of herself, always following him around. She turns up everywhere."

"Oh dear. I see. Do you think they . . ." I prompted, knowing full well they'd had an intimate relationship, but Mary Alice didn't know what I knew.

Her jaw stiffened, and I could see the muscles rippling over it. "It was a mere dalliance, a one-night stand, several years ago. It wasn't the first time Ralph had strayed. My husband was quite irresistible to women."

I definitely had to agree with her on that point, but it was no excuse for infidelity.

"I saw her throw a drink in his face at the party," I said casually.

She gave me a knowing smile. "He probably told her to shove off. To leave him alone. He didn't want anything to do with her."

This was the complete opposite of what Victoria had said. I wondered, not for the first time, if he'd been arguing with Mary Alice in his room the night he'd died, if he'd finally told her the truth about Victoria and the child.

"Did you speak with your husband after the party?"

"No. I left early. I was exhausted. I went to bed. Why do you ask?"

I shrugged. "You don't share a room. I thought perhaps you had told him good night. My late husband and I didn't share a room, either, but we always bade each other good night."

She scoffed. "I'm not sure what that has to do with anything, but no. I did not tell him good night."

"I see."

She narrowed her eyes. "I tell you that sheriff needs to look no further than Victoria Clement to find Ralph's killer. I heard her threaten him."

"When was this?"

"Earlier in the week, when we were at Archibald's ranch. She just showed up . . . or perhaps they agreed to meet, I don't know. I had stepped outside for some air and saw them by the barn. It seemed they were in an argument, and she shouted that he would "regret this decision" and stormed off. I thought that was the end of it, but then she was at the party snuggling up to him."

"Until she threw the drink in his face," I reminded her.

"The woman is unstable," she said. She pulled a handkerchief out from beneath the cuff of her sleeve and dabbed at her eyes.

"Again, I'm so sorry, Mary Alice. Is there anything I can do?"

She pressed her fingers to her temples and squeezed her

eyes shut for a moment. "If you don't mind, I feel a headache coming," she said.

"Of course," I said. "Is there something I can get you?"

She shook her head.

"Please let me know if you change your mind." I stood up, but she remained seated. I quietly left the room, my thoughts awhirl with what she'd just revealed about her husband's relationship with Victoria. It was quite different from what Victoria had said.

So, who was telling the truth?

My next task was to search Mr. Stewart's room, which was right next door to Mary Alice's. I reached into my pocket to pull out the heavy keychain that bore all the room keys. I had made a habit of carrying it with me at all times, should there be reason to get inside one of the rooms. Mr. Pettyjohn had his own set of keys, but alas, he often spent much time looking for them. Maggie, too, had a set, of course, to open the rooms for the maids to clean.

The sound of footsteps on the stairs caught my attention. Speak of the devil, it was Maggie, followed by Cordelia and Bijou. Bijou ran to me and danced on her hind legs, hoping for some attention.

"Hello, little sprite," I said.

"Hello, ma'am," Maggie greeted me. Her expression was somber, probably on account of the recent happenings with the death of Ralph Stewart. She was a sensitive soul who seemed to carry everyone else's burdens alongside her own. I thought she and Andrew a good and loving couple, both of them highly sympathetic and extremely kind. I liked them both very much.

"Were you going up to our rooms?" Cordelia asked.

"No." I tilted my head toward Mary Alice's door, then lowered my voice. "I've just been to see Mary Alice."

"How is she holding up?" Maggie asked.

I shook my head. I then nodded toward Mr. Stewart's room and urged them to follow me in. I tried my best to keep the keys from making noise. The walls in the hotel were thin, and I didn't want to disturb Mary Alice.

Once inside, I answered Maggie's question in a hushed voice. "She is not doing very well, as you can imagine."

"The poor dear," she said.

"Why are we in here?" Cordelia asked.

"The sheriff has asked me to help him to investigate the murder," I said. "Well, he didn't really ask me. I made a very strong suggestion."

"That's wonderful," Maggie said. "I hope you can get to the bottom of this before next week so we can continue with the festival. It would mean so much to Victoria."

"Yes," I said. "Though, we might have a problem as it relates to Victoria," I added.

"How so?" Maggie asked.

"I spoke with her earlier. About her relationship with Mr. Stewart. Her account was very different from Mary Alice's. And I think she may have lied to me. When I asked her if she'd been up in Ralph's room on the night of the murder, she said she hadn't been there, but Mr. Valdez said he heard a woman arguing with Ralph in his room. Mary Alice said she hadn't seen Ralph after the party, that she'd gone to bed. If she's telling the truth, it must have been Victoria. Mary Alice also claimed she saw them in an altercation earlier in the week."

"Did Mary Alice seem to know anything of the child?" Maggie asked.

"No. I'm not sure if she knows about him, and I certainly didn't want to be the one to bring it up."

"Andrew said he would facilitate a meeting between the boy and Mrs. Stewart," Maggie said.

"But what if Victoria is the one telling the truth, and Mary Alice was the one arguing with Ralph? What if he'd told her about his son?" Cordelia said.

"Right. Either woman could be lying. Both certainly had reason to be very angry with him. And then there is Mr. Valdez. He admitted to me that he had come to La Plata Springs intent on seeking revenge for his brother's death. He said he wished he had killed Ralph. I was hoping to find some clue in here as to what happened that night."

I scanned the place. Like all the rooms in the hotel, it was elegantly furnished. This particular room had a more masculine flair, like my own bedroom, with a double-sized walnut sleigh bed and a large walnut wardrobe opposite it. A rolltop desk littered with papers sat in the northwest corner next to a generously sized window that was now shut. More papers lay strewn on the floor beneath it. It was almost as if the papers had been swiped off the desk or the breezy winter air had blown through the open window. The chair had been rolled out some distance from the desk. The bed was rumpled, as if someone had been sitting on it or lying on top of the covers. A book and more papers lay on the bed.

I went over and picked up the papers. It was business correspondence that seemed to have something to do with the mines in California. The book was a copy of *Walden or Life in the Woods* by Thoreau. I thought it a strange selection for Mr. Stewart, a man who seemed to have been in pursuit of monetary wealth, but perhaps he was trying to change his ways.

"The sheriff said the window had been forced. And look here." Cordelia pointed to a jagged piece of wood along the frame.

"Yes, but he also said the cause of death was poison," Maggie chimed in.

"Right," I agreed. "When Mr. Stewart left the party, it seemed he wasn't feeling well. Someone could have poisoned him at the party."

"He came up to his room—" Cordelia continued.

"Andrew was with him but then left," Maggie added.

"Yes, so he came inside," I said. "One of the women, perhaps Mary Alice or Victoria, came to the room. They entered. There was an argument. Mr. Stewart, suffering from the effects of the poison, forces the window open—"

"But did Ralph fall out of the window, or was he pushed?" Maggie said. "Maybe the dose of poison hadn't taken effect fast enough for the murderer. They panicked and then—"

The sound of scratching distracted me from my train of thought. "Where is Bijou?"

The two women looked around. The scratching continued.

"It's coming from under the bed," Cordelia said.

I rolled my eyes. "Oh dear. Bijou must be after a mouse or something. The vermin in this hotel will be the end of me!" We had been battling rodents since the moment I'd stepped foot in the hotel. First rats, which were gone now, thank goodness; then squirrels, which admittedly were a lot cuter but a nuisance nonetheless; and now possibly mice or some other vile creature, which might be much harder to eradicate. I'd have to send Mr. Johns up here to investigate, but for now, I wanted to continue with my own investigation.

I wandered over to the desk and perused the papers strewn across it. Some were deeds to property here in Colorado. There were several bills and other correspondence. A folded piece of paper shoved into one of the small cubbies of the desk caught my eye. I pulled it out and opened it up. The signature grabbed my attention. It read, Cherrie Fontaine.

I scanned the note:

Good sir,
You will find that it is not I that am a threat to your good fortune, but perhaps you should cast your eyes upon Dr. Briggs. Your mother's adoration of the man makes her blind to his wicked ways. She is completely under his spell. I have been a good and faithful friend to your mother, and she has been a good friend to me. I assure you, I am not your enemy in this matter.

"What do you make of this?" I held the letter out to them. They came over, and Cordelia took it from my hand. Maggie looked over her shoulder.

"Cherrie Fontaine," Cordelia said. "Why would Ralph consider her a threat to his 'good fortune'?"

"And what about the doctor?" Maggie asked. "I have to say, the man does make my skin crawl. It's the way he is with Mrs. Stewart. All sweet and nice one minute, and then quite cruel the next."

"Cruel? In what way?" I asked, setting the letter on the desk.

"It was something I witnessed while I was bringing a fresh basin and pitcher of water to her room when they first arrived. He had requested it. The door was open, and I was about to walk in when I heard her whimpering. He was standing over her, holding something over her head. I think it was a medicine bottle. He said, 'Tell your son to stand down or you'll get no more of this.'"

"More of what, the medicine?" Cordelia asked.

She nodded. "I can't be absolutely positive, but I think so. She seems to be in a lot of pain at times, and at other times, she is quite dull. And of course, she's been in a terrible way since Mr. Stewart—"

"Yes, of course," I said. "The poor woman."

Cordelia had wandered over to the window again, examining the sill.

"But what did he want Ralph to 'stand down' about?" I said, my mind still focused on what Maggie had said. "Could the doctor have had reason to kill Mr. Stewart?"

Bijou toddled out from under the bed, obviously having lost interest in whatever creature, real or imagined, she'd been occupied with.

Cordelia picked at the loosened fragments of wood at the windowsill. "What if Mr. Stewart had succumbed to the poison and whomever was in here with him hauled his lifeless body to the window and then threw him out to cover up the fact he'd been poisoned?"

"Mary Alice or Victoria surely wouldn't have the strength to do that," Maggie said.

Bijou raised herself up on her hind legs and rested her paws on my skirt, wanting to be picked up. I was about to oblige when something wrapped around her paw stopped me cold. It was a gold chain.

"What is—" I unwrapped it from her paw and held it up. It was a chain with a medal of the Virgin Mary attached to it. The same one I saw Cristoforo Valdez wearing at the party. "Mary Alice and Victoria certainly wouldn't have the strength," I agreed with Maggie, "but a man would."

Bijou scampered toward the door, which we had left ajar. I went over to close it but stopped when something caught my eye. It was the hem of someone's skirt. I peered around the door to find a very startled Cherrie Fontaine.

Chapter Thirteen

"Miss Fontaine. May I help you?"

Her sage green eyes were wide with surprise. "I was just
— I was just coming to . . . to fetch something for Mrs.
Stewart. Some of his business papers."

"Right," I said, trying not to sound skeptical. If I
hadn't left the door ajar, she would have needed a key.
How much of our conversation had she heard?
"Come in."

Timidly, she stepped inside. She nodded a greeting to
Maggie and Cordelia.

"Well, I must be going," Maggie said. "I have much
to do."

"Thank you." I gave her a smile.

"I'm afraid the papers are a bit of a mess," I said to
Miss Fontaine with a tilt of my head toward the desk.

"Yes," she agreed with a slight upturning of her lips.
"Mr. Stewart's desk always looked like that. It drove his
mother to distraction. She has always insisted everything be
neat as a pin."

"Well, there must have been a method to his madness," Cordelia said.

"How is she doing?" I asked. "I haven't been by to pay my respects. I didn't want to disturb her."

She shook her head. "Not well. She hasn't been out of bed since . . . well, you know."

"Please let me know if there is anything I can do."

She smiled and went over to the desk. She started straightening the papers and then stopped short when her gaze fell on the letter she'd written.

"I hope you don't mind," I said, "but as you may or may not know, the sheriff has been laid low by an accident at his home. He's staying here at the hotel, and I'm afraid he's quite incapacitated. He's asked me to help him with the investigation into Mr. Stewart's death."

She looked at me quizzically, probably wondering what sort of qualifications I, as an actress and now hotel owner, would have.

Reading the situation, Cordelia stepped in. "Arabella is quite the sleuth. She's helped him before."

"Oh, I see." She continued to neaten the pile. "I'm sure Mrs. Stewart will appreciate that. She's quite keen to have the murderer brought to justice, as you would imagine."

"Yes," I agreed. "I found something I wanted to ask you about."

"Of course." She set the pile back on the desk. "I'll do what I can to help."

"In the letter you wrote to Mr. Stewart—" I indicated the pile of papers with a nod of my head "—you mentioned that you were not 'a threat' to Mr. Stewart. What did you mean by that?"

Her shoulders stiffened. "Oh." She batted a hand in the air, attempting nonchalance. "I've been with Mrs. Stewart for quite a long time. When her daughter, who was my age, died, she became overly attached to me. Mr. Stewart sometimes got jealous of her affection for me."

"And what did you mean about Dr. Briggs perhaps being a threat to him?"

As if deciding how much to divulge, she pulled her lower lip between her teeth. "Dr. Briggs is very controlling. Mrs. Stewart won't make a single decision without consulting him, and sometimes I feel he doesn't have her best interest at heart. He is a doctor, not a businessman."

"So, you feel he is not qualified to weigh in on matters of the family business?" I asked.

"Exactly. He and Mr. Stewart were often in disagreement. Mr. Archer also isn't too fond of Dr. Briggs for the same reasons. Though, Mr. Archer and his nephew didn't really get along, either. By appearances, Mr. Stewart was a very charming man, but he really wasn't the nicest person. Anyway, all the dissention made Mrs. Stewart anxious. She felt quite caught in the middle."

I nodded in understanding. "I'm sure she did."

"Now that her son is gone, she will be entirely reliant on Dr. Briggs. Not only for her medical care but for everything." She picked up the pile of papers and gave me a polite smile. "I need to get back to her. She doesn't like it when I am away from her too long. Especially right now."

"Of course, of course," I said. "Miss Fontaine, I'd like to speak with Mrs. Stewart. When would be a good time?"

"She is usually quite alert in the evenings, as her dose of laudanum is wearing off before I give it to her again before bed."

"She takes it quite often, then," I said.

"Yes," she said. "That's another reason Mr. Stewart did

not care for Dr. Briggs. He thought the doctor used the medicine to better control Mrs. Stewart."

"I see," I said, her statement giving me pause. "Very well, then. I'll come by this evening."

She nodded and left the room.

"It sounds like Mr. Stewart didn't care for Dr. Briggs or Miss Fontaine," Cordelia said.

"Yes. I didn't realize Mrs. Stewart was so reliant upon them. She seems such a formidable woman, but if she is in such discomfort as to have to take the amount of medicine she seems to take . . ."

"Poor woman. Her son's death must have hit extremely hard in her weakened condition."

"Well, I think we've seen what we can see in here for now," I said, surveying the room. "This—" I held up the medal and looked down at Bijou, who gave me a canine grin "—is a very good find."

Clarence appeared at the doorway. "There you are, ma'am." He was quite out of breath.

"Yes, Clarence, what is it?"

"It's Miss Mayes and Miss Chatterley, ma'am. I delivered your notes. Miss Chatterley, she said couldn't come."

"Oh? That's fine, tell her we can meet at another time at her convenience. Is Miss Mayes on her way?"

"No, ma'am. She said Miss Chatterley is in a right state, and she was going to tend to her. They said you should come to Miss Mayes's shop, ma'am."

I let loose a sigh. It would have been so much more convenient if they had come here, but I did want to speak with them. It seemed I was going to the dress shop. "Thank you, Clarence."

He tipped his hat and left.

I turned to Cordelia. "Care to join me?"

She nodded. "I'll go upstairs to get our coats and hats."

"Right. But first I need to go to the sheriff to tell him of the latest developments."

She nodded. "I'll see you in our rooms."

We parted ways, her going upstairs and me going down.

When I entered the sheriff's room, he was dozing. Holding Bijou in my arms, I stepped in quietly and sat in the chair by the bed. He looked so beautiful in sleep, it was all I could do to not reach out and brush the hair off his forehead. I cleared my throat in an attempt to dismiss the impulse. His eyelids fluttered open. When he saw me, he pushed himself up to sitting.

"Sweet dreams?" I asked.

He blinked, trying to wake himself up further. "I wasn't asleep. I was just resting my eyes," he claimed.

I smiled inwardly. "Oh. I see."

"How goes it? What do you have to report?" he asked.

I told him about my conversations with Victoria and Mary Alice, and also what Cordelia, Maggie, and I had discovered in Ralph's room with dear Bijou's help.

He glanced at Bijou and chuckled. "I've always thought that little dog was just a funny-looking fluff ball with nothing between her ears—"

Clutching her to my chest, I sucked in a breath. "I won't hear you disparage Bijou—"

He held up a hand. "But I was wrong. She has proved quite helpful in the past, and now."

Satisfied he'd seen the error of his ways, I smiled. "Yes. I don't know what I'd do without her."

He had been referring to the last murder case in our town, and while investigating it, I had gotten into a bit of a jam when Bijou had come to my rescue.

Delighted that Clayton was looking at her, she jumped

from my arms and onto the bed. She curled up beside him, and he rested his hand on her back. It warmed my heart to see. Bijou always managed to charm everyone eventually. It was quite helpful because I realize that, at times, I come off a little—well, unsympathetic or aloof. I put it up to the fact I may have built a rather hard shell around myself because of my upbringing. It was purely for protection, but others often did not see it that way. Bijou's presence softens that edge and reminds me of the goodness in life.

"So Valdez lied about being in Ralph's room that night."

I nodded. "I believe so. They must have had some kind of struggle, and Mr. Valdez's necklace came off. That's the only scenario I can think of. Why else would it have been there?"

"Right. But it still doesn't prove he killed Ralph."

"And then there's the note from Mrs. Stewart's secretary about Dr. Briggs." I then gave him a detailed account of the conversation I'd had with Miss Fontaine.

"I did get the sense Dr. Briggs was more than just Mrs. Stewart's physician," the sheriff said. "She is quite changed since I saw her last. She was always such a commanding presence."

"I wonder how ill she really is," I mused. "I'll talk to the doctor."

"Tread lightly, Arabella. The more you nose around, the more threatened the killer will become. And that could make for a dangerous situation."

"I will show the utmost discretion." I tried to assure him, but he had a very dubious expression in his eyes. "What?"

"You have a way of being—"

I opened my eyes wide in surprise. Was he about to criticize me in some way? I girded myself for his next few words. "Yes?" I prompted.

"Direct."

I blinked in confusion. "Is that a bad thing? I see no need in beating around the bush."

"A little subtlety is all I am after."

I raised my chin, somewhat affronted. Clayton Marshall had a way of being *direct*, too.

"I can be subtle," I protested.

"I'm sure you can. Put those acting skills to good use."

"Now you go too far, Mr. Marshall. I do not have to *act* to be subtle."

He laughed, making those delightful sapphire eyes twinkle. My heart lurched. "I'm just teasing you, Arabella. But, truly . . . do be careful."

I sniffed. "Of course. I'm not stupid."

"Oh, you are far from stupid. Just a little reckless at times," he said with another chuckle. I playfully slapped him on the shoulder and he grabbed hold of my hand. His palm felt rough, strong, and warm. Those breathtaking eyes gazed deep into mine. "I mean it, Arabella. Be careful."

Bijou, roused from her little nap, stood up and placed her front paws on Clayton's chest, breaking the spell that had us entranced. I pulled my hand away, and Clayton gently placed both of his on either side of Bijou's head.

"Take care of your mistress," he told her, stroking her ears. She lurched forward and licked him on the chin.

"Come, Bijou," I said. "Let's let the sheriff rest."

Unsettled with what had just transpired between us and the overwhelming and confusing feelings it caused in me, I left without saying goodbye. I reminded myself I had no time, nor inclination, for entanglements.

Chapter Fourteen

Back in our rooms, Cordelia greeted me with my coat and hat in hand. She was ready to go. After I had sufficiently bundled up, I reached for the leash that hung from a hook next to the door. I attached it to Bijou's collar and then put on my gloves.

Out on the street, we headed south toward Miss Mayes's shop. I pulled the collar of my coat closed against the cold, wishing I had remembered to wear my scarf. Despite the amount of snow on the road and on the ground, the townsfolk were bustling about as usual. Paths had been cleared to storefronts, and a track of wagon wheels had been etched into the road.

The air was crisp and cold and smelled of pine and burning fireplaces. Bijou happily trotted between us, stopping occasionally to sniff at something. In the distance, I viewed the open area next to the church where a Christmas tree had been erected, but it was sadly devoid of decorations. Constance and Miss Mayes had been responsible for that job, as they comprised the decorating committee. I sighed, further determined to find the killer so we could bring the festival back to life.

As we passed one of the local saloons, I saw Mr. Valdez and Dr. Briggs in the alleyway between the saloon and one of the other businesses. They seemed to be arguing.

"Look, Cordelia." I indicated toward the men with a tilt of my head. Her eyes widened.

We stood there watching the interplay. Dr. Briggs leaned forward, his mouth moving rapidly, his eyes flaring. I couldn't hear what he was saying, but his expression definitely carried a threat.

Suddenly, Valdez shook a finger in his face and then stormed off. He headed toward the river.

Dr. Briggs watched him go. He ran a hand through his hair, and then, to my horror, he looked over at us. Caught completely off guard, I lifted my hand in a half-hearted wave. He strode over.

"Dr. Briggs," I said, trying to infuse cheerfulness into my voice.

"Ladies."

"Fine day," Cordelia said, obviously feeling as awkward as I did at having witnessed the disagreement.

"Was that Mr. Valdez?" I asked. I would love to know what they had been discussing.

"Yes," he said with a scowl.

"Everything all right?" I ventured cautiously.

His lips turned up into a forced half smile. "Of course. Good day." He tipped his hat and walked on.

"Goodness," Cordelia said. "I wonder what that was all about."

"I don't know," I said, wondering the same thing. "But I aim to find out. Earlier, I saw Dr. Briggs at Mr. Valdez's door."

"Perhaps he was looking for him," Cordelia offered.

"Apparently," I mused.

We passed by Constance's newspaper office, which was right next door to Miss Mayes's dress shop. Through the window, I saw the printing press, her desk—which looked to be an unholy mess—stacks of papers, books, and other paraphernalia haphazardly crowding the shelves on either side of the room. It was dark inside.

When we stepped into the dress shop, the tinkling of a string of bells attached to the doorknob announced our arrival. This abode was definitely in sharp contrast to the printing office. It was neat, light, airy, and gloriously feminine. Three gorgeous dresses of the latest fashion adorned dress forms that stood in the window. A large counter stood to the right of the door, and behind it, a rainbow array of beautiful bolts of fabric lined the shelves, along with myriad ribbons and thread spools, and other items required for sewing and dressmaking. Not only did Miss Mayes design and make dresses for the wealthier clientele of the town but she provided the needed supplies for the less well-off to make their own garments. She was a smart businesswoman, and her store was thriving. Having purchased two of her dresses so far, I felt the quality rivaled those of my dressmaker in New York.

From the back of the shop, Miss Mayes emerged. "Ah, there you are, Mrs. Pryce. Hello, Miss Danson," she greeted us. She came over to help us with our coats and hats. She hung them carefully on hangers and placed them on a rack that stood adjacent to the window.

"I have your new coat for you." She nodded toward a box on the counter. "You can take it to try it on at your convenience, and if there is anything to be altered, let me know."

"Thank you," I said.

"Come in back with me. I have fruitcake!"

"Delightful." I raised my eyebrows at Cordelia, pleased that Miss Mayes seemed to have finally forgiven me.

"What is it you wished to speak with us about? Does it concern the festival?" Miss Mayes asked.

"Sort of," I said. "It's— Well, it's about Mr. Stewart's murder."

"I see. I'm sorry we couldn't come to the hotel. Constance has taken a strange turn and said she didn't feel well enough to go there. It's quite unlike her. I can't imagine what's gotten into her."

I bit my lip. I could. Darn that Percival. She probably didn't want to come to the hotel for fear of seeing him again. But a few days ago it had seemed like she'd put the sighting down to too much wine.

"Come on back," Miss Mayes said. She flipped the "open" sign on the door to "closed."

We entered the back room to find a modest parlor. It was small and furnished with two armchairs, a hard-backed chair, a small writing table, and a wood-burning stove that was more than adequately heating the place. Atop the stove, a tea kettle rumbled.

Constance was sitting in one of the armchairs, biting a fingernail. When she saw us, she looked up with surprise. "Oh good, you're here," she said, a look of concern on her face.

"Yes. Hello, Constance. I hear you're not feeling well?"

She shook her head. "It's my nerves. They're all a jumble."

"I'm sorry to hear that."

"I'm preparing some chamomile tea," Miss Mayes said. "I thought it would calm her. Would you like some?"

Cordelia and I both said we would.

"I was glad you asked to speak with us," Constance said, "because I wanted to speak with you as well. I was going to go to the sheriff, but as he's laid up at the hotel . . . well, I didn't want to bother him."

Was she trying to preserve my feelings by omitting that she didn't want to come to the hotel?

"Anyway," she continued. "I assume you're helping the sheriff with the murder case? You have such a talent for sleuthing. If anyone can get to the bottom of this terrible tragedy, it's you."

I smiled, pleased with her vote of confidence.

"Do you think you're up to it?" Miss Mayes arched a brow.

I couldn't tell if she was still feeling frosty toward me or if it was her pragmatic nature showing itself. I opted for the latter.

"Well, I was hoping for some help," I said. "You two have been here in La Plata Springs for a long time. Constance is always a wealth of information," I said, avoiding the word *gossip*. "And you . . . you are also a good resource because of your knowledge of all the townsfolk—"

"You mean because I am related to Archibald and Ralph," she added dryly.

"Well, yes, actually." I decided for the straightforward approach with her. "I thought you'd have intimate knowledge of the family and who their enemies might be."

Satisfied with my answer, she bobbed her head in agreement.

I turned to Constance. "What is it you wanted to speak with me about?"

"I saw something at your hotel when I woke up very

early that morning after the party. It concerns Ralph . . . and . . . and . . ."

"Oh?" I said with a slight degree of relief. Perhaps her upset had nothing to do with Percival.

Constance nodded. "And Cristoforo Valdez."

"What did you see?" Cordelia asked.

"I was coming down the hallway and into the lobby to exit out onto the street when I saw Mr. Valdez coming through the doorway that leads from the annex to the hotel."

"What time was this?" I asked.

"I believe it was around three thirty. I couldn't sleep and wanted to be home in my own bed."

Or she didn't want to run the risk of encountering Percival again.

"Hmm. He might have been visiting one of Kitty's girls," Cordelia supposed.

"So, what you're saying is that he would have seen Mr. Stewart's body," I said. "The doctor put the time of death at five or six hours before he was discovered. That would mean around midnight."

Around the time Mr. Valdez said he went up to the second floor to speak with Ralph but heard him arguing with a woman, I thought to myself.

"Yes," Constance confirmed.

Miss Mayes poured the hot water over the tea strainer that sat on the rim of the teapot and the lovely aroma of chamomile filled the little room. The teacups clinked against the saucers as she set them on a tray, as well as a plate with several slices of fruitcake.

"And Mr. Valdez didn't alert anyone," I realized aloud. "It was Maggie who came to our room at around six o'clock to tell us about Mr. Stewart."

"Interesting," Cordelia said. "But Mr. Valdez didn't

mention anything about seeing the body in the annex when you spoke to him, did he, Arabella? Why would he have omitted that?"

"Either he was guilty of the crime or he was afraid someone would think he was, I'd imagine," Miss Mayes said, bringing over the tray. "The animosity between him and Ralph was well-known."

We each took a cup and saucer. I sipped at the piping hot liquid, and it warmed me all the way through.

"What can you tell us about it?" I asked Miss Mayes.

She sat down and took the last teacup and saucer on the tray and held it in her lap. She offered me a slice of fruit-cake, which I readily accepted.

"Not much," she said. "I know Enrique Valdez invested a good deal of money in the mine in La Linda."

"Do you know anything about Mr. Valdez's claim that his brother held Mr. Stewart responsible for the explosion?" I asked.

"It's ridiculous," she said. "He can't prove anything."

"He claims Enrique investigated the accident and found Mr. Archer and Mr. Stewart had been negligent."

"That's not true," Miss Mayes said. "Is it, Constance?"

Constance was in the midst of noisily slurping her tea and stopped abruptly when we all turned our eyes to her. She lowered her cup to the saucer in her lap. "That is what Enrique claimed. Far be it from me to gossip, but Enrique was not an honest man. And Cristoforo . . . well, he's a criminal."

"A criminal?"

"Yes." Constance nodded. "A murderer. It was reported in Valencia, a small village near La Linda, that he'd killed a man."

Chapter Fifteen

I nearly choked on my tea. "Cristoforo Valdez killed a man?" This was surprising indeed. "What do you know of it?"

Constance shared a glance with Miss Mayes and then continued. "Apparently, he found one of his friends, a vaquero, in bed with his wife. There was a fight. Next day, the man was dead."

"What was the cause of death?"

She shook her head. "It was a bit of a mystery. Could have been from injuries from the fight. Some say it was poison."

"No one knows for sure," Miss Mayes added.

"I'm sorry, Constance," I said. "I don't mean to be rude, but how do you know all this?"

"When I first started as a reporter in '72, I was looking for a story. I'd heard about the new mine in La Linda and went there to write about it. That's when I first met Archie —er, Archibald. I also met Enrique and Cristoforo but just in passing. Word about town was Enrique was a thief and

Cristoforo a killer. Bad *hombres*, as the townspeople referred to them."

"What do you know about Enrique being a thief?"

"He claimed he owned the land where Archibald wanted to build his mine. Enrique agreed to sell the land to Archibald for a good price if—"

"Mr. Archer? But what about Mr. Stewart?"

She exchanged a look with Miss Mayes. "Bertha was not keen on her brother buying the land. She wanted Archibald to return to California, but he wanted to pursue his interests here."

"Mrs. Stewart? Why did she have a say?" Cordelia asked.

I took a bite of the fruitcake, and my tastebuds sang. It truly was delicious.

"From what I can surmise," Miss Mayes said, "when their father, my uncle, passed, he gave Bertha a larger role in the executorship of the estate. She was always Charles's favorite."

"She sent Ralph to oversee the project," Constance said.

I doubted that went over well with Mr. Archer. His young nephew, who was probably around twenty at the time, barging in on his business deal? It must have been humiliating. I recalled Miss Fontaine saying Mr. Archer and Mr. Stewart didn't get along—that Mr. Stewart was difficult.

"I see. But back to Enrique and Mr. Archer? Before Mr. Stewart arrived . . ." I prompted Constance, wanting her to continue.

"Oh, yes. The deal between them was that Enrique would sell Archibald the land if he could partner with Archibald. Enrique knew nothing about mining. Anyway, I have it on good authority the land was actually owned by a very old man who had no family. Enrique befriended the man and then ran him off his own land."

"That's terrible," I said. "What became of the old man?"

She shrugged. "Some say he went to New Mexico."

"What do you know about the mining accident?"

Constance gave a dramatic sigh. "It was a terrible tragedy. But mining by nature is a dangerous business. Mine shaft collapses are not uncommon."

"So, you don't believe Mr. Valdez's claim that his brother blamed Mr. Archer and Mr. Stewart? That he had the accident investigated?"

"There may have been an investigation, but if so, nothing came of it," Constance said.

"The mine was dangerous so Archibald and Ralph shut it down, which was the right thing to do," Miss Mayes added.

"Do the Archers and Stewarts still own the land?"

"As far as I know," she said.

"And Enrique disappeared," Constance said. "He left La Linda. We did not hear of him or see him again until 1882 when he came to La Plata Springs. He stayed for about a week and then returned last year."

"And that's when he died," I stated.

Constance nodded.

"Why did he come back?" Cordelia asked quietly, as if deep in thought.

Constance shrugged. "I'm not sure. Perhaps he wanted to invest in the mines of La Plata Springs?"

Cordelia scoffed. "Do you really think he would want to partner with Mr. Archer again? After what had happened before?"

I took in a deep breath and let it out. "Not likely. You say nothing came of any investigation?" I asked.

"Nothing," Constance reaffirmed.

I bit my lip, thinking. Enrique had disappeared after that. I wondered if Mr. Stewart and Mr. Archer paid him off. Or perhaps he was blackmailing them—money in exchange for keeping the findings of the investigation secret. After all, he would have needed the money having lost his land, his only asset. And if Mr. Valdez believed Mr. Stewart was responsible for Enrique's death, perhaps there was something to his claims. Perhaps Enrique had come back for more and needed to be stopped. Permanently. If that were the case, then Mr. Valdez was grounded in his belief Mr. Stewart, or perhaps Mr. Archer, was responsible for his brother's death.

And what about his medal I found in Mr. Stewart's room?

"Back to Cristoforo returning from the annex with poor Ralph's body lying on the ground," Constance said. "Given what we know of the history of the relationship between the Valdezes and the Archer/Stewarts, and from the death of Cristoforo's wife's lover, I think it's entirely possible he could have poisoned Ralph."

Miss Mayes nodded in agreement. "And the fact he was coming from the annex after Ralph fell from the window— maybe to make sure he was dead—definitely puts Cristoforo in a bad light."

I had to agree. "Yes, it certainly does."

Once I had settled the box containing my new coat under my arm, Cordelia and I stepped out of the dress shop to find that it was snowing once again. It came down in big, fat flakes. The air was still, cold, and silent. Bijou danced on the leash, jumping up to catch the snowflakes in her mouth. She wandered a little too far to the left of the shoveled pathway and found herself in a snowdrift up to her ears and unable to move. She looked up at us with such confusion on her little face that we couldn't help but laugh.

"Come on, you silly little beast." Cordelia leaned down and picked her up, for which Bijou was dearly grateful. She smiled in her canine way.

We hurried toward the hotel, lest we became soaked, and once inside, we removed our coats and hats and shook off the snow.

Cordelia's cheeks were pink from the cold, and her face glowed with health. It was good to see her not looking so pale and wan as she had in years past. She still spent a good deal of time with her books, but she seemed to enjoy the outdoors in a way she never had in New York. Her walks with Bijou had become more and more frequent. They both seemed to get great enjoyment from the exercise. I could use more of it myself, but things at the hotel and the planning of the festival had kept me too busy.

When we entered the hotel, Kitty and Sally Dean were speaking with a man standing at the reception desk, his back to us. When he turned around as we approached them, my heart sank to the pit of my stomach. It was Atticus Brooks. My nemesis.

"Mrs. Pryce," he said, opening his arms wide as if he were genuinely glad to see me. Which he wasn't. He was only glad to see me for the opportunity to torment me, an act he had been no stranger to over the years. He was dressed with his usual garish flair in a bright turquoise waistcoat and brown velvet jacket. His mustache was trimmed too far above his lip, giving it the appearance of a black worm.

I tried to give him a convincing smile, but I found it hard to make my lips work. It took all my acting skill to greet him properly. "Mr. Brooks. I'd heard you were headed this way. Welcome back."

"Thank you, my dear. I only wish it were under better circumstances. I am aggrieved to hear about poor Ralph. He was such an industrious young man and the apple of his mother's eye. Such a shame. And it happened in *your* hotel." He arched a brow at me.

I glanced at Kitty and Sally Dean, whose eyes were wide, looking at me as if I were in danger of standing in the way of an oncoming train—which in all fairness, I figuratively was now that Mr. Brooks was here—but the expressions on their faces made me think they knew something I did not.

Mr. Pettyjohn cleared his throat to get my attention and then tilted his head toward the end of the reception desk, indicating he wanted a word with me in private.

"Excuse me," I said to Mr. Brooks, forcing a polite smile.

Mr. Pettyjohn and I stepped away from the group while Cordelia engaged Mr. Brooks and the other two in conversation.

"Thank goodness you're here. We've had a bit of a problem," Mr. Pettyjohn said under his breath.

"What is it?" I whispered, giving Mr. Brooks a sideways glance, hoping he couldn't hear us.

"There's been an incident. In Mrs. Stewart's room. And I'm afraid it's made her quite unwell."

"What happened?" I asked.

"Someone broke into her suite."

"What? You aren't serious?"

"Unfortunately, I am. Dr. Briggs had been tending to her but stepped out, and I'm afraid she was quite alone—"

Fearing the worst, my breath froze in my lungs. "Is she all right?"

"I believe she is unharmed. Dr. Briggs is with her now."

"I'll go see her."

"Is Bertha unwell?" Mr. Brooks strode over to us. Apparently, the man had the ears of an elephant. Cordelia, Kitty, and Sally followed.

"She's a little . . . well, a little under the weather," I said, not wanting to give him further fodder for his sensationalist stories. It was bad enough that Ralph had come to his demise here. Add to that yet another crime against the family . . . A thread of anxiety wound itself tightly around my chest. How would I be able to control the narrative of what had transpired here?

"Oh dear," he said. "I was hoping to pay my condolences. And I suppose there will now be no festival?"

"That has not yet been determined," I said, trying to remain confident.

He emitted a dramatic sigh. "I know the yearly spectacle means so much to her. And she so generously donates to the affair. I was quite looking forward to experiencing it myself."

"Why don't we get you settled into your room," Cordelia said, rescuing me. "Perhaps Mrs. Stewart will be well tomorrow and you can visit with her then."

"Yes," he said. "But do let her know I've arrived."

"Of course, Mr. Brooks. We will tell her," she said. "Now, Mr. Pettyjohn, let's give Mr. Brooks one of the *finer* rooms on the second floor."

That seemed to please the vulture for the time being. I gave Cordelia a grateful smile.

"If you will excuse me," I said.

As I mounted the stairs, I peeled off my coat and gloves, removed my hat, and made my way up to the third floor. The door to Mrs. Stewart's suite was ajar due to the fact the doorframe, where the lock connected into it, was splintered and broken.

I gently knocked and stepped inside. Dr. Briggs was pacing the room.

"Is she all right?" I asked. "Was she harmed?"

He stopped pacing. "No, but she was frightened."

"Did she see who broke in?" Cordelia asked.

"The person was wearing a cloak and had their face hidden."

"Was anything taken?"

He rubbed his forehead and sat down on the plush, Jacobean-revival chaise lounge. "I'm afraid they've taken the bank book and some of Bertha's jewelry."

"Oh my," I said, sorry she had been robbed but also now worried about the reputation of the Arabella. Atticus Brooks would have his day in the sun, to be sure.

I would have to tell Clayton, too, but dreaded it. He was already having difficulty staying put in order to heal. This would just increase his desire to get up and set things right in his town.

"May I see Mrs. Stewart?" I asked, glancing at the partially open bedroom door.

"She's sleeping. I gave her a sedative. Miss Fontaine is with her."

"Cornelius? Cornelius, who's there?" Mrs. Stewart's weakened voice came from the room.

He went to the doorway. "It's Mrs. Pryce. She—"

"Send her in," she said.

"Bertha, I'm not sure that's—"

"Send her in. I wish to speak with her."

The doctor turned to me. "I don't advise this. She hasn't been making much sense since the death of her son. She's very confused."

"I'll keep it brief," I assured him.

I quietly opened the bedroom door and slipped inside. Miss Fontaine was sitting in a chair next to the bed, a book in her lap. She must have been reading to Mrs. Stewart.

The room was overfull with Mrs. Stewart's belongings. I wasn't surprised. When she had arrived, Mr. Johns and Clarence had to haul up a number of trunks. The woman obviously loved her creature comforts.

The bureau was littered with medicine bottles in various shapes, sizes, and colors. I noticed a beautiful beaded reticule on the dresser, as well.

When Mrs. Stewart saw me, she opened her eyes wide. "Mrs. Pryce," she said with some urgency in her voice.

"Hello, Mrs. Stewart. I came to check on you."

"It was him. It was that man. Cristoforo Valdez." She pointed to the door. Her ice-blue eyes were glassy and weepy from the laudanum.

"The person who broke in here?" I asked, a little confused. The doctor had said she couldn't identify the thief.

"He killed my Ralph!"

I glanced at Miss Fontaine, and she rose from the chair, indicating I should take it in her stead. I smiled and complied. She went to the bureau, and when she took up the beaded handbag lying there, I thought I saw something that, strangely enough, looked like a twig fall out of it, but I couldn't be sure. I was about to alert her, but she slipped out of the room. I got up to see what the item was, but Mrs. Stewart thrust her hand out toward me.

"Where do you think you're going?" she demanded.

I blinked in astonishment at her authoritative tone. "I . . . I was just—"

She tried to raise herself to sitting, but it seemed she was too weak.

I went back to the chair. Seeing her struggle, I wanted to offer comfort. "It's all right, Mrs. Stewart. Just lie back and relax."

She fixed a steely-eyed glare at me. "Don't tell me to relax. My son is dead. How can I relax?" She let herself fall back onto the pillow with a mixture of frustration and disgust on her face. "You really must take more precautions for the welfare of your guests at this hotel," she snapped. Suddenly, her eyes grew heavy, and it seemed she was fighting to keep them open.

"Yes," I said, withering inside. Her sharpness reminded me all too much of my mother. A woman embittered by loss and someone who wielded an excessive amount of control over the lives of her loved ones. Being subjected to Mrs. Stewart's harshness brought up all those feelings of anger, worthlessness, and self-pity. I tried my best to snuff them out. "I'm so sorry for all of your trouble."

"We should have remained at Archibald's ranch, weather be damned," she slurred. "Where is the sheriff? I would like to speak with him. He needs to arrest Cristoforo Valdez."

"Mrs. Stewart, why do you think Mr. Valdez killed your son?"

"Isn't it obvious?" she said, voice raised. Her rheumy eyes flared with indignation, sending a spike of trepidation straight to my stomach. When at her finest, I'm sure this woman could strike fear into anyone. She was indeed quite formidable, as Percival had said.

"You heard him threaten my boy." She weakly shook a finger at me. "He said, 'This isn't over.' You must have that man arrested!"

Even though I didn't like the way she was speaking to me, I had to concur. Mr. Valdez had lied about being in Mr. Stewart's room the night of the murder, he'd been seen with the body in the annex and hadn't alerted anyone, and if Mrs. Stewart was correct in identifying him, he'd broken into her room. There was no denying he looked guilty.

Mrs. Stewart lowered her hand and held it over her face. All the severity in her demeanor had vanished. The poor woman was indeed distraught, and it grieved me that she had come to such unhappiness here under my roof.

I reached out and gently patted her leg. "Don't you worry any further, Mrs. Stewart. We will find out who did this to you . . . and to your son."

Chapter Sixteen

I went to the sheriff's room to find Dr. Tate helping him from the bed with one hand and holding two wooden crutches in the other.

Clayton's face was etched with pain, but those indigo eyes shone with sheer determination.

"It looks like you're making progress," I said by way of politeness. I did not think he seemed ready at all for the crutches, but who was I to tell him what to do? I'd tried that before, and it hadn't turned out well. Mr. Clayton Marshall had a stubborn streak.

"We are just testing the waters a bit," Dr. Tate said. "I'd like to see if he can support himself on the bruised leg." He was a head shorter than Clayton, and as he was a much older gentleman, he didn't seem strong enough to support him should Clayton lose his balance and fall.

I quickly went to their aid. I took hold of Clayton's elbow and lifted it around my neck. I steadied him with my other arm around the back of his waist. He glanced down at me and held me in that sea-swept gaze. The warmth of his body pressing against mine made my heart thud uncomfortably in my chest. I looked away for fear of being lost in those stormy eyes. Now was not the time for such frivolities.

"How does the leg feel?" the doctor asked.

"Sore, but standing on it is manageable," Clayton said, trying to sound convincing, but his pinched expression said otherwise.

The doctor placed one of the crutches under Clayton's arm, and he handed me the other. Once they were secured under both the sheriff's arms, he hopped forward and then quickly sucked in a breath, obviously in pain.

Dr. Tate frowned. "I'd much rather you be in a wheeled chair."

"No, I'll be fine with this. I want to get stronger."

"See if you can move forward. More carefully this time," the doctor said.

Clayton set all of his weight on the less injured leg and stifled a groan. He clearly wasn't ready for this.

"All right, then," Dr. Tate said. "Let's get him back to the bed."

"I can do it, Doc. Just give me a minute," he snapped. He swung the tip of the crutches forward and then hopped on his good leg to meet them. He managed all right, but his face had gone white.

"Very good, Sheriff," Dr. Tate said. "But that's it for now. You can get up for a little while every few hours to build back the strength in that leg. I don't want you overtaxing it. It will slow the healing process."

Though I knew it was difficult for him to accept this, he reluctantly agreed to go back to the bed, but he insisted on sitting instead of lying down. After we got him settled, I pulled a chair up to his bedside. The doctor was placing his medical items back in his bag, preparing to leave.

Clayton seemed much more comfortable now, so I thought it a good time to divulge the latest news.

"I think I know who killed Mr. Stewart," I said.

"You do?" they asked in unison.

I told them about the break-in in Mrs. Stewart's room and the missing bank book. "She identified Cristoforo Valdez as the thief. And we found his medal in Mr. Stewart's room. I think you need to make an arrest."

"It's going to be hard for me to do that from here," Clayton said.

"I suppose I could do it," I offered.

He opened his eyes wide with surprise. "Oh no, you don't. Not alone."

As much as I hated to admit it, the sheriff was right. I would be no match for Mr. Valdez should he try to flee.

"What if the doctor accompanied me? I could also have Mr. Johns help. He's strong as an ox."

The sheriff gave a reluctant shake of his head. "I don't know, Arabella."

"She's right," Dr. Tate said. "We should at least bring him to you for questioning. Mr. Johns and I will see that no harm comes to Mrs. Pryce."

"All right." Clayton raised his hands in surrender. "Bring him to me."

———

Once I had retrieved Mr. Johns, the two of us went back to Clayton's room to fetch the doctor.

"Let's try the saloon first," I suggested. "Mr. Valdez spends a lot of time there."

The Bella, as usual, was full to bursting at this hour of the afternoon. I spied Mrs. Edwards-Stewart and Miss

Fontaine sitting at their usual table. Andrew, Victoria, and Maggie sat near one of the windows. Sally was serving them their supper.

Kitty approached us. "Afternoon," she said, a look of curiosity on her face at my two unlikely companions. "Stopping in for a bite or a beer?"

"Neither right now, Kitty," I said. "Have you seen Mr. Valdez?"

She shook her head. "He was in here earlier, but I haven't seen him since."

"Thank you." I turned to the doctor and Mr. Johns. "Let's check with Mr. Pettyjohn."

We went to the lobby, and I approached the reception desk.

"Have you seen Mr. Valdez?" I asked.

"No, madam," Mr. Pettyjohn said.

"He hasn't checked out, has he?"

"He hasn't paid his bill nor returned his room key, so my guess is that no, he hasn't."

I turned to Dr. Tate and Mr. Johns. "Perhaps he is in his room."

Together, we went back down the hallway. I knocked on Mr. Valdez's door, but there was no answer.

"Mr. Valdez?" I called out.

Nothing.

I took the hotel master key ring from my pocket. I found the key to his room and unlocked the door. The bed was unmade and all his belongings were gone. I checked the wardrobe, and it was empty. Something peeking out under the left side of the bed caught my eye. I went over to it and picked it.

It was a hooded cloak.

I held it up for the others to see. "Dr. Briggs said that

Mrs. Stewart mentioned the person who'd broken into her room was wearing a cloak."

My gaze traveled to the small writing desk. Upon it stood a half-empty bottle of whisky and two glasses. One of the glasses was empty and the other was half-full.

"He's gone," I said.

"We'll have to find him," Dr. Tate nodded. "We'll check the train depot—"

"But the train heading to Denver isn't running because of the avalanche up north," Mr. Johns reminded us. "And the one heading west isn't due to leave until later tonight. I doubt he'd be cooling his heels at the train station."

"Good point," the doctor agreed.

"We could also check the livery," I suggested. "He might have left by coach, or even on horseback, though that's less likely due to the weather." I set my hands on my hips, looking around the room. A puddle of dark liquid on the corner of the desktop stopped my gaze. I went over to it and peered closer. There were fragments of what looked like hair in the liquid. I touched it with my finger, and when I pulled it away, I gasped.

It was blood.

———————————

Dr. Tate, Mr. Johns, and I left Mr. Valdez's room and made our way to the lobby. "I'll get my coat and hat and meet you back here," I said.

"Arabella." Cordelia appeared from behind me. "You look flustered. What's going on?"

I tilted my head toward the stairway. "Follow me up. I have news."

143

Whispering, I told her of my mission and that Mr. Johns and Dr. Tate would be accompanying me.

"I'm coming, too," she insisted. "Safety in numbers."

She did have a point. "All right, then," I agreed.

When we reached our room, I noticed Percival's signature chill in the air, along with the lingering smell of pipe smoke. My gaze traveled to the love seat under the bay window to find it was occupied by his transparent form. He tapped his fingers on the armrest impatiently.

I stifled a sigh. I didn't have time for Percival's games.

"Cordelia, be a love and get my coat and hat from my wardrobe?" I asked.

"Of course," she said and left the parlor to go into our rooms.

"What is it, Percival?" I asked, equally impatient.

"I have information."

"Really? What kind of information?"

"I was passing through the hallway to go out to the river when I saw Cherrie Fontaine leave Mr. Valdez's room. I thought you should know because you told me to be on the lookout."

I blinked in astonishment. "Cherrie Fontaine? How strange. When was this?"

"About an hour ago. I came looking for you, but you were with your sheriff—"

I gritted my teeth. "I've told you, he's not my sheriff."

"And then you were with the doctor and Mr. Johns. And as you don't want me around when you are in the company of others—"

"All right, Percival. I understand." I held up a hand to silence him. "Was Mr. Valdez in his room at that time?"

"I don't know." He pressed his hand to his forehead as if it pained him.

"Are you all right?" I asked.

He lowered his hand. "I'm perfectly fine."

Just then, Cordelia entered the room with our coats and hats, and Percival popped out of sight.

"It's so cold in here." She shivered. "I think we need a fire burning all day long."

I smiled. "You're probably right. I will talk to Maggie about it."

Seeing us getting bundled up in our coats, Bijou started barking. She was obviously hoping for a walk in the snow. I considered not taking her but felt sorry for the little girl. Between the two of us, Cordelia and I could keep her wrangled in and safe, should there be any altercations between the men.

We met them in the lobby and then made our way outside. The late-afternoon air was crisp and cold, made more so by the sun dipping below the mountains and casting a shadow upon the town. But at least it wasn't snowing.

We headed south down the main street toward the livery, which was located at the very south end of town. It was an Archer establishment, of course, and run by Mr. Bob Parkhurst. Smoke was issuing from the roof of his forge, as he kept the coals burning throughout the day.

When we finally arrived, a bit winded from trudging through the thick snow on the street, I was glad to enter the warm, three-sided forge where Mr. Parkhurst was busy fashioning some horseshoes.

When he saw us, his dark-skinned face split into his usually friendly smile. "What brings you fine folks to my forge in this cold weather?"

"Hello, Mr. Parkhurst," I said, rubbing my hands together. Bijou tugged herself away from Cordelia's hold on the leash and ran over to Mr. Parkhurst. Grinning, he bent down and picked her up. Her coat was wet from the snow.

"Good day to you, Miss Bijou," he said, looking down into her face. She was smiling from ear to ear. He chuckled, scratching her behind the ears.

"Mr. Parkhurst. We are looking for someone. A Mr. Valdez. Has he been here to buy a coach ticket or to perhaps buy a horse?"

He shook his head. "I haven't seen anyone. It's a mighty cold day. Not many people out today."

"And you've been here all day?"

"I did go to the bank to make a deposit, but I don't think I was gone for more than fifteen minutes."

"Thank you, Mr. Parkhurst."

I glanced over at the horse pens. Mr. Parkhurst—or rather, Mr. Archer—kept about a dozen horses at the livery. Sitting on an acre of land, the livery was comprised of a large barn with six stalls on either side of it and another building that housed hay, wagons, and other conveyances. Each stall in the barn had an outdoor run, where most of the horses were, at the moment, enjoying the last rays of sun. Mr. Archer kept the horses there for potential sale or for the residents of La Plata Springs to lease as beasts of burden or an economical means of transportation. I myself had leased a horse for a few hours at a time for my riding lessons with Clayton.

All the horses on the west side of the barn were looking in the direction of one interior stall. The horse occupying that stall, a beautiful chestnut with four white socks, stood oddly still, leaning its weight on its back haunches. Its neck was arched, and it seemed to be looking at something from one of its large and expressive eyes. It emitted a low, snorting sound.

"What's wrong with that horse?" I asked Mr. Parkhurst.

He looked over at the animal. "Looks scared," he said. He set down his tools, and we followed him over to the barn. Once inside, we went to the aforementioned stall and peered over the door.

My breath caught in my throat. It was Mr. Valdez. His legs akimbo, his eyes wide and staring, he lay motionless on floor of the stall. In his left hand, he clutched the handle of his leather travel bag. A superficial gash oozed on his forehead.

"Oh my heavens!" Cordelia clasped both hands over her mouth.

Mr. Parkhurst opened the stall door, and Dr. Tate pushed through, rushing over to Mr. Valdez. He knelt down and held his fingers under Mr. Valdez's nose. He then took a pulse reading at his neck.

"Is he . . . ?" I couldn't make myself say the word.

"I'm afraid so," he said. "Mr. Valdez is dead."

Chapter Seventeen

"He must have been stealing a horse to get out of town," Cordelia said.

"He obviously didn't want to wait for Mr. Parkhurst to return from the bank," the doctor added. He took the bag from Mr. Valdez's hand and handed it to me. I opened it and started to go through it. There was a change of clothing, some toiletries, and other personal items. My gaze fell on the tiny edge of a piece of paper peeking out from the bottom panel of the bag. How odd. I reached in, and though it took some effort, I carefully pulled the panel up. Lying inside were several bundles of cash.

"It has a false bottom," I murmured. As a child, I had been in a play where the antagonist of the story, a thief, had just such a bag.

"What are you going on about?" Dr. Tate asked.

"Neither Mrs. Stewart's bank book nor missing jewelry are here, but look at this," I said, holding the bag open for the group to see.

"Wow. That looks like a substantial amount of cash," Mr. Parkhurst said.

"Yes, but I don't think Mr. Valdez killed Mr. Stewart."

"What do you mean, Arabella?" Cordelia asked.

"Look." I pointed to the gold chain around his neck. The medal rested on his throat. "He was telling the truth about not being in Mr. Stewart's room the night of the murder. How could he be wearing his medal if I have it?"

Cordelia frowned. "Where did the medal we found in Mr. Stewart's room come from, then?"

Mr. Parkhurst glanced around our small group. "What's this about?" I relayed the details of our searching Ralph Stewart's room. "Maybe the medal belonged to Mr. Stewart," he said.

I shook my head. "His wife said they were not religious."

"It could have belonged to the person who last stayed in the room. Before Mr. Stewart," Mr. Parkhurst guessed.

"No," I said. "Maggie is meticulous in her cleaning. Even if one of the other maids cleans a room, she always gives it an inspection. She makes a point of looking under the bed. You wouldn't believe what she has found under them on occasion—clothing, jewelry, books. She even found a gun once."

Dr. Tate looked at the medal. "I saw one of those in Archer's Dry Goods the other day. I was shopping for some supplies for the infirmary."

"You don't say?" Cordelia said. "Was it exactly the same as this one?"

"I couldn't say for certain, but they sure look the same."

My mind was racing now. "Mr. Valdez wore it quite prominently. Anyone who spoke to him would've seen it.

What if someone purchased the one in the shop and planted it in Mr. Stewart's room to make Mr. Valdez look guilty of the murder?"

"But why would they shove it under the bed like that?" Cordelia said.

I shrugged. "Whoever planted it surely didn't want Mr. Stewart to see it."

The doctor released an audible breath. "I've got to get Mr. Valdez's body to the infirmary to better examine him."

"I'll hook up a wagon for you," Mr. Parkhurst offered.

"Do you have something we can drape over the body?" Dr. Tate asked. "I don't want to alarm anyone in the street."

Mr. Parkhurst nodded. "Sure do. I'll have it all ready for you in a minute. If you'll excuse me," he addressed Cordelia and me.

"Of course," I said. "We have to get back to the hotel to inform the sheriff of this development."

I felt bad for thinking Mr. Valdez guilty of the crime, but from the testimonials and evidence I'd gathered, it had seemed to make perfect sense that he would want to kill—and was capable of killing—Ralph Stewart. He'd even said he wished he'd been the one to kill him. I was back to square one in my investigation. If we didn't find the murderer soon, we wouldn't be able to continue with the festival and Andrew would miss the opportunity to facilitate an introduction between Charlie and his grandmother, and to reunite him with his mother. And Mrs. Stewart would possibly tarnish the name of the Arabella—with the help of Atticus Brooks at that.

I simply had to find Mr. Stewart's killer.

We stayed while Mr. Parkhurst, Dr. Tate, and Mr. Johns loaded Mr. Valdez's body into the wagon. Dr. Tate handed me Mr. Valdez's bag. "You'll have to give this to the sheriff."

I nodded.

"If it is murder, that is evidence," the doctor added. "And his family will need to be alerted."

I nodded. "Yes. Thank you."

We watched Dr. Tate drive the wagon away.

Suddenly, I realized I was very cold. I had been in such a state of shock at finding Mr. Valdez's body I had quite forgotten the freezing temperature. I looked over at Cordelia, whose face was pale, her lips a deep shade of lavender. Little Bijou, wet from the snow, shivered at my feet. I picked her up.

"You poor thing," I said, holding her trembling little body close to my chest. "Let's get you back into the warmth."

Mr. John's began to peel off his coat. "Here, Mrs. Pryce, you look like you need this."

I held up my hand. "Absolutely not, Mr. Johns. You keep your coat on. We'll just hurry back to the hotel."

He settled it back around his shoulders, and we took off for the hotel, walking as fast as we possibly could.

Cordelia and I went immediately to our rooms to change out of our cold, wet clothes. Our skirts had become quite frozen with our walk in the snow. On our way upstairs, we ran into Maggie.

"My goodness!" she said. "You ladies look affright. And poor little Bijou, she is soaking wet."

"I'm afraid we were outside too long," I said, not wanting to go into the details.

"Let's stoke the fire in your rooms immediately," she said. "Come on now, we need to get you all warm."

She hustled us up the stairs, and when we arrived at our rooms, she went straight to the fireplace. The fire had dwindled in our absence, leaving warm gray coals. With Bijou still in my arms, I went to the bathing room to gather a towel. I wrapped my shivering little *chouchou* in it and went back to the parlor. Cordelia had moved Bijou's bed in front of the fireplace and I settled her into it.

With Maggie's ministrations, the fire quickly came back to life. She stood and wiped her hands on her apron. "You must get out of those dresses," she said to both of us and peeled off my coat. She then helped Cordelia. She hung the coats on the hooks that had been hammered into the fireplace mantel on each side of the grate for just such a purpose.

After she helped us with our hats, she shooed us off to our rooms.

"Thank you, Maggie," I said. "That will be all."

"I'll have Lottie brew some tea," she said, not willing to give up on her mission of restoring warmth to us, both inside and out.

"Very well, but have her bring it to the sheriff's room. We are going there directly after we change our clothes," I explained.

"Will do," she said. She bent down and pushed the edges of the towel farther under Bijou's little body. "There you go, girl. We can't have you getting sick. Your mistress would be lost without you."

I smiled at her tenderness. "Quite," I agreed.

Cordelia and I hurried down the stairs to the sheriff's room, Mr. Valdez's bag tight in my grasp. I knocked on the door and pushed it open as soon as the sheriff called out to enter. I stopped short, surprised to see Mr. Crawford of the Post Office & Telegraph Exchange sitting in the chair next to the bed. He had a kindly face, with fleshy jowls covered by pork-chop sideburns. He rose from the chair at our presence.

"Hello, Mrs. Pryce. I thought I would come to see how the sheriff was feeling," he said with a sheepish look on his face.

A glance at the thunder in Clayton's eyes made my heart sink to the pit of my stomach. "Is everything all right?" I asked.

"Close the door," Clayton said. His gaze was fixed on me, and I had the sinking feeling I was in trouble, but I hadn't a clue as to why.

Cordelia quietly closed the door behind us. Her eyes met mine, and she grimaced, sensing, as I did, things were not well and that we, or rather I, might have something to do with it.

My stomach fluttered but not with the familiar butterflies that occurred in the sheriff's presence on occasion, like when those heart-melting eyes held mine captive. This time it was with fear. Something was terribly wrong.

"I could have you put away for obstruction of justice. What you've done is at best is a misdemeanor and at worst a felony," he said sharply.

"I . . . I don't understand," I said.

"You forged my signature on a wire sent to Chicago."

I gulped, my stomach now doing somersaults. I glanced over at Mr. Crawford. His regarded me with a sympathetic look in his eyes, and I daresay a little bit of guilt. A few months ago, I had been determined to find the killer of my friend's husband. During my investigation, I had told Mr. Crawford the sheriff had given me authority to sign the wire, and he hadn't questioned me about it. But in reality, Clayton had warned me off the case, as he felt I was too close to the parties involved and it was too dangerous. He'd threatened to lock me in my rooms. And it wouldn't have been the first time. When I'd first arrived in town, I was accused of murder and the evidence had been stacking up against me. He had also assigned a watchdog to keep me imprisoned—Mr. Johns, one of my own employees, no less —which was completely humiliating. I was not a fragile flower in constant need of protection.

I went over to the chair, sat down, and set Mr. Valdez's travel bag on the floor next to me. "I can explain."

Clayton's eyes flared with rage. "You committed a crime. What's to explain?"

"I was following a lead and needed to know about the Clark case in Chicago. I was only trying to help."

"You made Mr. Crawford here an accessory to the crime," Clayton said, his voice low and, honestly, quite terrifying. "Don't you ever think of anyone but yourself?"

His words pierced through my very heart, nearly taking my breath away.

I directed my gaze to Mr. Crawford. "I . . . I am so sorry. I didn't realize."

"You have really overstepped your bounds, Arabella," Clayton said.

While I knew I was in the wrong, my intentions had been good. I had wanted to help my friend, and I also had wanted to help Clayton. I'd just gone about it the wrong way.

"But she figured out who killed Mr. Townsend," Cordelia said, attempting to come to my rescue, though from the look on the sheriff's face, I feared it may have been in vain. "About the same time you did," she added. "You must admit she's very good at crime solving."

"But she has no authority to do so!" Clayton said

loudly, making me flinch. He had been annoyed with me on many occasions, but I had never heard him raise his voice.

I straightened my spine and hardened my face, but inside, I was wilting. I'd made a terrible error in judgment. I had committed a crime, and worst of all, I had disappointed the sheriff, whose good opinion I desired, much to my irritation. I swallowed and tried to collect myself. "I apologize, Clayton. It was wrong of me."

"Your apology does not correct forgery, Arabella."

I looked straight into those stormy blue eyes and raised my chin. "What do you aim to do about it?"

He looked away from me. "I don't know yet."

An uncomfortable silence filled the room.

"Well, I should be going," Mr. Crawford said. He looked over at me. "I didn't mean to cause any trouble, ma'am. The sheriff and I were talking about the Clark case, and it just came up, and—"

I raised a hand to stop him. "No apology necessary, Mr. Crawford. The fault was mine. You did nothing wrong."

He pressed his lips together and nodded. "Good day, then."

He left, and Cordelia, who was, I am sure, much distressed with the overwhelming tension in the air, slipped out after him. The silence continued. Clayton, still fuming, wouldn't look at me.

"I have some news you should know about," I said, my voice barely louder than a whisper. My hands trembled with anxiety at his coldness, and my heart wrenched in two. I didn't have many friends in town. Yes, the residents had all been very polite and treated me kindly, but it was hard for me to let my guard down and really let people in. I had begun to let the sheriff in, but now, instead of me closing the door on him, he had closed it on me, and to my utter surprise, it left me bereft.

He slowly turned his head to look at me, and when his eyes met mine, they were not only filled with anger but something more devastating. Hurt. A lump formed in my throat.

"Mr.—" I cleared my throat. "Mr. Valdez is dead."

He raised his eyebrows.

"We found him in the barn at the livery. There was no obvious cause of death. Dr. Tate has taken his body to the infirmary to attempt to discern how he died."

Clayton let out a deep breath.

"He was wearing this around his neck." I held up the medal.

Clayton took it from me and examined it. "But you found his medal in Ralph's room."

"I found *a* medal." I pulled the second necklace from my pocket. I had retrieved it from my drawer after I'd changed out of my soaked dress. He took that one, too, and studied them.

"They're identical," he said.

"Dr. Tate said he's seen them for sale at the Archer's Dry Goods."

"Why would Valdez have two of the same exact medals?"

"Right," I said. "It does seem odd. I suppose he could have purchased another as a gift for someone. But his business here was with Mr. Archer and Mr. Stewart. It wasn't a pleasure visit."

"Someone could have planted the medal in his room to make it look like he killed Ralph."

"That's what I was thinking. He had his travel bag with him, too." I picked it up and set it on the bed. "I expected to find the jewelry and the missing bank book in there, but all I found was clothing, toiletries, and a large sum of cash beneath a false bottom." I opened the bag and showed it to him.

The muscles in his handsomely square jaw, still tight with ire, rippled under his skin. "Leave the bag with me," he said. "I won't be requiring your help any longer."

My stomach clenched. "But you're still not well. How can you—"

"I'll manage." He looked away from me, which was a relief in a way. I could no longer bear the disappointment I saw in his eyes. He focused his attention on the bag. "Send Mr. Johns in. I'll have to deputize him."

My jaw dropped. "But Mr. Johns is my employee. You can't just steal him out from under me—again. And besides, he wasn't very vigilant the last time you deputized him." When Mr. Johns had been assigned as my body-guard, he'd fallen asleep at my door. Then he'd fallen down the stairs, twisting his ankle. He'd been put out of commission as soon as he had started in his new, albeit temporary, role as deputy. "He doesn't have the where-withal for—"

"At least he isn't reckless or dishonest," he shot back, his hot gaze meeting mine. "I'll have to make do. Now, please send him in."

"What about deputizing Andrew?" I suggested, thinking him much more suitable. He had his own motivations for bringing the killer to justice and reuniting Charlie with his mother. He would be a far better candidate.

"Andrew doesn't have the stomach for it. Besides, he's too close to the case. He and Ralph were like brothers. He won't see things clearly."

"But I can," I said in a last-ditch attempt.

Looking away from me once again, he said, "Send in Mr. Johns."

I couldn't think of anything else to say to convince him he could trust me. I had completely ruined what we'd been building. My stomach curdled in a kind of nausea that was worse than any caused by intestinal sickness. His disappointment in me made me feel physically ill. It was one of my worst fears come to pass. I had lived my life performing. Shining. Succeeding. Making people love me—or the image they had of me—if only for a moment in time. And I had failed in Clayton's eyes. It was almost too much to bear.

A prickling at the back of my eyes stung my nose, and my mouth had gone dry. Tears threatened to surface, and I fought to keep them back. It was ridiculous that I felt this way. I couldn't allow it. I *wouldn't* allow it.

I reminded myself of my mission here. To serve my time here in La Plata Springs. To bring the Arabella back to her stately self, sell her, and get back to my life in New York, far from this provincial town.

I stuffed the painful feelings back into their box and closed the lid tight. I would not be defeated by them.

I stood up. "Sheriff Marshall, I apologize for my actions. I didn't mean any harm. I will send Mr. Johns directly." Without another word, I left the room.

Once in the hallway, I closed the door behind me. The prickling in my eyes started again, and I closed them tight, willing the tears away. I had disappointed one of my only friends in La Plata Springs, and for that, I was truly sorry. As much as it pained me, I realized I might never regain his respect or trust, and that was something I would have to learn to live with.

But I wouldn't disappoint the potentially bright future of a little boy who faced a life without a family, like I had.

Yes, I'd had my mother, but the relationship had been trans-actional. It was clear Victoria Clement would do anything to be reunited with her boy again, and I hoped upon hope she was not guilty of killing her boy's father.

I would do what I could to find the guilty party and bring the festival back to life so Charlie could be with his family. But I only had a few more days to make that happen.

Chapter Eighteen

DECEMBER 10, 1885

The next day, I requested that Maggie and Andrew meet me and Cordelia in our rooms.

"Thank you for coming," I said as they entered. Once we were all seated, I began. "We've hit a bit of a snag in our investigation into the murder of Ralph Stewart."

"What happened?" Andrew asked.

"Mr. Valdez is dead."

Maggie gave an audible gasp, her hand over her mouth.

"We are waiting to hear from Dr. Tate regarding the cause of death, but it's pretty clear that Mr. Valdez did not kill Mr. Stewart."

"You're certain?" Andrew said.

"Yes," I said. I turned to Maggie. "Before the Stewarts checked in, did you clean the room assigned to Mr. Stewart, or was it one of the other maids?"

"I cleaned it myself, ma'am. I cleaned all the rooms that

were to be occupied by the Stewart party. I wanted to make sure it was done absolutely right."

I smiled at her pride of workmanship. "Thank you, Maggie. That means a lot to me. Did you happen to clean under the bed?"

"Oh, yes, ma'am. There is always so much dust in the rooms. And I always check to see if the former occupant left something. You'd be surprised what we find under those beds."

"Yes. As I thought. So you didn't happen to see a gold medal on a chain under the bed in Mr. Stewart's room?"

She shook her head. "No, ma'am. I made sure it was spotless before Mr. Stewart occupied it."

I then explained to them how we'd seen Mr. Valdez wearing the medal and how we'd found a duplicate in Mr. Stewart's room after the fact.

"Do you think someone planted it there?" Andrew asked.

"Yes. Someone, most likely the real killer, wanted us to believe Mr. Valdez killed your cousin. Cordelia and I have compiled a list of possible suspects."

Cordelia held up her notebook and then set it back down in her lap to read it aloud. "First, we have Mary Alice Edwards-Stewart. She indicated her husband had a history of infidelity. She knows about Victoria, but it's not clear if she knows about the child. She could have been the woman Mr. Valdez heard arguing with Mr. Stewart in his room the night of the murder."

"We also have to consider Victoria," I said.

Maggie and Andrew looked at each other in surprise.

"Why would she kill Ralph?" Andrew asked. "They were going to be together. He was going to leave Mary Alice."

"Not according to Mary Alice," I said. "She claims Mr. Stewart told Victoria he wouldn't leave her and it was over between him and Victoria. So, she also could have been the one arguing with Mr. Stewart in his room."

"And she did throw a drink in his face at the party," Cordelia reminded us. "She was clearly upset with him."

"Mary Alice claimed she heard Victoria threaten Mr. Stewart earlier in the week. Something to the effect of 'You will regret this decision,'" I added.

Andrew shook his head. "She wouldn't jeopardize being reunited with Charlie. She wouldn't do something so stupid."

"We have to consider all possibilities," I said. "We also probably need to look into two others."

They all looked at me expectantly. With a tilt of my chin, I signaled to Cordelia to continue. "Dr. Briggs. Cherrie Fontaine indicated there was some kind of power play between Mr. Stewart and him. According to her, Mr. Stewart was concerned, and perhaps threatened, by the amount of control Dr. Briggs had over his mother. She's become quite frail and quite dependent—"

"On the laudanum he plies her with," Andrew finished.

I sighed. "I'm afraid so. He also claimed that a bank book and jewelry had been stolen from Mrs. Stewart's room. It was broken into earlier today. He said Mrs. Stewart told him the perpetrator was wearing a hooded cloak."

"But then Mrs. Stewart claimed she saw that it was Cristoforo Valdez," Cordelia said. "And we found a cloak in Mr. Valdez's room."

"But his bag did not contain a bank book or the missing jewelry."

"So, we don't know who might have stolen them?" Maggie asked.

"Right," I said.

"Who is the other person we need to investigate?" Maggie asked.

I caught Andrew's gaze. I hadn't shared this suspicion with anyone yet. "I think we have to consider Mr. Archer."

"My uncle?"

I gave a shrug of apology. "I spoke with Miss Mayes. She filled me in on some of your family's history. She claims your uncle does not have as much power, or as much control, over his businesses as he portrays."

Andrew furrowed his brow. "What do you mean?"

"She suggested Mrs. Stewart has more than equal standing in the running of the family estate and the businesses. She sent her son to clean up the mess at the mines in La Linda. Perhaps she'd given him a larger role."

Shock registered on Andrew's face. "You think Boss stole the bank book? And could have killed Ralph?"

I shrugged. "Perhaps. Maybe your aunt and Ralph were keeping something from him in regard to the finances of the estate? Or maybe that's just what he presumed?" I bit my lip, wondering if I should continue with my train of thought. "What if Mr. Stewart was somehow a threat to Mr. Archer's control over the business dealings here in La Plata Springs? What if Mr. Stewart stood in the way of—"

He opened his eyes wide. "Now, hold on. My uncle is a lot of things, and he can be a real . . . well, you know. But he is not a cold-blooded killer."

"Did your uncle ever complain about your cousin?"

"No. Not to me, at least."

"Did your cousin ever complain about your uncle?"

He huffed. "Yeah, but we all complain about Uncle Arch. He's pretty demanding and wants things his way. Why do you think everyone calls him Boss?"

I pressed my lips together. "Exactly. Your aunt is ill. And with Ralph out of the way . . ."

"Your uncle would be the only direct family member left. He would inherit everything. Unless you do," Cordelia said.

He shook his head. "I know I stand to inherit some money but certainly not the businesses."

"Andrew, maybe you could talk to your uncle. See what you can find out about the family estate? Maybe start with how it pertains to your inheritance. After all, you're entitled to know," I said. "Regardless of the murder case, you're a young man—an engaged young man. You need to plan for your future." I looked over at Maggie and smiled. She blushed a lovely shade of ripe peach.

"I'll do it," he said. "But I still maintain my uncle wouldn't have killed Ralph. He just wouldn't have."

From the hurt in his voice, I know he couldn't imagine Mr. Archer doing such a thing. The man had raised Andrew since he was a small boy. But the only person who Mr. Archer might confide in about such matters would be Andrew—certainly not me or anyone else on the festival committee.

"There is one more person we haven't considered," Cordelia cut in, bringing us back to the subject at hand.

"Who?" Andrew asked.

"Cherrie Fontaine," I said.

"Cherrie? Why her? You don't think she had motive to kill Ralph, do you?" Andrew asked.

"I'm not sure," I said. "Yet, in my brief conversation with her, I gathered she did not care much for Mr. Stewart. And I've seen her skulking around the hallways. There's just something about her behavior I find odd. What do you know about her?"

"Not much," he said. "Except that she's been in my aunt's service for some time. She's quiet as a mouse, though. Bookish. Meek."

"Yes. But we need to consider everyone who had an issue with Ralph."

The room filled with silence again, everyone immersed in their own thoughts. I cleared my throat. "I have something else to tell you," I said quietly. "The sheriff does not want me investigating the murder anymore."

"Why?" Maggie asked. "He certainly can't do it. He can barely walk."

"Why did he tell you to stop?" Andrew piped in.

I smoothed my skirt over my thighs with the palms of my hands. "He— Well, he's concerned about my safety." I thought it best to omit my previous transgression and the fact the sheriff may well never speak to me again. Or that he might possibly arrest me for forgery and interfering with an investigation, for which I could very well end up in prison.

Maggie's mouth dropped open, and her eyes shone with indignation. "This doesn't have anything to do with you being a woman, does it? If that's the case, then I'm going to give him a piece of my mind!"

I raised my brows, surprised by her outburst. It was not a typical response from her. She was usually so timid. "No," I said. "That has nothing to do with it. But in the meantime, he's deputized Mr. Johns."

Andrew slapped his hands against his thighs. "Johns? The man can barely keep himself organized. He's a nice fellow and all, but he's a brick short of a load—"

"Andrew!" Maggie scolded.

"He doesn't have the mind for investigating a crime," he finished.

"I agree. He's a dedicated and able bellman and handyman, and he'll do anything you ask of him, bless his heart, but I fear we will never find the culprit with him in charge."

"What do you aim to do?" Andrew asked. "We only have a couple more days before my uncle calls off the festival. Victoria will be crushed. Charlie will never meet his family."

"I know." I held up a hand. I then glanced over at Cordelia, and she gave me a nod, prompting me to finish. "We are going to continue."

Andrew let out a sigh of relief.

"But it has to appear I am not doing anything in regard to finding the killer. We will have to be discreet."

"We can do that," Maggie stated eagerly.

"What would you like us to do?" Andrew asked.

"I'd like for you to see what you can find out from your uncle about the details of the estate and the businesses your family owns, as well as his relationship with Mr. Stewart."

I turned to Cordelia. "Would you go to the dry goods store and ask Mr. Emerson who recently purchased one of those religious medals?"

"Yes, I'll go right now."

"Maggie, I'd like for you to keep an eye out for anything in the Stewarts', and the rest of their party's, rooms that you think might be a clue."

"I can do that," she said with a look of determination on her face.

I sucked in a breath, suddenly remembering something. "The suicide note! It was clearly a fake. If we could compare handwriting samples . . ."

"But doesn't the sheriff have it?" Cordelia asked.

"Yes." I tapped my fingers together. "I'll see if I can glean from him its whereabouts. I'll have to be subtle. In the meantime, Cordelia and Maggie, see if you can somehow get handwriting samples from the Archer/Stewart party."

Cordelia gave me a dubious look, and I knew what she was thinking. Subtlety was not my strong suit.

"Very well." I clapped my hands against my thighs. "We all have our assignments." I stood up, and the rest of them did the same.

Bijou jumped up from her bed and ran to the leash hanging on the wall, wanting to go outside. Her enthusiasm drew my attention to the door. It stood ajar. Whoever had entered last must have left it opened. An uneasy feeling crept into my bones. I hoped our conversation had not been overheard. But we were on the top floor. Who would have reason to come up here?

The question gave me some relief, but still, it would not be good if our covert plans had been discovered. Not good at all.

Chapter Nineteen

My trio of spies departed. Still somewhat disconcerted about the slightly opened door, I shut it behind them.

I then went to the desk. I was glad I had remembered the suicide note found in Mr. Stewart's room. But how was I going to persuade the sheriff to turn it over to me? He certainly would not, considering he probably wouldn't even speak to me, much less give me any kind of information pertaining to the murder. I grabbed a piece of paper and set to doodling, as it sometimes helped me to think.

A sudden chill filled the room.

"Hello, Percival," I said, without even lifting my pencil, or my eyes, from my doodles. I sensed he was in the mirror. I was getting used to the visceral response my body had in his presence. It grew keener by the day, it seemed.

"It's a shame you and your sheriff have had a falling out."

I looked up into the mirror. His back was facing me as he was sitting on the corner of my desk, looking down at my geometric figures. I turned to my left and looked into his transparent eyes, which bore a look of smugness. Or was it triumph? I recalled his odd behavior when we were cloistered in the closet. He seemed to be quite himself now, without the oppressive air he'd demonstrated before. I was quite glad of it.

"He's not my sheriff, and yes, it is a shame. It's entirely my fault, and I feel just terrible about it. I wish I wasn't so impetuous sometimes. But I need to get back into his good graces. Not only because I need some information from him pertaining to the case but because I want to be friends again. I hate when people are disappointed in me. It's quite crushing. Like I have a lead weight on my heart."

"I didn't know you cared about him so much."

"Don't be silly. I don't like it when anyone is mad at me, you know that."

"But you aim to continue your investigation, even though he asked you not to?"

"Yes. It grieves me that I may have done permanent damage to my friendship with the sheriff, but I don't want Mr. Archer to cancel the festival."

"I saw some of your merry troop of festival planners leaving a moment ago."

"Yes. Since I cannot officially investigate Mr. Stewart's murder, I've enlisted them to help me gather information and, hopefully, some evidence."

He pulled his pipe from his pocket, and with a snap of his fingers, the bowl glowed orange. Instantly, the pleasant smell of earthy tobacco filled the air. A sense of calm washed over me. As vexing as he could be at times, Percival also had the ability to soothe me. "I wouldn't have thought Miss Fontaine would be assisting you."

"Miss Fontaine? No. She's not a part of the investigation. Other than answering some questions. Why would you say that?"

He shrugged. "I saw her on the third-floor landing, near the stairs. I assumed she'd been in your rooms."

My brows pulled downward. "No . . ."

"Right. Oh well." He gave a little chuckle. "I seem to see her everywhere. Earlier, I saw her coming across the river on the footbridge. I was out at my favorite spot. You should accompany me sometime."

"Yes," I said absently, continuing with my doodles.

A smoke ring encircled my head. Percival obviously wanted my complete attention. I ignored his silent request.

"Speaking of Miss Fontaine," he persisted. "I've remembered something."

"About what? Mr. Stewart's murder?"

"No. From some years ago. At Boss Archer's the night I departed from this world. She was there, of course. With Bertha."

"When was this?"

"About this time of year in '82."

"What do you remember about it?"

"I saw her speaking with Enrique Valdez in a most coquettish manner."

"She was flirting with him?"

"Yes. He was quite enamored with her. He was a bit of a ladies' man, I recall. Spent a lot of time in the company of Kitty's girls."

"How odd. Miss Fontaine does not seem the flirtatious type. She has a quiet seriousness about her. She reminds me of how Cordelia used to be before we came to La Plata Springs."

"They were huddled in a corner table with a bottle of wine."

I blinked. "Astonishing."

"It seemed Enrique got a little fresh with her, and she didn't like it. He'd had hold of her wrist. I went over to see if I could help."

"How chivalrous of you. What happened?"

"She was quite upset. I told the gentleman to leave her alone. He resisted at first. Jumped up from his seat and grabbed me by the lapels. Told me to mind my own business. Luckily, I was able to talk him down. Having seen the altercation, Boss Archer came over to us and asked what was going on. I explained what happened, and he asked Mr. Valdez to leave. Valdez eventually skulked away."

"I see. Good on you, Percival."

"Yes."

"What happened then?" I asked.

"The poor young lady was unnerved, as you might imagine. But she thanked me and then left. I myself was a little rattled, so I sat down and enjoyed the wine. They hadn't touched it. I was tiring of the crowd and relished a little quiet. I asked Boss to join me, but he said he had to get back to his guests."

"You are quite the knight in shining armor," I said with a grin, teasing him. My thoughts went back to what he'd told me of Miss Fontaine's behavior. I did not know her very well at all, but what Percival had said about her flirtatiousness seemed very out of character. "I'm not sure this has anything to do with Mr. Stewart, but thank you for your insights, Percival."

"You're welcome, my dear. It's odd, but the Stewart family—and Miss Fontaine—returning to La Plata Springs has seemed to awaken something in me. I can't imagine why, and I'm not exactly sure what it is."

"That is strange," I mused. "I wonder, Percival. You said

you have not seen Mr. Stewart's spirit here. Is that still the case?"

"Yes. No trace of him."

"What about Enrique? Since he died here in this hotel, have you ever seen him?"

He shook his head. "No."

"I see. Well, I might pay Miss Fontaine a visit."

"So, you really are not going to heed the sheriff's order to cease your investigation?"

I sighed. "A little boy's future is at stake. I think that is more important than what Mr. Marshall might think of me."

A smile crept across Percival's handsome, transparent face. "Yes, far more important."

I narrowed my eyes at him. I couldn't figure out if the grin was for the sake of the boy or because I might get into even more hot water with the sheriff.

I stepped into the hallway and dug my keys out of my dress pocket. I locked the door to our rooms securely and turned to go down the stairs when I noticed some dirt on the rug next to the doorway. Someone must have tracked it in from the street.

I would have to alert Maggie, or one of the other maids, so they could clean it up later, but for now, I was focused on finding Miss Fontaine. There was no answer at her room on the second floor. I then went back up to the third floor to Mrs. Stewart's room. Dr. Briggs answered the door.

"Hello, Dr. Briggs. How are you?"

"I'm doing well, Mrs. Pryce. Won't you come in?" He opened the door wider.

"Oh, well, thank you. I won't keep you long. I was just looking for Miss Fontaine."

"She isn't here. She left to go to the telephone exchange. She was making a call for Mrs. Stewart."

"Thank you, Doctor. Maybe I'll catch her in the street," I said. I caught a glimpse of a suitcase lying on the sofa behind him. "Are you packing to leave?" I asked, my heart in my throat. They couldn't leave yet. It was too soon.

"Just getting things organized for when we do leave. Though, I think it may be soon."

"But didn't the sheriff say you all had to stay in town?"

He gave me an indulgent smile. "He asked us to, but he has brought forth no real evidence or charges. And don't forget, this is a company town. Archibald's town, and the sheriff works for him. Archibald and Mrs. Stewart have the final say in all matters pertaining to the town."

"Even the law?" I asked, a little surprised at this declaration.

He held his arms out, palms up. "It seems so."

"I see," I said with some apprehension. Things were certainly run differently out here in the West. But seeing that Mr. Archer owned the town, or most of it, I suppose they did wield all the power.

The doctor continued. "Mrs. Stewart is quite anxious about seeing Ralph buried, and she wants him buried in Denver."

"Oh, not California?"

He shook his head.

"Her late husband was originally from Denver. He is buried there in the family plot. She wants them together."

"Of course. That makes perfect sense. Tell me, when are you planning to go?"

"We've heard there is another storm in Denver, so we

173

will leave as soon as it has passed. The train tracks have been cleared from the avalanche near there, but we don't want to risk being caught in the storm. Especially in Bertha's condition."

"Right." I gave him a polite smile. It seemed my time to find Mr. Stewart's killer was running out. And quickly. "Thank you, Dr. Briggs."

I glanced out the window behind him and noted the cloud cover. This room faced the mountains to the northeast. There was also a nice partial view of the river and the dense forest to the west of it. Denver was hundreds of miles away, but it looked as if we may be in store for a storm as well. I hoped those clouds would deliver a mountain of snow, if only to keep Mrs. Stewart here a bit longer.

I was about to turn for the door when I saw a man and woman emerging from the woods hand in hand. She was dressed in a scarlet overcoat and hat, and he was wearing a long, dark coat. They were looking adoringly at each other and laughing. A pang of longing struck me.

How nice it must be to have someone to indulge in a secret rendezvous in the woods.

I shook myself out of my silly sentimental musings. I said goodbye to Dr. Briggs and left the room.

I considered paying Clayton a visit, to see if I could charm him into forgiving me and letting me continue with the case. I would love to get ahold of the supposed suicide note. But I thought it best to give him some distance for the time being, knowing I was the last person he wanted to see at the moment. It could wait until after I spoke with Miss Fontaine.

I made a quick trip back to my rooms to gather my coat and hat. Fishing my keys out of my pocket, the blob of dirt on the rug at my door caught my attention again. I bent down to get a closer look at it. Enmeshed in it was a tangle of tiny, dark, fibrous seed pods. I wrinkled my nose. I took my handkerchief out of my pocket and scooped the dirt into it. When I went back into the parlor, I shook the handkerchief into the wastebasket.

I bundled up and made my way downstairs to the lobby. It was bustling with activity. As it was cold outside, I supposed the guests had chosen to mingle in the lobby or the saloon, which I quite liked. It was nice to see folks so comfortable in the hotel. A positive experience would prompt others to spread the word about the Arabella. It would be good for business.

I passed through the lobby and out the doors onto the street. The frigid air sucked the breath right out of me. I headed down the street to the south, toward the telegraph exchange.

Sure enough, Miss Fontaine was leaving the building. She stopped on the front stoop to put on her gloves.

"Miss Fontaine," I called out and hurried toward her.

She lifted her head and gave a tentative smile when she saw me. "Hello, Mrs. Pryce. What are you doing out here? It's so cold."

"Yes." I rubbed my gloved hands together. "It is, but I fancied a walk. It's nice to get some fresh air. Even if it's cold. What brings you out of doors?"

"Dr. Briggs wanted me to wire the Albany Hotel in Denver for our upcoming stay."

"Oh, yes. He said you'd be leaving us soon."

She nodded. "As soon as the weather clears near Denver."

"I see. I'm sorry to see you go."

"Dr. Briggs thinks Mrs. Stewart needs to put all this behind her. For her health. Besides, the only time she comes here anymore is for the festival. And it looks like that might not be happening anyway."

A sinking feeling hit my stomach. Those orphans simply had to come to the festival. Charlie needed to meet his grandmother. The festival had to happen, and Ralph Stewart's killer had to be brought to justice.

The idea that she would undoubtedly never forget her son came to his end at my hotel, and the fact that Atticus Brooks would certainly cast blame on the Arabella in a story, was nothing compared to the fate of that little boy.

"Of course," I said, feeling even more desperate to put things to rights. "Miss Fontaine, would you like to join me for some tea and biscuits down at Gilroy's Bakery?"

She smiled, and her eyes crinkled in the corners with delight. The effect was quite charming. She always seemed so serious; it was good to see her brighten up. "Yes. That sounds marvelous."

I hooked my arm through hers. "Shall we?"

Chapter Twenty

Miss Fontaine and I entered the bakery and were assailed with an infusion of most welcome warmth and the beautiful aroma of baked bread and cake. Betty Gilroy stood behind the counter arranging several loaves in baskets and setting them on top of the counter. The display case to her right was filled with various cakes, pies, and my favorite biscuits. My mouth watered.

"Good day, ladies," she said, her ruddy complexion coloring even more with her wide smile. Her coarse red hair peeked out from under her cap, framing her face in a halo of errant and wiry curls. "What can I get you?"

I deferred to Miss Fontaine, who ordered coffee and a piece of mahogany cake. I ordered a cup of my usual Earl Grey. Since my arrival in town, she had kept it on hand for me, and I deeply appreciated her thoughtfulness. I also asked for one of the delectable fat buttermilk biscuits smothered in blackberry jam.

"I'll brew a fresh pot of tea and boil some coffee. It will

only take a minute," Betty said. She indicated we should take a seat.

Three small tables sat in the front portion of the bakery, and we took the one closest to the counter, away from the cold window.

"Are you still helping the sheriff to find Mr. Stewart's killer?" Miss Fontaine asked.

"Yes—Well . . . –yes." A pang of guilt stabbed at my belly at going against the sheriff's demand that I stop.

"Have you had any luck?"

"Not really, no. I was pretty certain it was Mr. Valdez, but evidence proves it wasn't him."

"What evidence?"

I explained about the medal.

A look of surprise crossed her features. "I see. Yes, I suppose that does put him in the clear. Poor man. He died in the stable? Was he kicked by a horse?"

"No. There was no evident cause of death. There was a wound on his forehead, but it didn't seem bad enough to have killed him. I have not heard from the doctor yet regarding the results of his examination."

And I doubt I will, if the sheriff has anything to say about it.

"Ah. Yes. Well, it could have been anything, I suppose. From what I understand, his brother died of an ailment of the heart. Perhaps it runs in the family?"

"Yes." This was the perfect lead-in to my previous conversation with Percival. "Were you acquainted with Enrique Valdez?"

She sighed. "Not really. I knew he had invested in Mr. Stewart's mines—well, Mr. Stewart and Mr. Archer's mines. It didn't end well."

"So I've heard," I said. "Yet, I understand he came to a

party that was given by Mr. Archer at his house about a year ago."

She rolled her eyes. "Yes. Uninvited. Apparently, the man was a constant thorn in Mr. Stewart's side."

"Hmm," I mused. "I've heard that, too. So, is that when you first met Enrique Valdez?"

She shook her head. "No. I first met him at another party, about three or four years prior, I don't remember. It was about the time things between them all had soured."

"After the collapse."

"Yes."

I waited for her to offer more information, but she just looked at me with a pleasant smile on her face. I wanted to get to the part where she and Enrique had sat down to share a bottle of wine at that first meeting, but I wasn't quite sure how to proceed.

"Was he not invited to that party as well?" I asked.

"I believe he *was* invited to that party. I think Mr. Archer and Mr. Stewart were trying to talk him into staying with their mining company."

"Did you happen to speak with him at that particular party?" I ventured.

She pulled back her chin in question. "Why would I have spoken with him? I told you, I barely knew the man."

Interesting. Either Percival misremembered or she was lying.

"Besides—" she waved her hand in the air "—he left early. It seemed he'd caused some trouble."

"What kind of trouble?"

"It was with Mary Alice."

"Mary Alice? Really?"

She nodded. "Yes. I think he had designs on her."

"Goodness!" I was not expecting that. Or was she trying to deflect from what really happened?

"She went to Mr. Stewart and complained that Mr. Valdez would not leave her alone," Miss Fontaine continued.

"What did he do?"

She gave me a small smile. "Sadly, nothing. He told her she was imagining things, that she thought too highly of herself."

"That's not very nice."

She shook her head. "No. He was never very kind to her."

"But she claimed Mr. Stewart loved her."

She shrugged her shoulders. "I think that is what she wanted to believe. But in her heart, she knew he didn't. She confided in me from time to time. She was very unhappy in the marriage."

"And what about Victoria? Do you believe Mr. Stewart was going to leave Mary Alice for her?"

"I'm not sure. I do know Mary Alice feared it. She did not want to be displaced in the family. She would have done anything to stop that from happening."

Anything? Interesting.

"Why was it so important to her?"

She blinked at me and gave me a curious smile. "Why, money, of course. And if Mr. Stewart left her . . ."

"Does she not come from money?" I didn't know why I had assumed she did. Perhaps because Miss Mayes said Bertha Stewart had arranged the marriage. Many wealthy families often brought their children together. Though, I married far above my station.

"She does. But her family lost their fortune. They owned

a textile manufacturer, and the company failed due to poor management. It's up to her to support them now."

"Ah, of course." I knew all too well the pressure she was under, having had to support my mother and me at a very young age. *Too young*, I thought with disdain. It was shameful how my mother put the onus on me. The responsibility had been soul-crushing.

Betty arrived with our tea and treats. We waited silently while she set them on the table.

"Thank you, Betty," I said. I took a sip of my tea. It was piping hot—just how I liked it—and the wonderful flavor of bergamot danced on my tongue.

"You let me know how everything tastes, will you?" Betty asked. "Mr. Gilroy has tried a new recipe for the biscuits, and I've made some alterations to the cake. We like to keep things fresh."

"We will," I assured her. She left us to our conversation.

Miss Fontaine stared into her coffee cup, transfixed on the contents.

"Is everything all right?" I asked.

"Yes, it's just—" She brought the cup to her lips and took a sip. "I, well, I saw something that— Well, if you are pursuing your investigation into Mr. Stewart's death . . ."

I raised my brows, anxiously awaiting what she would say next.

"I hate to say anything. Mary Alice is my friend, but . . ."

"What is it?"

She took in a breath and let it out. "Mrs. Stewart wanted to meet with Mary Alice and me the afternoon before the party. She wanted to discuss plans for the winter festival. As you know, Mrs. Stewart had put Mary Alice in charge of refreshments for everyone at the General, for after the tree-trimming ceremony."

I nodded. Mr. Archer had wanted his family to host the orphans and any tourists for hot cider, cookies, and games for the children at his hotel.

"Go on," I prompted.

"We were sitting in the parlor of Mrs. Stewart's rooms. The fire had gone out, and Mrs. Stewart was cold. Dr. Briggs had gone to get some firewood from your maid."

"And?"

"I asked Mrs. Stewart if she wanted to get into bed to get warm, but she said no, so I suggested a blanket for her knees. Mary Alice volunteered to go into the bedroom and get one for her. Then Mrs. Stewart said she wanted her wool wrap, so I went into the bedroom and saw Mary Alice—"

"You saw her . . . ?"

"I saw her take a medicine bottle from the bureau in the bedroom—Dr. Briggs has many in there for Mrs. Stewart—and put it in her handbag."

"What kind of medicine bottle?" I asked.

She shrugged. "I don't know. I couldn't make it out."

"Why didn't you mention this before?" I asked.

"I know I should have, but . . . I didn't think anything of it at the time. It's been bothering me, though. Besides, she might have just been taking some of Mrs. Stewart's laudanum for sleep."

"I see. Is Mary Alice in the habit of using laudanum?"

"No. She used it once and did not like the effect. She said she'd rather be in pain."

I nodded. I, too, felt the same way. I did not like the dull sensation the drug produced. Headache powders worked just fine for me, thank you very much.

"Then why do you think she took it?" I asked.

"I don't know. I just— Well, Mr. Stewart did die of poisoning, did he not?"

I blinked. "Are you saying Mary Alice gave him a fatal dose of this medicine?"

She sighed and picked at the cake with her fork. "I hate to think so, but as I mentioned, she was worried about that Clement woman taking her place. I feel bad about telling you this. As much as I like Mary Alice, my loyalty is to Mrs. Stewart. She's been so kind to me. She's employed me for a very long time. I think not knowing who killed her son is very difficult for her."

I reached out and put my hand over hers. "I assure you, I will do everything I can to help."

"Thank you," she said with a sweet smile.

I studied her face as she finally took a bite of the cake and then sipped her coffee. Aside from her striking features, there was a cool confidence about her that I quite liked. Even though she'd perhaps betrayed Mary Alice with the information she'd just given me, she seemed convicted in her desire to help Mrs. Stewart find solace in her time of grief.

I made a mental note to ask Maggie if she'd seen a bottle of medicine in Mary Alice's room. If what Miss Fontaine had just imparted was true, Ralph's widow had motive, means, and opportunity. The perfect combination for murder.

After we'd finished our tea and coffee, Miss Fontaine said she needed to go to the dress shop to buy some buttons to mend one of Mrs. Stewart's dresses.

"Of course," I said. "Don't let me keep you."

She reached into her handbag. "I'll just pay for the coffee and—"

"It's on me," I offered.

"Thank you." She turned to Betty, who was again arranging pastries in the case. "The mahogany cake was the best I've ever had."

Betty clapped her hands together. "That's wonderful. I'm glad you enjoyed it."

Miss Fontaine bade us goodbye, and I went to the counter to pay.

"Thank you, Betty," I said. "The new recipe for the biscuits is wonderful. Did I detect the addition of anise seed?"

She smiled. "Yes, you did. I'll tell Mr. Gilroy it has met your approval."

I opened my reticule to pull out some coins.

"Is that woman part of the Stewart party that's come to town?" she asked.

"Yes. She's Bertha Stewart's secretary."

She furrowed her brow and looked as if she wanted to say something.

"What is it, Betty?"

She shook her head. "It's nothing. Does she have a beau?"

I raised my brows. "Not that I know of. Why do you ask?"

"I saw her talking with a man down by the river. The conversation looked quite intense."

"Really? Do you know the man?"

"I think he's that doctor that's come with the Stewarts."

"Dr. Briggs?"

"Yes."

I shrugged. "Perhaps they'd gone for a walk."

"It seemed like more than just a casual walk."

"What do you mean?"

"I think they may have been quarreling, but it was hard to tell for sure. Perhaps it was a lovers' spat?"

I blinked. I hadn't even considered they might be involved.

"Well, to each their own, I suppose," I said, a little distracted by the idea. I supposed it would make sense. They did work very closely. It wasn't so unreasonable that an attraction might have formed, even though he was quite a lot older than she was. But who was I to judge? William had been my senior by a decade and then some.

I considered Betty's words. The two might have convened down by the river, but they'd shown no such ardent affinity for each other within the confines of the hotel. If they were involved, they obviously wanted to keep their affair a secret. But why?

Chapter Twenty-One

Newly fortified from the hot, strong tea and my belly full of warm biscuits, I made my way out into the cold to return to the hotel. I hoped the afternoon repast would give me the strength to face Clayton and try to make amends. The question was, did I share what I had recently learned about Mary Alice? If he knew I was still making inquiries, I'd have no chance of winning back his favor. I wondered how Mr. Johns was faring in his new role as deputy. Had he made any new discoveries?

Once back at the hotel, I stopped in to see Mr. Pettyjohn. He greeted me with a look of deep consternation on his face.

"Mr. Pettyjohn, what is it?"

"I'm afraid there's been a problem in the annex. The supports for the roof on the porch at Mr. and Mrs. Harrison's has snapped in two. The entire portico has collapsed. We've had to move the family into the hotel. As there are five of them, I've put them in one of the larger rooms."

"Oh my days! Snapped in two? How can that be?"

He gave a shrug. "I've sent Mr. Johns to help clear the rubble."

I dashed past the desk, turned the corner, and fled down the hallway toward the annex. Once outside again, I spied the mess. The Harrisons' unit was the farthest from the hotel, next to the alleyway between the hotel and the haberdashery.

Mr. Johns and some other men were tossing the broken pieces of roof and wood into a pile in front of the porch.

"Mr. Pettyjohn told me what happened," I said, addressing Mr. Johns. "Do you think this is from the weight of the snow on the portico?"

He shook his head. "No, ma'am. I've been making sure these roofs have been cleared of snow. But the support there —" he pointed to a sturdy-looking four-by-four "—was busted in two."

"Well, how did that happen? Has the wood been weakened in some way?"

He rubbed his chin. "No, ma'am. I checked that support myself when I put it up. It looks like someone took a sledgehammer to it."

"You mean, it was done deliberately?"

"I don't know how it could have snapped in two on its own, ma'am."

My mouth dropped open. This was the third time that someone had vandalized the hotel since I'd come to La Plata Springs. The first was the river rock in the stove at the wedding reception I'd hosted for Eliza and the late Mr. Townsend, and now this. Not to mention the hole in the second-floor outhouse that we'd had to repair a couple of months ago. Why was someone doing this to me?

"I'm sorry, ma'am," Mr. Johns said, obviously reading the shock on my face.

I shook my head. "It's not your fault, Mr. Johns. Thank you for your help."

I went back into the lobby, my heart heavy with dread. Who was out to make me fail with the hotel?

Only one person came to mind. The man who'd been pestering me to sell it to him. Archibald Archer.

As much as I wanted to find him and give him a piece of my mind, I knew it would have to wait. Time was running out before Mrs. Stewart left town.

I reasoned that I would have plenty of time to deal with the matters of the hotel, but the murder case could not wait. A child's welfare was at stake.

I pulled in a breath and attempted to reorganize my thoughts. I would set the matters of the hotel aside for the moment. I'd put off speaking with the sheriff, too, as I was not in the best frame of mind and wanted to be at my sharpest when dealing with him.

"Mr. Pettyjohn, see if you can find some more men to help Mr. Johns with the fallen portico," I instructed. "We need to get that fixed so that the family can move back in. I'll pay them handsomely."

"Yes, madam," he said.

"Do you know where Maggie is?" I asked.

"I last saw her going upstairs."

"Thank you."

I searched all the second-floor rooms, but she was nowhere to be seen. She must be tending to Mrs. Stewart's suite or Dr. Briggs's suite on the third floor.

As I climbed the stairs, I noted raised voices coming from above. When I reached the third-floor landing, I saw that the door to Mrs. Stewart's room was slightly ajar.

"You can't do this, Bertha!" a male voice boomed. I couldn't be sure, but it sounded like Mr. Archer's voice.

"It's done, Archibald. It was completely within my power." Mrs. Stewart's tone, though somewhat weaker than usual, still bore an air of authority.

"But now that Ralph is gone," Mr. Archer said, "I am entitled to resume my rightful place as head of this family. You should never have taken that from me."

"I did not take it from you! Father made me executor of the estate because your greed has made you reckless. As you proved in the disaster of La Linda. Father was probably turning in his grave—"

"But you put Ralph in charge of *my* project at La Linda! I can't tell you how humiliating it was to answer to *my nephew.*"

"He had a better head for business. And we had to clean up your mess."

"I've made this family a great deal of money, Bertha. You know that."

"Yes, but you don't manage it well. I'm sorry. It is done. Upon my death, Louis will become executor of the estate."

"This is outrageous!"

"You will still be in charge of La Plata Springs, the mines, the bank, the construction company, and any of the other businesses that we've acquired here. You're good at that. Spending money."

Construction company? I hadn't heard about that one.

"I've had to spend that money to make money. That's how it works. But now I will have to beg *a lawyer* for it?"

"Someone has to keep you reined in."

Huh. I guess that's something we have in common, Mr. Archer. Having our money held hostage by a legal professional. How ironic.

"This isn't right," he repeated.

Then footsteps neared the door. He was leaving. I scurried over to Dr. Briggs's room and knocked on the door. When Mr. Archer appeared in the hallway, I turned to face him.

"Oh, Mr. Archer. I didn't realize you were at the hotel," I lied.

He didn't say a word. Just glared at me, crammed his hat on his head, and went down the stairs.

The door to Dr. Brigg's room opened and Maggie stood there bright-faced. "Oh, hello, Mrs. Pryce."

"Hello, Maggie," I said absently. My mind was still whirling with the conversation I'd just overheard.

It was clear now that Mr. Stewart had stood in the way of Mr. Archer's inheritance, as well as any power he'd had within the family. He'd thought he'd become the executor, or "head of the family," once his nephew and sister were gone.

Perhaps he'd tried to expedite the process.

"Mrs. Pryce?" Maggie said, interrupting my thoughts.

"Oh, yes. I was looking for you." I peered into the room. "Dr. Briggs isn't here, is he?"

"No ma'am."

"Good." I entered. My gaze immediately fell to the desk and bureau which were littered with medicine bottles and other various medical equipment.

"Maggie, did you happen to see a medicine bottle in Mary Alice Stewart's room, by chance? Perhaps a bottle of laudanum?"

"No, ma'am, I haven't. Just here in the doctor's room and Mrs. Stewart's room."

"Oh. I see." I perused some of the bottles on the bureau. Underneath some of them were handwritten dosage instructions. I supposed if she had taken one of Mrs. Stewart's bottles of laudanum and used it to poison her husband, she either disposed of it or returned it to Mrs. Stewart's room, or even brought it here, to throw off any possible suspicion. There would be no way of proving that she had done it.

"Have you noticed anything out of the ordinary?" I asked, in reference to her assignment that she look out for any kind of evidence in the four rooms the Stewarts and their party occupied.

"Wait a minute," she said, pressing her index finger to her lower lip. "I did notice a bottle of some kind in Mrs. Edwards-Stewarts room. But I don't think I was supposed to see it."

"What do you mean?"

"Well, I know you have a strict policy of not opening the drawers of the bureaus or the wardrobes in the rooms while a guest occupies it—for privacy and all—but, you see, the drawer at the bottom of the bureau was partially opened, and there were some undergarments hanging out of it. I didn't like that it wasn't tidy, so I folded the garments back in it and was ready to close the drawer when I saw the bottle. I'd not seen one like that before."

"Really? What did it look like?"

"The label was quite beautiful with a fashionable lady on it. I think it was some kind of wine. Some kind of brain or nerve tonic."

I scrunched up my nose. Something about what she'd said was familiar. *Brain or nerve tonic.* "Oh!" I suddenly remembered. "Was it Coca Wine by any chance?"

"Yes. I believe that's it. Sounds like chocolate wine." Her features twisted into a grimace of distaste.

"It's a remedy for a number of ailments," I said absently, recalling that I knew an actress in New York who used it regularly—too often, in fact. Especially before a performance. She claimed it cured any kind of cold or illness, anemia, mental fatigue. It contained a medicine that was in a number of different tinctures and potions, and even soda drinks. Cocaine. The wonder drug of the age.

"Hmm. Thank you, Maggie," I said absently. *Coca Wine.* I supposed it wouldn't be that unusual for Mary Alice to possess a bottle of Coca Wine. But why keep it in a drawer? And a bottom drawer, no less. As if she was hiding it.

I wondered if ingesting too much of the tonic would be fatal. The actress I knew who used it had collapsed before a performance once. The doctor had put it down to exhaustion, but now I wondered if her collapse had been caused by too much Coca Wine.

Once I got back to the lobby, I took in a deep breath and steeled myself for what lay ahead. My impending and necessary visit with Clayton. I needed to see if I could make things right with him.

I took off my coat and hat, and hung them on the circular coat rack near the staircase. As I left the lobby and walked down the hallway toward the sheriff's room, I ran a hand up the back of my coif to settle any stray hairs and smoothed down my skirt. Once at his door, I took in a deep breath and let it go, readying myself for the visit.

I gently knocked. The sound of footsteps neared from inside the room, and the door flung open.

My heart sank as I stared into the face of Atticus Brooks.

"Mr. Brooks," I choked out. I looked over his shoulder to see Clayton sitting in a chair next to the wood-burning stove. His crutches leaned against the wall next to him. He glanced my way, and I gave him a tight smile.

"May I come in?" I asked.

Mr. Brooks looked to Clayton for permission. He gave a brief nod, and Mr. Brooks opened the door wider for me to enter.

I swept past the hack writer, doing my best to ignore his smug countenance. The man made my skin crawl.

"I came to see how you were feeling," I said to Clayton, taking the chair next to him.

He looked at me with those soulful eyes. In them I saw pain, and I knew that pain had been inflicted by me.

"Better," he said. "I'm getting used to the crutches. The doctor said as soon as I am steady with them, I can get back to work."

I gave him a smile, but my mind was full of doubt and worry. Should he have to apprehend someone, or defend himself, how would he do so? Men could be so stubborn. I hoped the temporary deputy would arrive from Denver soon. Clayton clearly needed help. At least I could do—or rather, orchestrate—some of the investigative footwork for the time being.

"That is good news," I said.

"The sheriff has been briefing me about Ralph's death," Mr. Brooks cut in, making me flinch. "Poison, he tells me. And then his fall from the window. Tragic."

"Yes."

"Such a pity it happened here at your hotel," he repeated, taking a jab at me. His mustache twitched upward. "And so unfortunate for the dear orphans if the festival is canceled. I know you must be relying on the Archer/Stewart funds for that, given the financial woes of the Arabella."

I sucked in a breath. How had he learned about the hotel's financial situation? Certainly not from anyone in my employ. The only person I knew of who had that information was Mr. Archer. I gritted my teeth. He had no right to impart such personal information to anyone, much less a newspaper writer who had a personal vendetta against me. Would he assume that I was penniless? It was, of course, far from the case. Well, at least temporarily. I dreaded the thought of him writing about all this. His last slanderous story about me had been retracted—his allegations against me for murder were obviously false—but Ralph coming to his end here was blatantly true. I would have no recourse.

"And I hear from young Andrew that you are helping the sheriff with the murder case," he added with a twitch of his overly waxed mustache. "It's too bad you have not made much progress in finding the killer."

I glanced over at Clayton, expecting him to inform Mr. Brooks that I *was not* working on the case, but he remained silent.

"It looks like you may have lost your touch, Arabella. You were so *brilliant* in clearing your own name. And in solving the murder of Mr. Townsend. I guess you just got lucky in those instances. Perhaps instead of attempting to run a hotel or floundering about town with your cute little detective hat on, you should stick to what you do best: playing pretend on the stage."

I opened my mouth to retort, but Clayton raised a hand in the air. "Whoa there, Mr. Brooks. I think that's a bit heavy-handed."

Mr. Brooks gave a tilt of his head. "Perhaps. My apologies, dear."

I clenched my fists at my sides at his barefaced condescension. The man was as low as a worm. No doubt his next story would disparage the hotel and highlight all my failures in La Plata Springs. A spike of anxiety ran through my veins at the thought.

But there was one bright spot in all this. It seemed that Clayton had not divulged my criminal act or my fall from grace as his temporary deputy. That gave me hope that he might not incarcerate me for the forgery—despite the fact that I had probably ruined any chance of continued friendship with him—and that he might still be reliant on me for information.

I raised my chin in defiance of Mr. Brooks's pettiness. "I have every confidence that Clayton will find the culprit."

"Let's hope so. And I hope this all gets cleared up soon. It would give Bertha such comfort to see her son's killer brought to justice before she leaves. As it stands now, I suppose there will be no festival?" he asked.

"That is to be determined," I stated.

He tsked with a click of his tongue. "I would hate to see it overshadowed by this terrible turn of events." He gave me a grimacing smile. "Well, I must be off. Mrs. Stewart has requested my presence. Good day," he said with a nod of his head, which I refused to acknowledge.

When he left the room, I rose and closed the door behind him, my blood boiling with rage. "Vile creature," I muttered under my breath and came back to sit in the chair.

"Are you all right?" Clayton asked.

Some of the tension eased from my body at his concern. "Yes. That man is like a persistent virus that won't leave me alone."

"He really does have it out for you. Why?"

I swallowed down my anxiety at the ugly truth of the matter. "My husband was a very powerful man. He knew everyone who was anyone in New York City . . . and farther afield. Mr. Brooks was invited to my husband's club for a game of cards. He cheated, and William caught him. As a result, Mr. Brooks was banned from ever returning to the club. After that, he wrote a less than favorable review about me in the paper—more than once. Through his connections with the editor of the paper, William saw to it that Mr. Brooks was fired. He has been out for revenge ever since, and now that William can no longer protect me . . ." A lump of sadness formed in my throat at his loss.

"I guess that is one of the pitfalls of being famous. It can make you vulnerable. Everything you do, good, bad, or —illegal—" A jab of guilt stabbed me in the heart at my counterfeit transgression as he continued "—puts you under a great deal of scrutiny."

I pressed my lips together and shut my eyes against the fact that he could very well have told Mr. Brooks about my error in judgment.

"Don't worry," he said, reading my mind. "I didn't say anything that would slander you."

I let out a sigh of relief. "Thank you, Clay. I really am so sorry. It was so stupid of—"

"I still haven't decided what I'm going to do about it," he cut in.

My hopes wilted. "I see."

An uncomfortable silence passed between us. He ran his hand down his thighs and then rested them on his knees. He was obviously still upset with me. I hesitated to impart the information I had gathered. If he knew I'd been working the case, he'd be furious. But what I had learned was so important.

"I'm sorry I've had to redirect Mr. Johns. We've had an issue in the annex and—"

"I know," he groused. "He told me. You have to make sure your tenants are safe."

"I'm still willing to help—"

"I can do it."

I reached out and put one of my hands over his. "Can you really?" I asked quietly. "Those crutches are clumsy at best."

He let out a breath and closed his eyes. It was difficult to see the defeat in his face. I pulled my hand away.

"The deputy from Denver is on his way," he said.

"When is he due to arrive?"

"Tomorrow. Given the storm doesn't delay the train from Denver."

"Oh. So soon." I cleared my throat. "Then there are some things you might want to tell him."

He slid a narrow-eyed glance my way. I diverted my gaze.

"What things? You haven't been . . . ?"

I took in a deep breath and let it go. "Do you want to know or not?"

"What I want to know is why you are so invested in this," he said with questioning eyes.

I clasped my hands in my lap and gave a shrug of my shoulders. "I suppose it's Charlie."

"What about him?"

I swallowed, not sure I wanted to bare my soul. I raised my eyes, sneaking a glance at him. He looked genuinely interested.

"I didn't have a very pleasant childhood. My mother was—well, let's just say ambitious. Because I had to support us—"

"As a child?" he interjected.

"Yes, I was onstage from the time I was ten. Anyway, I

missed out on a lot of things that a normal child experienced. I don't want that for him—for any child—but he's been put in my path, and if I can help just one . . . and Victoria wants what's best for him, unlike . . ."

"Your mother."

"She does love me," I retorted, suddenly feeling a little defensive, probably because I wasn't entirely sure of the truth of the matter.

"Of course," he said sympathetically, and then a look of resignation passed over his face. "Tell me what you know."

Relieved he'd changed the subject, I told him what Miss Fontaine had said about Mary Alice taking the bottle of medicine, possibly laudanum, from Mrs. Stewart's room.

"Why is that significant?" he asked.

"According to Miss Fontaine, she won't use the stuff herself. She also claimed that Mary Alice was terrified of Mr. Stewart leaving her for Victoria. She didn't want to lose her place in the family or the money that privilege brought with it. She was helping to support her own family."

"Okay."

"She could have slipped an overdose of the laudanum to her husband. Put it in his drink or something. Or she could've given him something else."

"Like what?"

"Maggie found a bottle of Coca Wine in Mary Alice's room."

"Coca Wine?" He scoffed. "Isn't that stuff harmless?"

I shrugged. "I don't know if it is or not. I just thought you should know Maggie found it in Mary Alice's room."

He didn't say anything more. Just tapped his fingers on his knees.

"I also overheard something that might be important." I

told him about the interchange between Mr. Archer and his sister. "Apparently, she holds all the cards," I finished.

His mouth turned down, and he nodded. "That explains a lot."

"What do you mean?"

"Archer. He's always so puffed up. Exercising control over everything. Or trying to. I suppose he's keeping up a facade."

"He assumed that since Mr. Stewart was gone, he'd gain control of the estate—or part of it. That would definitely give him motive to get rid of his nephew," I said. Then I remembered the suicide note. Since Clayton seemed willing to hear what I had to say, I decided to ask him about it. "Do you happen to have the note found in Mr. Stewart's room?"

"Yes. Why?"

I shrugged. "Just curious. Have you had Mr. Johns get handwriting samples from the suspects?"

His features registered surprise, and then his mouth tightened. It didn't seem possible, but apparently I'd aggravated him even further. "I'm working on it."

"Any matches so far?"

He scowled at me and didn't bother to answer my question.

He then placed his hands on either side of his legs and gingerly rose from the chair. Wincing, he came to full standing on his bruised "good" leg and reached for his crutches.

"What are you doing?" I asked.

"I'm going to see Archer."

"But how will you get there?"

He looked over at me as if I was daft. "The hotel has a coach, doesn't it?"

"Oh, of course. Yes, I'll have Mr. Pettyjohn find Mr. Ellis. And then we can—"

"We? No. You're not coming," he said, giving me a pointed glare with those stormy blue eyes.

I swallowed at his dismissive tone, but I was treading on shaky ground. It wouldn't be good to put up any kind of argument at the moment. "I'll get the coach for you."

I left the room with a stick in my craw and a pain in my heart.

Chapter Twenty-Two

As I watched Clayton struggle with the crutches, it was all I could do to not physically assist the man out of his room, into the lobby, and into the coach. But I was the last person he wanted any help from at the moment, even though I had just given him vital information about the case. I tried to ignore the stabbing sensation in my chest. Would I ever regain his good opinion of me?

I pushed out a breath. I would have to figure out a way . . . But in the meantime, I wanted to know what, if any, new information my troops had gathered.

At the reception desk, I scrawled off a note to Andrew asking him to meet me in my office in the annex. I also thought it might be a good idea to invite Miss Mayes and Constance, as they seemed to know a lot about the goings-on in town and had already provided some useful information about the Archer/Stewart clan. I placed each note in an envelope, sealed them, and then wrote WINTER FESTIVAL COMMITTEE on each one.

When I finished, I presented them to Mr. Pettyjohn. "Please have Clarence deliver these promptly."

"Yes, madam."

I sighed. It was no use trying to get him to stop calling me *madam*. It seemed to be ingrained in his mind. I would just have to get over my strange abhorrence of it.

I gave him a smile. "Thank you. Oh, has Cordelia returned with Bijou?"

"I have not seen her," he said.

"Very well. When she returns, would you ask her to meet me in the annex office?"

"Yes, madam," he repeated.

I then went up to my rooms to refresh myself before the meeting. When I opened the door, a rush of cool air danced over my skin.

"Percival?" He seemed to be nowhere in sight, but I could definitely feel him. Then his transparent form wandered out of Cordelia's bedroom.

"What were you doing in there?" I asked.

"Nothing," he said.

"You weren't snooping were you?"

"The woman has a lot of books." He placed his hands behind his back.

I slid him a warning glance. "Percival—"

"Don't worry. I didn't move anything. There is only a small vanity mirror in that room. I wouldn't be able to move anything except some toiletries, which don't interest me in the least. I was just trying to get to know her a little."

"For what purpose?" I inquired.

He shrugged. "Curiosity."

"I'm not telling her about you," I said.

He sighed, then released one of his hands and raised it to his face, palm up, fingers folded, and examined his fingernails, as he often did when trying to feign boredom or was annoyed. "What brings you up here?" he asked. "I thought you would be with your sheriff."

I narrowed my eyes at him. He was trying to get under my skin. "*The* sheriff, Clayton Marshall," I said, emphasizing that I had no ownership over the man, "has gone to see Mr. Archer."

"Up and about so soon?" he asked, his eyes brightening.

"Too soon," I added. "But since he has banned me from investigating, and Mr. Johns is attending to the fallen portico in the annex, he now feels the pressure of finding Mr. Stewart's killer on his own. Hopefully, the storm will not delay the train and the deputy will arrive tomorrow."

"I see. But as you have not banned yourself from the investigation, what have you come up with?"

"Well, I've learned a lot about Mr. Stewart's family, Victoria Clement, Cherrie Fontaine, and Dr. Briggs, but nothing concrete that connects them to the murder. Some of them have more motive than others, but it now seems that Mary Alice and Mr. Archer had the strongest motives."

"Archibald?" Percival frowned.

"Yes." I explained the situation.

"Interesting."

"Isn't it?"

"The man can be ruthless," he said.

"Yes. I think he might be behind some of the problems we've had in the hotel. But I can't prove anything. He's determined that I sell it to him. He might be sabotaging my renovation efforts to wear me down. But that is a matter for another time. We've got to ensure that the Winter Festival happens so that young Charlie can meet his grandmother and be returned to his mother. We are running out of time."

"Yes," he said. "What kind of relationship do you think Miss Fontaine and Miss Clement have?"

I blinked in confusion. "Why, none that I can tell. Why do you ask?"

"I saw them together in the saloon. Miss Fontaine was having breakfast, and Miss Clement joined her. They had a brief discussion. I know not what they talked about, but Miss Fontaine took something from her handbag and handed it to her. I couldn't see what it was. Then Miss Clement left."

"When was this?"

"Yesterday."

"Hmm. Well, perhaps I'll speak with her again. Do you happen to know where she is right now?"

"I imagine she's in her room. She rarely strays from it. I believe she is heartbroken over Ralph's death."

Or his rejection of her, if he did reject her, I thought. "Thank you, Percival."

He gave me a nod and popped out of view, the chill in the room evaporating.

On my way down the stairs, I ran into Maggie on the second-floor landing. "Could you meet in my annex office within the next fifteen minutes?" I asked.

"Yes, ma'am. I am just finishing up with Dr. Briggs's room. I had to get another towel."

"Great. See you then."

I went down the hall and knocked on Victoria's door. I heard rustling about. After a few moments, she answered. The complexion of her face startled me. Usually so bright and rosy, it was gray and wan. Dark half-moons rimmed her lower lids, and her hair was disheveled. She was wearing a dressing gown and was slightly bent at the waist.

"My dear, are you ill?" I asked.

She gave me a faint smile. "Yes, but it's nothing catching. Would you like to come in?"

I stepped inside and shut the door. Victoria ambled back to bed, clutching her abdomen.

"Is there anything I do for you? Do you need the doctor?"

She shook her head. "I've been down that road. There is nothing a doctor can do for me."

"I'm so sorry," I said, wanting to know what ailed her but felt it was presumptuous to ask. "Are you sure?"

She gave me that faint upturn of her lips again. "Yes. What I have is incurable. An ailment of the pancreas. That is why I need my boy to be taken care of. To have a family."

My heart wilted at this devastating news. "Of course. I understand. Did Mr. Stewart know of your condition?"

"Yes," she said quietly.

I shook my head. The situation was far worse than I had imagined. The boy would soon truly be an orphan.

"Does Andrew know?" I asked.

"No one else knows. Please don't say anything. It just makes people sad." Her lips turned up in a weak smile. "I can usually hide it well. I have good days and bad days. On the good days, I can function pretty normally. But on the bad days, like today . . ."

No wonder she'd kept to her room.

"What can I do to help?"

She gave a small laugh. "Make sure that Mrs. Stewart meets her grandson. Make sure that I can see my son one more time . . ."

My breath hitched in my throat. "I promise you. I am doing everything I can to make sure the orphans come to La Plata Springs before Mrs. Stewart departs. Are you sure you can't just tell her about Charlie?"

She shook her head. "She won't have anything to do with me. Mary Alice has completely poisoned her against me." She scoffed. "If only Mary Alice knew about Cherrie Fontaine. They wouldn't be such bosom friends."

"What do you mean?" I asked.

She winced and clutched at her stomach. I reached out to comfort her, but she held up her hand in protest. After a few seconds, she continued. "Ralph told me that he and Miss Fontaine had a brief affair before he became my patron. But it ended as quickly as it had started. He said he wasn't really all that interested in her, and she did not want to do anything to jeopardize her position with Mrs. Stewart, so they called it off. Mary Alice obviously didn't know about it. If she did, I'm sure she would've ended Miss Fontaine's employment. Instead, she's treated like one of the family."

Her bringing up Mary Alice reminded me of what the woman had told me about Victoria threatening Mr. Stewart.

"Victoria, I have to ask you something. You were seen out at Mr. Archer's ranch with Mr. Stewart and you were overheard threatening him: You told him he would 'regret this decision.' Can you tell me why you said that?"

Her face squinted up in confusion. "Who said that?"

I pressed my lips together, not sure I should divulge who my informant was. "Were you out at the ranch?"

She sighed and then looked away from me. "Yes. Ralph was being difficult. I thought he was going to go back on his word. He was worried about being cut off from the family —and their wealth—if he claimed Charlie and left Mary Alice. I was so frustrated with his indecision, I told him he would regret it if he backed out on me. That's when I told him I was sick. He later came around and apologized. He said he would go through with our plans."

"Did he change his mind again? At the party?"

"Not exactly. Like I told you, he hadn't told Mary Alice yet. He was putting it off until after the party. But I thought he was weakening again. His indecision made me lose my temper, and I threw the drink at him. Now I regret it. That was the last time I saw him." Shaking her head, she put her hands over her face.

"I see," I said quietly.

She lowered her hands and smoothed them over her face, wiping the tears away, and then continued. "If Mrs. Stewart could just *see* Charlie. He's a miniature version of Ralph. There would be no denying who his father is—was." The sharp edge of grief flitted over her eyes.

Seeing her pain, both physical and emotional, I realized there was no possible way this woman could have killed the father of her child. All she wanted was for Charlie to be cared for. Andrew was right. She wouldn't jeopardize that in any way.

"Are you taking anything for your ailment?"

She nodded and pointed to the bureau. I went over to it where I found a small medicine bottle with little twigs in it. Tied around its neck was a label. It read, *Take before sleep.*

"It's yarrow root," she said. "It's for menstrual cramps, which is not my problem, but I find that it helps."

"Yarrow root? I see. Where do you get it?"

"I usually get it from my doctor in Addison. But I ran out. Miss Fontaine gave me some. She said she uses it from time to time. She told me that her grandmother makes it. She is a medicine woman of sorts."

That must have been what Percival saw Miss Fontaine giving her. And the substance I saw fall out of her handbag in Mrs. Stewart's room.

207

"Really? Her grandmother is a medicine woman. How fascinating," I said.

She closed her eyes and winced. Shivering, she sank onto the bed. "I'm sorry," she said. "I need to rest."

I went over to her and helped her get into bed. Once she was settled, I pulled the covers up to her neck. I then went to the wood-burning stove and stirred the coals with the fire poker until they glowed orange. I placed a few more pieces of wood on them and then closed the stove door.

"There," I said, satisfied with my efforts. "That should help."

I was about to ask her if I could bring her some water, but her eyes were closed and the steady rhythm of her breathing told me she was already asleep.

My heart wrenched in two—for her and for her boy.

Chapter Twenty-Three

An hour later, the festival committee, which was now my little troop of spies, was gathered in my office—all but Maggie who was finishing up in Dr. Briggs's room still.

Miss Mayes had come in looking fresh and elegant as always. She greeted me with a warm smile, and my heart lifted. We were on good footing again, and it filled me with relief. I didn't need more than one person upset with me at a time. Mending my relationship with Clayton would be much more difficult, but I was determined to make him my friend again.

Usually so cheery and ready for a parlay of the latest town gossip, Constance seemed a little frazzled today. Her bright colors and flamboyantly styled dress were in sharp contrast to her countenance, which was pale and weary. She fidgeted in the chair. Could she be worried about seeing the ghost of the Arabella hotel?

Hopefully, Percival would not make an appearance. If he wanted to remain my friend, he would do well to stay away. If he did not, I feared I would have to have an honest conversation with Constance, to assure her that she was not losing her wits, but I did not relish the prospect. I tried to assure myself that I could not read the woman's mind and she might be nervous about something else entirely. I hated to show all my cards, lest I be seen as the necromancer of La Plata Springs.

"Thank you for meeting me here today," I said to the group. "I thought it would be a good time to go over anything we might have discovered pertaining to Mr. Stewart's and Mr. Valdez's deaths. Cordelia, what did you find out from Mr. Emerson?"

Notepad and pencil in hand, Cordelia cleared her throat. "There was a silver religious medal, similar in style to the one Mr. Valdez wore, in the case at the shop. I asked Mr. Emerson if he sold any of them in gold lately. He said he'd had one in the case, but it was sold a few days ago."

"Did he know who purchased it?" Cynthia asked.

Cordelia shook her head. "He'd had to make a trip to Addison to get some things for the store. He left Tilly, a young woman who works for him, in charge. She sold the gold medal."

"Have you spoken with this Tilly?" I asked.

"As soon as Mr. Emerson returned, Tilly left town. Her sister, who lives in Pueblo, had just given birth. She went to see the baby. Mr. Emerson said he wasn't sure when she'd be back."

My spirits flagged. I doubted she would be back before Mrs. Stewart and her clan departed.

Just then, Maggie came into the office. "Sorry I'm late."

"It's fine, Maggie. I know how busy you are. We were just discussing the gold medal. I'm afraid we still don't know who recently purchased it from the dry goods store."

She nodded and closed the door behind her.

"Andrew? Have you had a chance to speak with your uncle?" I wasn't sure how to proceed with him. I didn't know if he knew that the entire estate would be under the control of the family lawyer when Mrs. Stewart passed on. I hated to step on any toes.

"Yes. I went to the mine and told him I wanted to discuss my future. He wasn't really in the mood to talk, but we've scheduled a time to meet at the General later today."

I wasn't surprised Mr. Archer was a bit broody, given what I'd overheard earlier. "Good," I said. "Constance, what about you? Have you learned anything from the townsfolk that might pertain to the case?"

Her eyes wandered the room, and her face was pinched. She looked pensive and unengaged. I wondered if she'd heard me, or anything of the conversation, really.

"Constance?" I tried to get her attention.

She turned to me with brows raised in question.

"Have you discovered anything from the townsfolk that might give insight into Mr. Stewart's or Mr. Valdez's deaths?" I repeated.

She snapped out of her preoccupation with the ether. "Well, not really. But, Martha—you know, the laundress—she was down at the river to get some stones. Says she likes to pound the dirt out of things with them. Anyway, she saw Dr. Briggs go over the bridge and into the woods. He was carrying his medical bag. But why would he take that to the woods?"

"When was this?"

"She said it was yesterday, I think."

"Maybe he was taking some exercise?" Cordelia suggested.

"Yes, it could be as simple as that," I concurred. But, then, to Constance's point, why bring the medical bag?

"That would explain the dirt I found on the floor of his room," Maggie piped up. "I wish people would use the doormats we have set up at every single entrance of the hotel. It would make things a lot easier for my maids," she said with a scowl.

Maggie mentioning the soiled floor reminded me of the dirt I'd seen at my doorway. I hadn't thought much of it at the time. Several people had come up to my room for the meeting I'd called. But I suddenly remembered that Percival said he'd seen Miss Fontaine lurking on the third-floor landing the other day—that he'd thought she'd come from my rooms after our last committee meeting. He also said he'd seen her go into the woods earlier that day.

"Some folks have no manners." Constance shook her head. She seemed to have completely recovered from her vigilant scanning of the room.

I breathed a sigh of relief. I did not want to have the spiritual phenomenon discussion with her unless it was absolutely necessary. And if I were to willingly divulge my secret to anyone, it would be Cordelia, but I didn't see that happening, either. I shook myself from vulnerable thoughts of my ghostly abilities.

"Maggie, do you have anything else to add?" I asked.

She shook her head. "I'm afraid not. Poor Mrs. Stewart. I know she plans to leave soon, but she's quite frail. She still hasn't gotten out of her bed."

"Yes, but she is quite determined to leave," Miss Mayes said. "I popped in to pay her a visit before our meeting." She looked over at Maggie. "She might appear frail, but I assure you, that woman is tough as nails. And when she sets her mind to something—"

Andrew and I exchanged a glance. I knew he was

concerned about the fact that we were running out of time, too.

"Very well," I said, standing up. "Please let me know if you learn anything new."

Constance stood up and straightened her curls. "Well, I must dash. I have a lunch date with Mr. Brooks. It's so nice to be in the company of another wordsmith."

My heart seized. I hoped she wouldn't divulge anything that might disparage me or the hotel to Mr. Brooks. Unintentionally, of course.

"How wonderful," I said, biting back my irritation. "But remember, Constance, discretion please."

She straightened her shoulders. "Oh, don't you worry, Arabella. You can count on me."

"Perhaps you might find out if he's gathered any information that would be useful to us?"

She smiled. "I'll be sure to let you know if he has."

I opened the door for her and ushered her out, hoping that neither I nor my hotel would be the subject of public damnation.

Cordelia and I remained in the office after everyone had left. Sitting near the little pipe stove with Bijou in my lap, I ran my hand down the back of her head and her body in long, deliberate strokes, thinking about what we'd just learned from the others. The information Constance had given about Dr. Briggs going into the woods, and Percival's witnessing Miss Fontaine doing the same continued to play in my mind, but I wasn't sure exactly why. What were they doing back there?

Cordelia was scribbling notes on her notepad.

"Have you ever been in the woods?" I asked her.

She raised her head but stilled appeared deep in thought. "Pardon?"

"Have you ever been in the woods? You know, crossed that little bridge? I see people using it sometimes. Is there something of interest back there?"

"Yes, I've taken Bijou there from time to time. There are some walking trails. I don't know if they were created by human foot traffic or animals, but they go quite far back. It's especially lovely in the fall," she said.

"I'd like to see it. Care for a walk?"

At the word *walk*, Bijou raised her head.

"Yes, that would be lovely." Cordelia stood.

I set Bijou on the floor, and she immediately started to dance, excited at the prospect of an outing. "We need to get your leash, girl," I said, watching her little performance with a smile.

Once we were adequately bundled up against the cold, we set out from the back of the hotel. Heavy clouds loomed above us, insulating the town like a giant cocoon. The air was crisp and cold, and our breath formed an icy mist in front of us.

"Are we expecting more snow?" I asked, wondering if the storm in Denver would be passing through. A surge of hope lifted my spirits. Hopefully the weather would further detain the Stewart party a few more days.

"It certainly looks that way."

Another troubling thought passed through my mind. "Would it deter the arrival of the children from St. Anne's?"

"I don't know," she said. "From what I've gathered, they travel here by coach and on horseback through the Wilmington Pass. It's a well-traveled route, and they've made the journey in all kinds of weather before."

"How do you know this?"

"Andrew told me."

Bijou, pulling on the leash, attempted to scamper ahead of us. She made a grand leap over one of the railroad tracks and then jerked backward against the strain of the leash.

"Goodness, girl. Don't hurt yourself." I chuckled at her enthusiasm, and she looked back at me smiling and wagging her tail.

We approached the little footbridge that crossed over the river. The water lazily gurgled beneath us, passing over the lumps and bumps of submerged rocks. It was clear as glass, and ice formations clung to the boulders at the river's edge.

Once we had crossed it, we picked up a small, snow-packed footpath that led into a copse of pine trees. The atmosphere cooled as we moved deeper into the forest. The tiny footprints of deer veered off the trail to the right and left. The beasts had probably been foraging for food.

Bijou trotted ahead of us, pulling the leash tight. She barked when a squirrel zipped up one of the pines to our left.

"Let's go this way," Cordelia said, pointing to the right of a fork in the path. "There's a beautiful clearing a little ways out."

She passed me, taking the lead. After a few more minutes of dense forest, we stepped into a sweeping meadow laden with snow. A row of naked Aspens lined one side of it, and ahead of us was a small lake. To our right, three deer were making their way across the plain, headed toward the mountainside flanking the meadow.

"This is beautiful," I breathed out, taking in the landscape.

"You should see it when it's covered in grasses and fall wildflowers. It's like a fairy land." Cordelia's eyes lit up.

Why had I not experienced this before? I had been so caught up in the hotel and other matters that I hadn't taken the time to get into nature and enjoy its splendor. I vowed not to make that mistake again. As long as I was here, I might as well enjoy what La Plata Springs had to offer.

The little trail we were following skirted the edge of the trees. Dead foliage poked through the snow on either side of it. Some of the foliage did not appear to be completely dead, though—only gone to seed, waiting for the warmth of spring. I stopped when I saw something that looked vaguely familiar. The plant had a single stem, then a burst of seed pods fanned out from it. I had seen these pods before . . . In the patch of dirt outside my parlor door!

As I was again recalling what Percival had said about Miss Fontaine loitering on the third-floor landing, Cordelia called out to me. "Come on, Arabella! There's a great view just over there." She pointed to a cropping of boulders ahead. We continued along the trail, as neither one of us desired to trod through the snow and ruin the perfectly pristine blanket covering the meadow.

Something in the thicket of trees caught my eye. The transparent figure of a man stood amid the pines. Percival. Had he followed us, or was he also wandering the woods? I knew he liked to sit by the river, but he'd never mentioned that he went farther afield.

I took a deep breath, determined not to let his presence deter me from the serenity produced by the beautiful wintry landscape. We walked on.

When we reached a clump of boulders, Cordelia took a seat on one of them. Her face was flushed pink from the exertion and the cold. She looked positively radiant. "Come sit," she said, patting the boulder next to her. "Just look at this!" She spread her arms wide.

I took the proffered seat, and Bijou strained at the leash, wanting to continue. "Okay, girl. I'll take you off the leash, but you mustn't wander far. I don't want to lose you." I unclipped the metal fastener.

We sat in silence listening to the faint whistle of a breeze through the pines and the flitter of small wildlife in the forest. A sudden calm washed over me, and I closed my eyes, relishing the serenity. I didn't recall ever feeling quite so peaceful. My life in New York and my life since I had arrived in La Plata Springs had been fraught with chaos. I hadn't realized it until now, when everything stopped. Closing my eyes, I inhaled deeply and slowly let it out, basking in the quiet.

I hadn't been aware of how much time had passed with my eyes closed, but when I opened them, I turned to Cordelia, who also had her eyes closed. I scanned the area. Bijou was nowhere to be seen.

"Cordelia." I laid a hand on her arm. "Where's Bijou?"

Her eyes fluttered opened. "What?"

"Where's the dog?"

"Bijou!" she called. "Come here, girl!"

"Bijou!" I echoed. My heart raced, the previous calmness I'd enjoyed gone like the snap of my fingers. I scanned the trees, looking for Percival. He might have seen where she'd gone, but I didn't see him, either.

"We should check the forest," I said. "She might have gone after a squirrel."

I lifted my skirt as I trudged off the little path through the calf-deep snow. It slipped down into the tops of my boots, sending an icy chill through me.

"Bijou!" I called again. How would we ever find her? The snow was so deep in some areas, it was taller than she was. We might never spot her.

The echo of our voices in this small canyon rang through the air. A lump formed in my throat at the thought of never seeing my little canine companion again.

Suddenly, my gaze caught a small clearing amid the trees. Percival, in his ghostly form, stood near it, his hands folded in front of him. At his feet, Bijou was rooting around in something.

"Bijou!" My heart sang with relief at finding her. Hearing her name, she lifted her head. Her snout was covered in something black.

"There she is!" Cordelia's voice rang out behind me.

"What have you gotten into?" I said, rushing toward her, the snow making my progress laborious. When I finally reached her, she was standing in what looked to be ashes and char from a small fire. Bits of wood burned that had turned to charcoal littered the area. Bijou's feet were covered in it.

"Oh dear, you silly dog!" I said. I glanced at Percival. He made no movement, just looked at me with that droopy-eyed transparent gaze. I smiled at him with gratitude for finding my little friend.

I bent down to attach her leash. As I was about to stand, I noticed her foot was resting on something that looked like it had once been paper. On closer inspection, I saw bits of charred leather near it, and next to that was a sheet of paper that was only half-burned. I picked it up.

It was some kind of ledger. I blinked, trying to read the neat handwriting. There were several entries that I could make out, and two of them stopped me short. The name read CSB Manufacturing, and there was one entry for last month and one for this month, both in the amount of $225 dollars.

"Cordelia, look at this."

She came to look over my shoulder. I held my finger under the company name and ran it over to the expenses column.

"My goodness, that's a lot of money," she said.

"There is one for last month, too."

Cordelia's eyes widened. "This must be the bank book that went missing."

"Yes. But who took it, and why was it burned?"

Chapter Twenty-Four

Back at the hotel, we ran into Kitty who was just coming through the interior door from the Bella Saloon.

'Hello," she said, giving us the once-over. "Don't you look cold. Your skirts are soaking wet. And look at Bijou!"

The dog's ears, tail, and short little legs were decorated with frozen patches of snow. She ran to Kitty and jumped up, setting her front paws on the woman's skirt.

"Bijou!" I called out. "Get down. You'll get Kitty's dress wet."

"Ah, it's fine," she said, bending down to give her a pat. "My goodness, she's shivering."

"Yes, we are going up to our rooms to change and sit in front of the fire."

"I'll bring some tea and some of Lottie's scones. She's been practicing. This batch is quite good. She used some dried black currants and cinnamon."

"That sounds wonderful," I said. "How is everything here?"

"It's been pretty quiet."

"How is everyone in the Stewart party? Have you seen them?"

"I think Mrs. Stewart is still in her room. That secretary of hers has been bringing her meals."

"Yes. And Mary Alice?"

She tilted her head. "She's in the saloon with the secretary."

"I see. And how is Miss Clement?" I had asked Sally to tend to her. She had such a gentle nature and was always so willing to help. I had explained that Victoria was merely a little under the weather but did not divulge her secret.

"I think she's perked up a little. Hasn't left her room, but the last time Sally was in with her, the woman had gotten herself dressed."

"Good. Thank you, Kitty."

We were about to go up the stairs when we saw Dr. Briggs striding into the lobby from the hallway at the back of the hotel. His cheeks were pink from the cold. He was carrying his medical bag.

"Dr. Briggs," I greeted him.

He tipped his hat and then took it off. "Mrs. Pryce." He then nodded to Kitty and Cordelia.

"Were you out on a call?" I asked, tilting my head toward his bag.

"Oh." He lifted it up and then chuckled. "Just out for a walk. I don't like to be without it. Force of habit, I suppose. Never know when you might come across someone in need of medical attention. Especially in a mining town."

I nodded. "Of course. That makes perfect sense." I paused a beat, then said, "Dr. Briggs, about the bank book that went missing—"

His brow furrowed. "Yes?"

"I think we may have found something." I glanced over

at Cordelia, then produced the charred piece of paper. He looked at it and then up at me.

"Where did you find this?" he asked.

"In the woods," Cordelia said.

"As you can see, it was burned. There were some remains of leather on the remnants of the fire. Do you think it could be Mrs. Stewart's bank book?" I asked.

"I suppose it could be," he said, further studying the paper.

"Do you know of a CSB Manufacturing?"

He shook his head. "No. Never heard of it."

"Oh, well, thank you. I'll show this to the sheriff," I said, taking it back from him.

"Yes, yes, of course," he agreed.

"If you will excuse me," Kitty said, "I'll get that tea started for you."

I nodded. "Thank you, dear."

She smiled and headed toward the kitchen.

"Mrs. Pryce, have you seen Miss Fontaine?" Dr. Briggs asked, his tone even more serious than usual.

"She's in the saloon with Mrs. Edwards-Stewart," Kitty said over her shoulder.

"Thank you," he said and gave me a tight smile. "Good day."

Cordelia, Bijou, and I went up the stairs. Once in our rooms, we took off our gloves, coats, and hats.

"When are you going to take that ledger paper to the sheriff?" Cordelia asked.

I took in a breath and let it out. "Soon. I'm just getting up the nerve."

"Look," she said in a placating voice. "You were just taking a walk in the woods. Anyone could have found that burned-out fire and piece of paper. You just happen to know that Mrs. Stewart's bank book is missing. It doesn't necessarily indicate that you are still investigating."

Cordelia's rational thinking made me smile. She was right of course.

"If you'd like, I could take it to him," she offered.

I shook my head. "No. I'll do it. But later. I want to get changed and warmed first."

As much as I dreaded the possibility of further angering Clayton, I also felt pulled to see him. I so wanted to make things right between us, but I didn't really know how to start. Whenever William and I'd had a disagreement, we'd carried on as if nothing had happened, and soon, it dissipated and we were back to ourselves. But this was different. Clayton felt I had betrayed him. And as much as I hated to admit it, I had.

We each went to our bedrooms to change. As I was buttoning the buttons at the sleeves of a fresh blouse, the distinct odor of pipe smoke filled the air and the temperature of the room lowered. I turned to the mirror to find Percival watching me, holding his pipe to his mouth.

"Thank you," I finished with the buttons.

"What for?" he said, his teeth clenching the pipe stem.

"Pointing us in the direction of the burned bank book."

He shrugged. "I didn't do it. It was your little dog who found it."

"So, you were just following us?"

He lowered the pipe. "I wanted to make sure you came to no harm."

"How chivalrous." I smiled. "Just out of curiosity, had that happened, what would you have done exactly?"

"I have my ways of communicating. I would have alerted someone."

"Ah," I said. I took up the piece of charred ledger paper

I'd set on the bureau and studied it again. "Have you ever heard of CSB Manufacturing?"

He shook his head.

I continued my thought process. "If that was indeed Mrs. Stewart's bank book, the entry must have something to do with the family businesses. Perhaps the mine. It's such a large sum."

"Surely *you've* seen that kind of money. Why are you so intrigued by it?" Percival asked.

I tapped my finger on my lower lip. "I don't know. It just stands out to me."

A chuckle came from the mirror.

"What?" I lowered the paper.

"When you are deep in thought, you purse your lips. It's quite adorable."

"Do I?"

He gave me an endearing smile.

"Well, I'm still cold . . . and you're not helping," I said, diverting from the compliment. "I hope Kitty hurries with the tea. I'll see you later."

He popped out of the mirror, leaving me with my own reflection. I patted my hair into place and then left the room, entering into the bathing room. I knocked on Cordelia's door on the other side. There was no answer, so I opened the door and went through, going into her room and then into the parlor. I found her adding wood to the fire.

"Ah, it feels good in here." Crossing my arms over my chest, I rubbed my hands up and down my arms.

There was a knock at the door. "That will be Kitty with our tea."

I opened the door and was surprised to see Cherrie

Fontaine holding the tea tray, laden with teapot, two cups and saucers, and a plate of scones.

"Oh! Miss Fontaine," I said.

"I was coming up to speak with you and saw Kitty bringing the tray. I offered to bring it for her. The saloon suddenly got very busy."

"Oh, well, thank you, Come in." I opened the door wider to let her in. I gestured that she set the tray on the low table in front of the love seat. She and Cordelia exchanged a greeting.

"What did you want to see me about?" I asked her, indicating she sit on the love seat. I took the chair adjacent to it.

Cordelia finished with the fireplace and then sat next to Miss Fontaine. "Would you like some tea?" Cordelia asked. "I can fetch another teacup."

"No, thank you." Miss Fontaine raised a hand. "I just had some with Mary Alice. In fact, that's what I wanted to speak with you about."

"Mary Alice?"

"Yes. She confided in me something of a most disturbing nature."

"What is it?"

Cordelia poured me some tea and set it on the table in front of me. She then poured some for herself and added two sugars.

"She wasn't drinking tea," Miss Fontaine said. "She was drinking liquor. Had been all day. We were talking about Ralph. She was upset, said she couldn't live with what she had done."

"Done? You mean . . ."

I glanced at Cordelia, who'd just taken a sip of her tea. She coughed and patted her chest, obviously having swallowed wrong. Her eyes were wide at Miss Fontaine's declaration.

"She didn't say what it was that she'd done, exactly, but . . . with the medicine bottle she'd taken, it made me think—"

"That she killed him?" I asked.

She shrugged. "She also mentioned Victoria Clement. Said something about 'the money.'"

I tilted my head in question. "What money?"

"I'm sorry, I don't know."

The exorbitant amount of money in the expenses column of the charred paper came to mind.

"I see," I said. "Do you know anything about a company called CSB Manufacturing?"

She shook her head. "Never heard of it."

"Have you mentioned this . . . confession of sorts to the sheriff?" I asked.

"He's not in his room. One of the maids was cleaning it. Said he'd moved out. That's why I came to you."

Moved out?

"Oh." The words hit me like a punch in the stomach. I wasn't quite sure why it came as such a blow. The sheriff was back on his feet. Sort of. Even though it wasn't the most prudent thing to be on his own, Clayton did not seem the type of man to be reliant on anyone for anything. I knew it had pained him to be here, with us all waiting on him hand and foot. Yet, I couldn't help but think he left because of me, that he wanted to get as far away from me as he could.

I picked up my teacup and rested it under my nose. The warm, bergamot-scented steam caressed my upper lip and filtered into my nostrils. The familiar aroma eased the new tension behind my eyes but did nothing to soothe my heart.

I was just about to take a sip when there was another knock on the door.

"I'll get it," Cordelia said. She took another sip of her tea and rose to open the door. It was Clarence.

"Hey, Miss Danson. May I speak with Mrs. Pryce?" his teenaged voice croaked.

"Come in, Clarence," I said, turning in the chair.

He came in and whipped his bellman's cap off his head, leaving his sandy-blond hair in messy spikes. He tucked the cap under his arm. He nodded a greeting to Miss Fontaine.

"What can I do for you?" I asked.

"You need to come to the annex, ma'am. There's another problem with that collapsed portico."

I heaved a sigh. "Oh dear. Can it wait?"

"Mr. Johns says you need to come right away."

I set my teacup down, feeling deprived as I hadn't even had a sip. "Very well. Miss Fontaine, I apologize. It seems I'm needed elsewhere."

"Oh . . . Oh, I see. Well, I probably need to get back to Mrs. Stewart anyway," she said, a quick smile flitting across her face. "She needs me to write some letters for her—to inform friends and business associates about Ralph."

"Of course," I said, not envying the task. In writing those letters, she and Mrs. Stewart would be reliving the man's death all over again.

Chapter Twenty-Five

My heart filled with dread as I made my way to the annex. Once there, I approached Mr. Johns, who was standing near the rubble of the fallen portico. There was another man with him.

"Clarence said you needed to see me," I said.

"Yes, ma'am." He tilted his head toward the man. "This here's Matt Bryson. He's a carpenter."

He tipped his cap to me, and I greeted him with a nod. "What seems to be the problem?"

Mr. Johns fished some gloves out of his coat pocket and put them on his hands, which were red from the cold. "We tried to bolster the portico once more, but it just fell apart. I'm afraid the wood has rotted—likely from weather and termites."

"Which means, ma'am, that the other porch roofs are probably in the same condition," Mr. Bryson added. "As well as the roofs of the houses. It's only a matter of time before—"

"The others collapse," I finished. "So, all the house roofs and porticos need replacement?" I asked with my heart in my throat. I could not afford this at the moment.

"I can give them all a look," Mr. Bryson said, "to see just how bad it is. Some of them might be salvageable."

I heaved a sigh of disappointment. *When will I see the light of day?*

Mr. Johns offered me a sympathetic smile. "We'll see what we can do to prevent collapse of the other structures for the time being, but if we get just one more big storm, I'm afraid we'll have quite a mess on our hands."

I swallowed my trepidation at the prospect. "All right, Mr. Johns. Thank you."

I would have to go to Mr. Tisdale, William's estate lawyer, to beg for more funds, which would most likely mean trading a few more months here in La Plata Springs to secure them. My yearlong stay in the West was slowly turning into a year and a half. But what could I do? I'd never be able to sell the hotel in its present condition—and it wasn't safe for the current inhabitants. Those miners and their families, and Kitty's girls, needed safe accommodations. Or they would leave the hotel, taking with them the income I so desperately needed. Not to mention the income I might lose in the form of visitors for the Winter Festival if I did not find out the truth about Mr. Stewart's death.

Which meant I needed to tell the sheriff about what Cordelia and I had found in the woods, something I was not looking forward to. It seemed to be a significant piece of evidence and he had to know about it, but he would not be happy to think I was still investigating. Would he believe that Cordelia and I just happened upon it in the woods? It was the truth, but I knew it'd sound false to the sheriff's ears.

I shook my head, disgusted with my predicament, both with Clayton and the annex. My friendship with the sheriff might not be repairable, but the roofs in the annex certainly were. I would have Cordelia write a letter to Mr. Tisdale for me.

I trudged back upstairs to my rooms. When I stepped into the parlor, I found Cordelia lying on the love seat, her arm over her eyes. Bijou sat next to her, studying her intently.

"Cordelia? Are you all right?"

She lifted her arm from her face. "Yes. It's just a headache."

"Oh dear. I'm so sorry. It's been some time since you've had one."

"I know. I thought that perhaps the clean air here had rid me of them, but I suppose not."

I couldn't very well ask her to write the letter now. "Would you like me to get your headache powders for you?" I asked instead.

"Thank you, yes," she said, her voice weak.

Poor dear. These headaches often laid her very low. I hoped she would recover quickly.

I went to her room and got one of the small paper envelopes that held the cure. I took the glass sitting on her nightstand, and from the ewer on her dresser, I poured some water into it and then sprinkled the powders in.

"Here you are." I handed her the glass.

Her tea was unfinished, as was mine, and I'm sure it had gone quite cold. I eyed the tea tray with the teapot, sugar bowl, and cream pitcher. "I'll take this down to the kitchen. Would you like more tea?"

She shook her head. "No. Leave the tray. I'll take it down in a little while. I'll just lie here for a bit until the powders start to work. Then I will get up. I'm sorry I can't be of assistance at the moment."

"Don't worry about it. You'll be fit in no time."

She gave me a weak smile and flung her arm over her eyes again. I took a throw blanket from the chair in front of the fireplace and laid it over her, then stoked the fire to flame again.

Since I would be going to see Clayton, who was probably at his office, I put on my coat, hat, and gloves. I carefully placed the charred piece of paper in my handbag. Watching me readying myself for the cold, Bijou gave a little yip.

"All right, girl," I said, gesturing with a tilt of my head for her to come. She carefully jumped over Cordelia and followed me out the door.

We left the hotel and headed down Main Street. The late-afternoon sun had come out from the clouds, making the snow sparkle. Water dripped from icicles clinging to porch overhangs and the eaves of the buildings. The warmth of the sun had even encouraged the townspeople to come outdoors, either for a pleasant stroll or to run their various errands.

When I reached the front door to the sheriff's office and jail, I took a deep breath, steeling myself for my visit. Gathering my wits about me, I opened the door and went in.

Clayton was sitting at his desk, his broken leg propped up on the corner of it. He was going through a mountain of papers. Bijou scampered over to him and raised herself up on his chair. To my surprise, another man sat at a smaller desk on the opposite side of the room, next to the two jail cells.

"Oh, hello," I said.

The man rose to his feet. He was extremely tall and

broad shouldered. Younger than me by half a decade, I guessed. He had expressive dark eyes and a shock of reddish hair. His smile was quite dazzling. "I'm Dirk Fleming, deputy sheriff from Denver." He approached me with an outstretched hand.

I took it and found his grip to be solid and sure. "Arabella Pryce," I said.

He grinned. "As in the Arabella Hotel? I've heard a lot about you, Mrs. Pryce."

I glanced over at Clayton, who looked at me with a vague expression. I couldn't tell if he was upset to see me or not.

I turned back to Deputy Fleming. "Yes. You're here to help with Ralph Stewart's murder case?" I asked.

"Yes, ma'am. The sheriff's been briefing me on the situation."

"Wonderful," I said. At this point, any amount of help would be welcome.

I looked over at Clayton who had gone back to studying his papers. He still had not properly greeted me, which was not only hurtful but rude.

"Good afternoon, Sheriff," I said pointedly, intentionally not using his name in the familiar, as it seemed we were no longer friends. He glanced up at me, and I gave him my brightest smile, ever hopeful that I could charm my way back into his good graces.

His face remained placid. "Arabella." He refocused on the paper he held in his hand. "What can we do for you?"

"I was . . . I was coming by to see how you were doing. You didn't say goodbye when you left the hotel."

"Ah," Deputy Fleming said. "The sheriff said he'd been holed up at your hotel for a few days."

Holed up? Was it truly all that bad?

Clayton shot him a look, and the deputy blinked. "Right," he said and then cleared his throat. "I'll be going, then." He grabbed his hat and secured it on his head, giving me that dazzling smile again. He was absolutely charming. "It was a pleasure to meet you, Mrs. Pryce."

"You too, Deputy Fleming."

Still focused on the paper, Clayton said, "I didn't say goodbye because I thought you were busy. I didn't want to disturb you."

"Of course," I said. Trying to remain gracious at the wave of coolness coming my direction. I half expected Percival to be in the room with us, but he wasn't. "How's the leg? Are you still in pain?"

"It's fine. It doesn't bother me too much. These crutches on the other hand . . ." He gave them a sideways glare.

"I imagine they are very awkward."

He scoffed. "You could say that."

An uncomfortable silence ensued. I couldn't decide if I wanted to run out of there or say what I'd come to say. He had to know what Miss Fontaine had told me about Mary Alice and also about the bank book. Even if it meant he'd never speak to me again.

"Clayton, I . . . I need to tell you something."

He finally looked at me in earnest.

"I found— Well, Cordelia and I we went for a walk, and well . . . Bijou—"

At her name, she scampered over to me, begging to be picked up. I complied, happy for her soothing weight against my chest. Clayton raised his brows at me, waiting for me to continue, or to at least make some sense whatsoever.

"I think we found the missing bank book," I blurted out. "I wasn't looking for it, I promise. It's just that both Miss

Fontaine and Dr. Briggs had been seen going into the woods, and—"

He set the paper down and folded his fingers across his belly. "So, you were following a lead." I let go a breath and squinted my eyes shut. "No . . . Well, maybe, but it was just that I was more curious about the woods than anything. I've never been back there, and I'm sorry. It's just that, well, Victoria Clement is ill—very ill—and she so wants to see that her boy is taken care of and . . . and then Mrs. Stewart is thinking of leaving any moment now, and the festival—"

"Arabella."

I opened my eyes.

"There's no stopping you, is there?" he said.

I took in a breath and let it out. "I haven't done anything illegal."

"This time," he added.

"Right." I swallowed. "And I promise I won't ever do anything like that again." I traced an *X* over my heart. He still hadn't arrested me and thrown me in jail . . . yet. The longer he went without doing so, the better chance I had of it not happening. I hoped.

He blew a breath out of puffed-up cheeks. "What did you find?"

Happy that he was willing to hear me out, I set Bijou down and opened my handbag. I produced the charred piece of paper and handed it to him.

He quickly perused it. "It does look like ledger paper." He held it closer to his face. "CSB Manufacturing," he said under his breath.

"Yes. Do you know the company? It's an awfully large sum that seems to be paid monthly. I asked Dr. Briggs about it, and—"

He shot me a look with raised eyebrows. "You questioned Dr. Briggs about this?"

"Well, it's not like I interrogated him or anything. I just, well, he was the one who told us the bank book was missing in the first place, so I—"

He raised a hand to silence me and then rubbed his chin with his thumb and forefinger. "Thank you, Arabella," he said, a dismissive tone in his voice.

"You're welcome. What for? What are you thinking?"

He glanced over at me, as if trying to decide if he should divulge more or not. He didn't open his mouth to speak so I assumed not.

"Miss Fontaine has also said a few things I think you should know about," I added.

He shook his head, disbelief in his eyes. "So, this is you *not* investigating?"

I pressed my lips together. "I can't help it if people talk to me, Clayton. As proprietress of the hotel, it's only natural that I will hear about things that go on there—"

He rolled his wrist in the air, reluctantly indicating for me to continue.

"Remember how I told you about Mary Alice taking a medicine bottle from Mrs. Stewart's room? And the Coca Wine Maggie found in her drawer?"

"Yes," he said, barely hiding his impatience.

"Well, Miss Fontaine said that Mary Alice had been drinking quite heavily earlier today and confessed to her that she regretted what she had done. So, maybe it's possible that she poisoned Mr. Stewart. Has the doctor discovered what kind of poison he consumed?"

"No. Not yet."

"What about Mr. Valdez?"

"No."

"I see. I wonder what's taking him so long," I mused.

He set the paper down and looked up at me incredulously. "He's doing his best, Arabella. He's a country doc, not a trained coroner."

"Yes. Yes, of course," I said apologetically, not wanting to offend him further. I was grateful that he hadn't booted me out of his office yet, which I took as a good sign.

"Were you able to get any clues from Mr. Archer?" I asked, remembering that before he left the hotel, he'd said he was going to question him.

Clayton didn't answer my question. His gaze had returned to the charred piece of paper. He then pulled his foot off the desk and stood up, his balance teetering on his good leg.

"Where did you say you found this?" He held up the ledger paper.

"In the woods, out by the meadow."

"Which meadow?"

I stared at him dumbly. "I . . . I don't know. The meadow."

"There are a few around here," he said with a sarcastic tone, which I did not appreciate. "Which way were you headed? North or south?"

I blinked, trying to recall. I hadn't been paying attention. "I . . . I don't know."

"Never mind. I'll find it." He reached for his crutches.

"You're going out there? On crutches? It's too far."

"I'll take Queenie," he said.

I scoffed. "Right. And how are you going to get on her? Can you even ride with a broken leg?"

He shot me a pointed look. "I could ride with a broken back."

I sniggered. The man's pride was so deep it was amusing.

"Something funny?" he asked.

I shrugged. "No. But listen, you could be out there forever. Let me show you where it is. I can get there. I just can't explain *how* to get there."

He considered me for a moment and then pushed out a breath. "All right."

"Great!" I clapped my hands together, pleased that he'd agreed. Bijou barked at my enthusiasm. "I'll get a horse from Mr. Parkhurst at the livery."

"No. I don't want to take the time. We'll go tandem."

Tandem? I had experienced this two other times before with the sheriff and the lovely Queenie. The last time was when I'd injured my ankle when I'd fallen off a horse and caught my foot in the stirrup, and the first was at my humiliating entrance into La Plata Springs after he'd fished me from the river. Both occasions had left me feeling vulnerable and embarrassed. I didn't relish the idea, but at least it seemed that Clayton was finding me useful.

Bijou barked again, sensing we were going on an adventure of sorts. But I didn't think it a good idea to take her. It was cold, and she would just get wet again.

"Could Bijou stay here?" I asked. "She won't be any trouble."

"Sure," he said less than enthusiastically. He took his coat from the back of his chair and slipped it on. After grabbing his hat from the desk, he secured it on his head, and with the aid of his crutches, he went out to the hitching rail where Queenie was dozing in the sun. I followed behind. At our approach, the horse perked up.

Clayton unfurled the rein from the rail and brought her to stand at the corner of the porch leading into his office.

He handed me his crutches and then placed his left foot, the "good" foot, into the stirrup and swung the broken leg over Queenie's back. He winced as he settled in the saddle and then pushed himself over the back of the cantle of the seat. He bit his lip in obvious discomfort but settled again, leaving the seat empty.

"Come on," he said, waving his fingers with an upturned palm.

I wasn't sure how to proceed, and he wasn't offering any suggestions. On the prior occasions he had lifted me up and set me in the saddle as if I weighed nothing at all, which was both exhilarating and exasperating at the same time. But this approach to getting on board was one I hadn't experienced before. I figured the most graceful way to do this was to put my left foot in the stirrup and then twist my body so that my bottom landed on the seat. I would be riding sidesaddle in a way.

I put my foot in the stirrup and swung myself up, but I'd miscalculated and started to topple backward over the other side.

"Oh!" I screeched.

Clayton leaned forward and caught my fall with his arm. Dipped over Queenie's side, our faces were nearly touching. Our eyes locked, and my heart thumped so loudly in my chest I feared it vibrated through my body and into his arms. His scent, woodsy and faintly reminiscent of leather, enfolded me in a cloud of quiet security. Looking into his eyes, I could scarcely breathe.

Queenie, ever the patient equine, stood absolutely still despite the fact that the majority of our weight was straining to one side of her. Finally, Clayton pulled me upright in the saddle.

Completely flustered and still quite breathless, I stiffened between his arms.

"You all right?" he said, his voice low in my ear.

Unable to speak or even swallow, I nodded. This was absolutely ridiculous. I had to get control over my emotions. I closed my eyes, imaging myself onstage, taking command of my performance and the audience.

I cleared my throat. "Yes. I'm fine. Let's go."

He clucked to Queenie, and we were off.

Chapter Twenty-Six

As we walked down main street, my heart took up pounding in my chest again—not from the breathlessness the sheriff had produced but at the fact several people were staring at us.

To my chagrin, Cynthia Mayes was in front of her store talking with Constance Chatterley and none other than Atticus Brooks. All three of them turned to look at us with raised brows and open mouths.

Miss Mayes had at one time intimated that I'd had designs on the sheriff and commented on the way I looked at him. I, of course, told her that was preposterous. But seeing me and him like this would only strengthen her convictions. And then there was Constance with her penchant for gossip and Brooks's aim to malign me. This was a recipe for disaster.

My attention was pulled away from them as Deputy Fleming crossed the street and approached us. His face broke into an amused smile. He'd probably made the same assumptions as the others as the sheriff and I—I'm certain

—looked like two lovers out for a casual ride. Heat flamed up my neck and into my cheeks.

"Anything?" Clayton asked him.

"Nothing yet, Sheriff."

"Well, hopefully she'll get back to us soon. In the meantime, bring Dr. Briggs in. I need to ask him some questions. I'll be back shortly."

"Will do, sir." He tipped his hat to me with that ridiculous grin on his face. This was just beyond the pale.

"Dr. Briggs? Why do you need to speak with him?" I asked.

He didn't answer and I felt it best not to press. For the moment. Even though I wanted to know who the "she" was he referred to as well.

We crossed the road and passed through the little alleyway between Gilroy's Bakery and Archer's Shoe Emporium, leaving the main street and all the gawkers behind, much to my relief.

Once we crossed the footbridge over the river, we made our way into the woods. Neither one of us spoke. The rhythmic movement of Queenie's gate lulled me into a more relaxed state, despite the fact that Clayton's left arm crossed my body and rested on the saddle horn in front of me. His other hand rested on his leg. His closeness still made it hard for me to breathe, but I did my best to conjure the protective veneer I wore onstage. Notwithstanding my efforts at restraining myself from further inquiry, I found I couldn't quell my curiosity.

"Who was Deputy Fleming trying to reach?"

He hesitated, but then finally said. "Tilly Weston."

"Ah. About who purchased the medal we found in Mr. Valdez's room," I finished for him.

He didn't respond.

"Turn this way," I said, recognizing our path. I was gaining purchase with my emotions, and it helped me to think more clearly.

We entered the meadow, and the boulders near where we'd found the burned-out fire came into view.

"Head over there." I pointed.

His left arm pressed against my waist as he steered Queenie to the right. We rode on in silence, and I started to melt into myself and into the saddle. The late-afternoon sun shone brightly, but as it was starting to make its descent, the air had cooled. Without the eyes of the townsfolk on us, and all alone in this beautiful pristine wilderness, I found I didn't mind our close proximity. In fact, if felt quite natural.

Before I knew it, we were at the boulders. He pulled Queenie to a halt. "Where now?"

"In there." I pointed to the tree line. In seconds, we were at the spot.

Clayton swung his broken leg over Queenie's rump and jumped down from the saddle onto his good leg, his hands resting on either side of me. He groaned in pain.

"Was that wise?" I asked, looking down at him.

He raised his head and scowled at me. Setting his hands on my waist, he helped me down and then hopped over to the black coals and ash.

"How are you going to get back on?" I asked as there was no raised porch anywhere in sight.

He didn't answer but continued to peruse the area. He went beyond the fire and was looking amid the trees. Taking his cue, I did the same but in the opposite direction.

"What are we looking for?" I asked.

"I'm not sure yet."

We continued to scan the area, him hopping painfully on one foot and me not sure why we were out here.

"Got it," he said.

"What?" I went over to him.

He pointed at a footprint in the moist dirt. "Go to Queenie. In the saddlebag is a burlap sack. Please bring it to me. And also my canteen in the other saddlebag."

I did as he said and then handed the items to him. From the bag, he took a plank of wood framed with a ledge of about one inch. Then he took out a flat, spade-looking thing, and with his hand braced against a tree, he gingerly lowered himself to his good knee with a groan and began to dig around the footprint, careful not to touch it with the implement. After a few minutes of digging around it, he leveraged the flat tool against the ground and lifted the footprint out.

"The ground is still a bit frozen, so it will hold up for a couple of hours. We've got to get this back my office."

"Whose footprint do you think it is?"

"Dr. Briggs's."

"Why him?"

"You said Martha saw him come out here with his medical bag."

"Well, yes, but that doesn't mean he was here in this very spot."

He studied the block of dirt in his hands. "I think he came out here to burn the bank book."

"How are you so certain it was him?" I asked.

"The handwriting in the ledger matches the handwriting on the fake suicide note. And a sample of the doctor's handwriting Mr. Johns found in his room."

"So you think he killed Ralph?"

"I'm not sure. But I definitely think he stole the ledger."

I sucked in a breath. "But why?"

Suddenly, it dawned on me. *CSB Manufacturing.* Cornelius S. Briggs.

"Of course!" I said a little too loudly, sending a couple of birds flurrying from the trees. "He must have been embezzling money from the family. Why else would he burn the book? He was destroying the evidence."

"That's my guess." Clayton carefully lowered the block of dirt onto the plank and into the sack.

"And maybe Mr. Stewart knew. He found out the doctor was stealing from the family."

Clayton shook his head and let out a chuckle. Was he laughing at my conclusion?

"What?" I asked.

"Nothing."

"What's so funny, Clayton?"

"It's not funny. You just surprise me is all."

"Oh." I wondered if that was a good thing or not. "In what way?"

He handed me the sack so that he could get to his feet, which he did quite laboriously. He reached for the sack again. "Go get Queenie and bring her over to that stump there." He pointed to a tree stump in a small clearing.

I stared at him, waiting for him to answer my question, but it seemed he wasn't moved to do so.

"Go on," he said. "We need to get back to town."

I sighed and did what he said.

With Clayton's injuries, my clumsiness, and the awkwardness of the burlap sack, which we had to handle with great care, it took some time but we finally got ourselves on Queenie once again. I held the sack in my lap while Clayton steered with the reins.

"What did you mean when you said I surprise you?" I asked, still curious at his cryptic remark.

He let out another chuckle. "Another time, Arabella. Another time.

As we made our way back into town, I tried to make conversation. I so wanted him to tell me what he'd found so amusing, but the more I queried him about his silly statement, the more he clammed up.

When we stepped onto main street, all eyes were on us again, which was still a bit embarrassing, but I did my best to brush it off. It was no one's business what went on between the sheriff and me, and the people could think what they wanted. After all, I was used to public scrutiny, wasn't I?

When we finally reached the sheriff's office, he dismounted, this time with more ease. He took the sack from me, set it on the porch, and lifted me down from the saddle.

Once I'd touched down, I expected him to release me, but his hands stayed firmly on my waist. I peered up into those deep blue eyes, and the look in them sent my pulse racing. There was pain, confusion, and . . . longing. It seemed he was about to say something, but then he suddenly lowered his hands.

"Thanks," he said, his gaze sliding away from mine.

"What for?" I asked, a bit surprised. It seemed I'd done nothing but cause trouble for him.

"For coming out to find me that day. For putting me up in your hotel."

I offered him a slow smile, appreciating his gratitude. "You're welcome."

He picked up the sack and reached for his crutches,

which were leaning against the porch. I took the sack from him and we entered the office.

The deputy had his feet up on his desk, and Bijou, smiling from ear to ear, was curled up in his lap. Dr. Briggs sat on the cot inside the jail cell.

He leaped to his feet. "Sheriff, what is the meaning of this? Why did this man arrest me?"

Glancing at me, Clayton pointed to the desk, indicating he wanted me to set the sack there. Hobbling on his crutches, he approached the cell. "Take off your shoe," Clayton demanded. He secured the crutches under his arms to free his hands.

Dr. Briggs blinked in surprise. "What?"

"You heard me. Take it off."

The doctor rolled his eyes but did what he'd been told. He handed the shoe to the sheriff.

"Mrs. Pryce?" Clayton said, pointing to the sack. I brought it over to him.

He addressed Dr. Briggs. "You are quite close with Mrs. Stewart, aren't you?"

"Well, yes. Of course."

"She trusts you implicitly."

The doctor wrapped his hands around the bars in front of him. "Yes," he hissed angrily. "Why. Am. I. Here?"

"You kept the books for her, am I right?"

Dr. Briggs huffed under his breath. "What of it?"

"You reported to Mrs. Pryce here that Mrs. Stewart's bank book went missing."

"Yes. I did."

"You said Mrs. Stewart didn't know who took it. That the thief's face was covered," I added.

"Yes, but she later remembered that it was Valdez. She told Mrs. Pryce as much," Dr. Briggs said.

"Or perhaps you convinced her it was Mr. Valdez," I said. "But it was you. I saw you leaving Mr. Valdez's room. You put the cloak in his room to make it look like he was the one who'd stolen the bank book."

"This is ludicrous," the doctor said with a laugh. "Why would I take the bank book?"

Clayton removed the plank from the bag. The clump of dirt had crumbled a little from the ride, but the print was still intact. He held the shoe up to the print and showed it to the doctor.

"These look like a match, don't they?" he asked him.

Dr. Briggs scoffed. "What is this all about?"

"I've done a little research," the sheriff continued. "CSB Manufacturing. There is no such company, is there?"

Dr. Briggs's face froze. He looked away from the sheriff.

"You were stealing from the Stewarts," Clayton continued.

Dr. Briggs shook his head. "This is outrageous. You have no proof of anything."

"Ralph knew," Clayton said. "Did Valdez somehow know as well?"

Dr. Briggs turned his gaze back to him and narrowed his eyes. "What are you implying, Sheriff? That I killed them? You've got to be joking."

Clayton pulled a folded piece of paper from his coat pocket. He handed it to Dr. Briggs. "This is the note that was found in Ralph's room the morning after his death. Is that your handwriting?"

Dr. Briggs's eyes went wide. "Uh, well . . . I didn't write this note, if that's what you're saying."

"That is what I'm saying. Like most doctors, you carry a number of medicines with you, am I right? Medicines that cure but can also kill. Ralph knew that you were embezzling money from the family. He was going to expose you, so you poisoned him and then pushed him out the window. You wrote this fake suicide note."

"I didn't!" Dr. Briggs gripped the bars so hard his knuckles went white.

"I wonder, though," the sheriff said, "why kill Valdez? Dr. Tate found that Cristoforo Valdez had been poisoned as well."

Fear darkened Dr. Briggs's eyes, and he vehemently shook his head. "I didn't kill either of them, and I didn't write this note. I swear it!"

Clayton turned to Deputy Fleming. "Wire Denver. Tell them we have prisoner who needs to be set for trial."

"You have to believe me!" the doctor said, desperation in his eyes. He held up his hands in surrender. "All right. I'll admit I was taking money from the Stewarts. The night of the party, after Bertha and I left, Ralph came to her room to say good night. I was administering some medicine to Bertha in the bedroom, and I had left the bank book open on the desk. When I came out of the bedroom, he confronted me about those payments. He was acting strange, slurring his words, stumbling. He'd had too much to drink or something. He asked me about those payments. I told him they were for a drug manufacturing company that I had encouraged Bertha to invest in. I think he believed me, but he took the book."

"Did you follow him back down to his room?" the sheriff asked.

"No. I swear. Bertha was not feeling well. She was agitated. She wouldn't let me leave. You can ask her. She was up for hours. I don't think she fell asleep until three o'clock the next morning. And then you all woke us at around six thirty."

"How did you get the book back?" I asked.

He shook his head. "It was after you had us all up to your rooms," he said. "After Ralph had died. I went there immediately after you'd informed us of Ralph's death. I took it and kept it hidden until yesterday when I was able to destroy it."

"Why did you take it to the woods? Couldn't you have burned it in your rooms?" Clayton asked.

"Bertha often comes in unannounced. I couldn't take the chance," he stated matter-of-factly.

The sheriff regarded Dr. Briggs's haggard face for a few moments and then turned to the deputy and held up the plank for the deputy to retrieve. He set Bijou on the ground, stood, and came over and took it from him. Bijou sat patiently at my feet, looking up at me.

"We need to go to the hotel," Clayton said.

"You have to let me out of here," Dr. Briggs said. "I didn't do it!"

The sheriff ignored him. "Deputy Fleming, let's go. We need to have another word with the Stewart party."

"What did you find out from Mr. Archer?" I asked, hoping he would tell me something this time.

Clayton slid me a look. "We'll accompany you back to the hotel," he said. Apparently, he did not want to divulge his findings, if any, to me, which was annoying, but in all fairness, I was not supposed to be working on the case— even though I had provided valuable information and insights. I decided not to press.

"Come, Bijou," I said.

We left the office, and the sheriff proceeded to untie Queenie from the hitching post and led her up to the porch. I didn't think it was necessary for me to hitch a ride this time. The hotel wasn't very far away.

"I'll walk with the deputy," I said.

"Suit yourself." He handed Deputy Fleming his crutches to carry, and then he clambered on board and got himself situated with the reins.

He clucked to Queenie, and Deputy Fleming and I followed behind.

"So, what's it like owning a hotel?" The deputy asked me, his face bright with curiosity.

I smiled at him, and he smiled back, revealing a charming dimple below the left corner of his mouth. "Challenging," I said.

"I bet. How long have you been here?"

He wanted to engage in idle chitchat, which was sweet, but my mind was full to the brim with the murders.

"Not long. Only a little over five months."

"Really? You must have just recently purchased the hotel, then?"

"No. It's a long story. If you will excuse me, I need to ask the sheriff something."

I trotted away from him to catch up with Clayton, Bijou on my heels.

"What do you think about what Dr. Briggs said?" I asked. "About not killing Mr. Stewart and Mr. Valdez?"

"I'm not entirely sure. The man's a thief. Why wouldn't he be a liar?" Clayton asked.

I had to walk fast to keep up with Queenie's long legs. Deputy Fleming had quickened his pace and was again by my side.

"But if he was telling the truth about staying with Mrs. Stewart, he couldn't have killed Mr. Stewart," I said. "Didn't Andrew say he was with his cousin until around eleven that night? And Dr. Tate said that, based on the body temperature, Mr. Stewart had been dead for at least five or six hours. If Dr. Briggs didn't leave Bertha until three in the morning, then Ralph was already dead. He couldn't have killed him."

The sheriff tipped his hat to some young ladies passing by. They twittered with delight and then eyed the handsome deputy, who greeted them with a wide smile. They giggled behind gloved hands.

"I need to be sure," the sheriff said. "I need to speak with Mrs. Stewart."

Chapter Twenty-Seven

We reached the hotel and Clayton walked Queenie up to one of the three horse ties positioned on either side of the steps leading to the doorway. His dismount was a little less awkward this time, but I could tell his leg pained him. Deputy Fleming handed him the crutches.

I picked Bijou up and settled her under my arm as the deputy held open one of the large beveled glass doors of the hotel for the sheriff and me.

When we got to the reception desk, Mr. Pettyjohn greeted the two men with a smile. Well, not really a smile. Mr. Pettyjohn didn't smile, but it passed for a smile.

"Could you wait right here, Mrs. Pryce? Kitty said she needed to speak with you right away." He left the desk and went back toward the kitchen.

"Very well." I turned to Clayton. "How will you get up the stairs with those crutches?" I asked, my hands on my hips.

He smirked and slid a glance at the deputy. "Slowly."

He made his way to the stairs, the deputy following behind, just as Kitty came down the hall from the kitchen.

"Arabella, I think there's something you should know," Kitty said, her face eager with news. She glanced over at Clayton. "Sheriff, you will definitely want to hear this."

"My goodness," I said. "It sounds terribly important."

She nodded. "Could we go somewhere more private?"

"My office?" I suggested.

The four of us walked down the hallway toward the annex. Bijou opted to stay with Mr. Pettyjohn. He didn't really care for the dog, but Bijou liked to sit and stare at him—probably trying to persuade him to change his mind. I let her be.

We stepped out into the cold of the annex and then into my office.

Kitty closed the door behind us and set her eyes on the deputy.

"Oh, forgive me," I said. "Kitty, this is Deputy Fleming."

She nodded a greeting to him. "Welcome to La Plata Springs."

"Thank you. It's a lovely town," he said.

Kitty turned her gaze on me. "I think I may have eliminated one of your suspects."

"*Your* suspects?" Clayton said, giving me a pointed look. "So, you *were* still working the case, even though I told you not to? Does that mean you went looking for the bank book and didn't just happen by it like you said?"

"Oh—" Kitty's gaze darted back and forth between me and the sheriff.

"I did just happen by the bank book! And I got a confession out of Dr. Briggs, didn't I?" I said, probably a little too loudly.

"Dr. Briggs? Did he commit the murders?" Kitty asked.

"No," I said.

"We don't know for sure," the sheriff followed.

"All right, you two. Stop squabbling." Kitty's face clouded over with that familiar sternness that stopped even the most hardened cowboys and miners in their tracks. "My goodness, you sound like an old married couple."

I folded my arms over my chest, and the sheriff cleared his throat. "What did you want to say, Kitty?" he asked.

"It's about Mary Alice Stewart. She couldn't have poisoned Ralph that night."

"How do you know?" I asked.

She took in a breath. "Well, I was talking to one of my girls—I won't say who—but the subject of the murders came up. She said there was talk that Victoria or maybe Mary Alice was the guilty party, and—"

"It wasn't Victoria. I would bet my life on it," I said.

"Well, it wasn't Mary Alice, either," Kitty said.

"Are you ever going to actually tell us why you think this?" the sheriff asked, impatience in his voice. The area around his eyes looked tight. He definitely seemed to be in a lot of pain, which was no wonder with how much activity he'd had today.

Kitty pulled her lip between her teeth, and her gaze ricocheted between the three of us. "Because she was at the annex, with my girl."

"Why would she have gone there?" I asked. "She said she had gone directly to bed after the party. In her room."

The sheriff let out a breath. "Of course she said that."

"Why, 'of course'?"

Kitty raised a brow.

It suddenly dawned on me. She was *with* Kitty's girl.

"Oh, I see." I was surprised at this declaration but not shocked. I had known more than one person in the theater world who was sexually adventurous.

Now that we were all on the same page, Kitty continued. "My girl said that Mary Alice and that Fontaine woman parted company right after they left the party. Mary Alice came directly over to my place and was there 'til the wee hours."

"But wouldn't she have passed right by her husband's body in the morning on her way out?" I said.

"I have a back entrance to both my houses," Kitty said. "For discretionary purposes. Mary Alice left here at around five thirty in the morning and went back to the hotel through the rear door. Another one of the girls, who happened to be leaving the hotel, saw her, too."

"But Dr. Tate said poison killed Ralph," Clayton said. "Briggs mentioned that later that evening, Ralph seemed inebriated, was slurring his words, possibly from drink or maybe from the poison. She could have slipped him something earlier in the evening."

"I thought about that," Kitty said. "But she and . . . my girl . . . were also at the annex before the party."

"I never saw Mary Alice and Mr. Stewart together at the party, either," I chimed in.

"Well, that does seem to eliminate her for Ralph's death, but we still have Mr. Valdez," Clayton said.

"Why would she want to kill Mr. Valdez?" Deputy Fleming asked.

"He could have been blackmailing the family," Clayton said. "Maybe she did it to protect them."

I shook my head. "Miss Fontaine said Mary Alice was very concerned about her stake in the family, which would explain why she would want to protect their wealth. That might lead her to murder Valdez, but now that she is Mr. Stewart's widow, is she entitled to any of the family's money? Would she inherit from her late husband, or would she be turned out with nothing? It seems Mrs. Stewart has control of everything. If Mary Alice gets nothing, why would she kill Valdez?"

"You have a good point, Arabella," Kitty said. "I think you can rule out Mary Alice."

The sheriff cleared his throat, clearly still annoyed with me. "Thank you, Kitty," he said. "Is there anything else?"

She shrugged. "Not that I can think of at the moment."

"All right. Deputy Fleming, I want you to speak with Victoria Clement. Valdez said there was a woman in his room—"

"Maybe Victoria was in the room with Mr. Stewart, but she didn't poison him," I said. "I'm certain of it."

"She was also with him at the party. I saw it myself," the sheriff said, ignoring me. "She threw a drink in his face. Perhaps that's how the poison was administered."

"But it wouldn't make sense that she would kill him. She needed him for the sake of her son," I insisted.

"But if she didn't get what she wanted—" Clayton said.

"She didn't do it." I set my hands on my hips, frustrated that he didn't want to listen to me. I didn't really have any solid evidence for my conviction, but I knew it deep in my gut. "Mr. Stewart was Victoria's ticket to getting their son back. Even if Mr. Stewart wouldn't leave Mary Alice and marry her, he most likely would have provided for her and the child in some way. She wouldn't have killed him."

As I said the words, a twinge of sorrow pierced my heart. Victoria was fighting, perhaps with her dying breath, for the well-being of her son. Something that was quite different from my mother, who used me for her own welfare. Even though his circumstances at the moment were less than ideal, he was fortunate in his mother's selflessness.

Clayton's jaw flexed, and he gave me a look that made my throat close. Not in that knee-melting way that he sometimes did but in a not-very-nice way.

"Whether she is guilty or not is for me to decide," he said, shutting me out.

I narrowed my eyes at him. It seemed I was never going to get past my previous transgression, no matter how many times I apologized or how much I tried to help.

I pulled in a breath. "Very well, then," I said, pushing it out. "I'll leave you to it."

A range of emotions crashed through me—anger, frustration, hurt, despair. I had to get out of the room, had to get away from him. I brushed past the three of them, wanting to go to my rooms to get ahold of my emotions and sort myself out.

After all, I had a hotel to run. My sleuthing days were over once and for all.

I swept past the reception desk, my blood still boiling and the swirl of emotions making my head spin. I was about to climb the stairs when Mr. Pettyjohn called out my name.

"Yes," I said quite tersely.

"Mrs. Stewart has been asking for Dr. Briggs. I didn't see him return with you. Do you know where he is?"

"You'll have to ask the sheriff about that," I huffed.

"But she's requested I get the funds necessary from him

to purchase train tickets for her and her party. And also to arrange for Mr. Stewart's coffin to be transported with them. There's a train leaving for Denver the day after tomorrow. Six thirty a.m."

I heaved a sigh. The matter was out of my hands now. It made me sad that the festival would most likely be canceled and Charlie would not be reunited with his mother or introduced to his grandmother. He'd be orphaned and alone. My heart broke. I'd failed in my mission.

"Thank you, Mr. Pettyjohn. The sheriff should be coming out of the annex at any moment."

Of all the feelings wrestling within my body, the worst ones took precedence. Fear of failure. Defeat. Worthlessness.

Bijou had ambled over to me and reading my distress, looked up at me with sad eyes.

I should have stopped by the kitchen for some chamomile tea to calm my nerves, but all I wanted was to escape to my rooms and hide from the world for a while.

I finally reached the top of the stairs and opened the door to the parlor.

"I don't know why I try to help that man," I said to Cordelia who was still lying on the love seat. "It doesn't seem like he's ever going to forgive me. He'll probably arrest me after he gets this murder solved. *If* he gets this murder solved. And Mrs. Stewart plans to leave the day after tomorrow. Little Charlie won't—"

I looked over at her, and my heart stopped when I saw she wasn't moving. Her arm was hanging down the edge of the love seat, and her head was cocked at an unnatural angle.

"Cordelia?" I went over to her and nearly stepped on a puddle of vomit. "Oh my goodness! Cordelia!"

I shook her shoulder, but she remained unconscious. I vigorously patted her cheek. It was cold and clammy to the touch.

"Oh no! This can't be happening. Cordelia!"

Bijou jumped up on the love seat and licked Cordelia's face.

Coming out of the stupor of shock, I raced down the stairs.

"Mr. Pettyjohn!" I yelled as I wound down to the third floor, then the second. "Mr. Pettyjohn, we need Dr. Tate!"

I finally reached the first floor, but Mr. Pettyjohn was not at the reception desk. Luckily, Clarence was coming around the corner. I went to him and grabbed him by the shoulders. He flinched, his eyes wide at my frantic behavior. "You have to go get Dr. Tate. It's Cordelia. Something's wrong with her."

"Yes, ma'am," he said and ripped himself out of my grasp.

I fled back upstairs. Bijou was lying next to her, her paws resting on her hip. I placed a cloth napkin over the vomit and then lifted her upper body and scooted onto the sofa next to her, cradling her head in my lap. I placed my fingers under her nose, and the faint warm vapor told me she was still breathing but barely.

"Stay with me, Cordelia. Stay with me. Don't go," I said, my voice cracking. Cordelia had been my most loyal supporter for so many years. We were like sisters, or mother and daughter—each one of us playing mother from time to time—but most of all, Cordelia was my friend, my most faithful companion.

I held her tight, rocking back and forth. *Please God, don't take her from me.* I was not a religious woman, but if there was a God, I hoped he'd heard me.

It seemed like hours passed, but finally, Dr. Tate arrived, winded from his jaunt up the stairs. Clarence accompanied him but hung back in the doorway.

"I don't know what's wrong with her. I found her like this," I said, my voice coming out like a wail.

"Let me examine her," he said, patiently coming over to us.

"Be careful," I said. "She was sick." I indicated with a tilt of my head toward the napkin-covered mess.

He sidestepped it. "You're going to have to move," he said gently.

"Oh, of course. I'm sorry." He helped me lift her upper body, and I slid out from beneath her. He laid her back down and took her pulse.

"Thready and weak," he said. He pried open her eyes and looked in her mouth, then bent down and took a big sniff, which I thought was odd. He reached for the napkin I'd placed over the sick on the floor, removed it, and took another whiff.

My stomach roiled. What was he doing?

"That's what I was afraid of," he said.

"What? What is it?"

He didn't answer but rummaged through his bag. From it, he pulled a clear glass bottle with a beautiful cut-glass stopper. He opened it and set it against her mouth. He let a small amount trickle in.

"What are you doing? What is that?"

"It's an emetic. It will help clean out the poison. It's a good thing she got sick. It's probably why she's still alive."

My breath caught. "Poison? What poison?"

"I believe it is the same poison that was used to kill Mr. Stewart and Mr. Valdez. It took me awhile to figure it out, but I'm almost certain it's what killed them."

"What is it?"

"Water hemlock. I've seen it in the woods. Even in winter, the seed pods are deadly."

"Seed pods?"

Suddenly, Cordelia stirred. Her face contorted in discomfort.

"A wastebasket, please." Dr. Tate held out his hand. I hurried over to the desk and got the container from beneath it and handed it to him. In seconds, Cordelia was sick again, retching like I've never seen anyone retch before.

Dr. Tate held back the stray locks of hair that had escaped from her coif and placed them behind her ear. He then gently rubbed her back as she continued to empty her stomach. "That's good, Cordelia. I know it's unpleasant, but it's necessary," he murmured. My eyes brimmed with tears at her agony.

After some time, the retching slowed. Her countenance was pasty white, but she seemed more alert.

"I think it's passed, for the most part," he said. "Let's get her to her bed. She'll be more comfortable."

Together, we helped Cordelia to her feet and made our way into her bedroom. I threw back the covers, and we settled her in bed after I had taken off her boots.

"We should let her sleep," the doctor said. "I've done everything I can. The rest is up to her."

My hand flew to my mouth. "You don't mean she could—"

"I don't think so," he quickly cut in. "She's young and healthy, and I believe we caught it in time. She should be all right. We'll just have to keep an eye on her."

I nodded. "Thank you," I said, grateful that he'd come so fast.

"Send someone if she seems to be getting worse."

I walked him out of her room and back into the parlor.

"What has she eaten in the last couple of hours?" he asked, a perplexed look on his face.

I scanned the table in front of the love seat, looking for the tea tray, but it was gone. Only Cordelia's teacup remained.

"Kitty prepared some tea for us—said she was going to also bring up some of Lottie's scones."

His eye traveled to the desk, and he pointed. Cordelia must have moved the tea tray to the desk. The scones were untouched. As was my teacup. I hadn't had a chance to take a sip before Clarence told me I was needed at the annex. The doctor went over and picked up a scone. He took a whiff.

"What are you looking for?" I asked.

"Water hemlock has the faint odor of carrots," he said. He took the lid off the teapot and stuck his nose in it. He then looked up at me. "There it is." He held the teapot under my nose. Sure enough, the sweet aroma of bergamot and carrots hit my senses.

"You said something about seed pods," I said. "What does water hemlock look like?"

He took a piece of stationary from the leather stationary box on the desk and an ink pen from the oblong tray in front of it. He quickly drew a tall-stemmed plant with a spray of flowers spiking out in all directions.

"This is what the plant looks like in bloom," he said. He then drew the same stem and spray but with tiny, clustered seed pods where the blooms had been. "And this is what it looks like in the winter."

I sucked in a breath, my mind reeling, my pulse racing. "Oh. My. Stars," I said, staring into his kind eyes.

"What is it?" he asked.

I grabbed the back of the desk chair to settle myself, my legs threatening to go out from under me.

"Mrs. Pryce?" The doctor took hold of my arm.

I swallowed hard, trying to get ahold of myself. It was suddenly all so clear. I looked into the doctor's eyes. "I know who our murderer is."

Chapter Twenty-Eight

Dr. Tate and I stood in front of Mary Alice's door. I knocked.

The sounds of heeled shoes tapping across the floor echoed from within.

"Mrs. Pryce," she said when she opened the door. "What can I do for you?" She cut a glance at Dr. Tate, who nodded a greeting to her.

"May we come in?" I asked. "It's very important."

"I . . . I suppose." She opened the door wider for us to enter. "What is this about?"

Once inside I turned to face her. "It's about the deaths of your husband and Mr. Valdez."

"I see. Do you have news?"

"I think I know who killed them," I said.

She opened her eyes wide. "Oh? Well, then who?"

"Before I say, would you please open the bottom drawer of that bureau?" I tilted my head at the burled walnut chest of drawers.

"What?" Her brows pressed downward in confusion. "Why?"

I smiled. "Please bear with me."

She went to the dresser and opened the bottom drawer. Pulling her chin back in surprise, she pulled out the bottle of Coca Wine.

"This is Ralph's. What is it doing here?" she asked.

"Would you please hand it to me?" I held out my palm. She complied, her gaze darting back and forth between me and the doctor.

I took the bottle, uncorked it, and took a big whiff. The faint odor of carrots tickled my nose. "That's what I thought."

I handed it to the doctor, and he did the same. Our eyes met and he nodded.

"What are you doing?" Mary Alice asked.

"This contains the seeds, either crushed or whole, of water hemlock," the doctor told her. "It is a poisonous plant. One that was used to kill your husband and Mr. Valdez."

Her jaw dropped. "I didn't do it. I didn't even know that was there."

"I know," I said. "I believe it was planted."

"By whom?" she and the doctor asked in unison.

"Come with me," I said. "We need to go to your mother-in-law's rooms. But first, I need to have Clarence fetch Mr. Archer. He needs to be present for this."

Clarence didn't have to go far. He said he saw Mr. Archer go into the Bella Saloon with Mr. Brooks. I told him to bring him to Mrs. Stewart's room.

When I got back to Mary Alice's room, she, the doctor, and I made our way upstairs. I knocked on Mrs. Stewart's door, and Cherrie Fontaine answered.

"Hello, Miss Fontaine, may we come in?" I asked.

"Yes, of course," she said.

We walked in to find Clayton and Mrs. Stewart seated in the parlor. Mary Alice went to the sofa and sat down next to Mrs. Stewart. In a completely unexpected gesture, she took hold of the older woman's hand and held it in her lap. Mrs. Stewart looked just as surprised as I felt. She glanced at Mary Alice with questioning confusion but didn't pull away.

Suddenly, the temperature in the room dropped a few notches, and a chill ran up my spine. Percival's transparent form appeared behind the sofa, to the left of Mrs. Stewart.

My breath caught in my throat, and I coughed. Would the man ever heed my request to stop startling me? He crossed his arms over his chest, waiting for me to continue. I couldn't very well ask him to leave because what I had to say concerned him as well.

"Pardon me," I said, patting my chest and then clearing my throat. "I'm here because I know who poisoned Mr. Stewart and Mr. Valdez."

"Arabella—" Clayton started to stand, a look of grave annoyance on his face.

"Let her speak," Dr. Tate said.

Clayton reluctantly lowered himself in the chair again.

"Dr. Tate here just told me he has identified the poison that both men ingested. It's water hemlock, which can be found in the forests in this region." I glanced at the doctor.

"Yes," he concurred. "I discovered it in the stomach contents of both victims."

"And it was also intended for me," I said. "And Cordelia."

"What?" Clayton's expression was no longer one of annoyance but of deep concern. My heart lifted at his protectiveness.

"Isn't that right, Miss Fontaine?" I said, giving her a pointed look. My fists clenched at my sides, and I could barely contain my rage. My dearest friend in the world had nearly died because of this woman. And what would have happened if I had drunk some? I wouldn't have been able to save her. We'd both be dead.

Miss Fontaine shook her head, a look of mock disbelief in her face. Her gaze bounced between me and the doctor. "Me? You can't be serious. Why would I kill Ralph? You should look no further than his wife." She pointed at Mary Alice.

"That's what you wanted me to believe." I held up the bottle of Coca Wine. "You knew Mr. Stewart used Coca Wine for fatigue. You spiked it with water hemlock, and then you planted this in Mary Alice's bottom drawer. You alluded to her as the guilty party every chance you got. It would make sense, the jealous and scorned wife. But she did not kill her husband or Mr. Valdez."

"You're saying I killed Mr. Valdez, too?" She blew out a snort. "I hardly knew the man."

"But you knew his brother," I said. "You were seen with him at a party a few years ago. In 1882. It was a party at Archibald Archer's mansion. You had planned to poison him that night, but your plan failed. Mr. Valdez did not drink the wine, did he?"

Her eyes blinked rapidly, and her mouth twitched. She didn't say anything, just shot daggers at me with her eyes.

"But someone else did." My gaze slid over to Percival.

"Someone who tried to protect you from Enrique Valdez's advances."

Percival's luminous eyes widened, and he placed a translucent hand over his mouth.

"That's right," a voice came from the doorway. It was Mr. Archer's. I wondered how long he'd been standing there. "I remember. Percival Blank was there. He'd intervened when Valdez got aggressive with you. After Valdez left, you left. Blank asked me to join him for a glass of wine, but I couldn't. The next morning, he was dead."

"You can't prove any of that," she said, her body shaking. "Again, why would I want to kill Enrique Valdez?"

"You did it for Mr. Stewart. Because you were in love with him," I said.

Her alabaster complexion blanched even paler, and then she let out a nervous laugh and looked over at Mrs. Stewart, who winced at the very idea.

Miss Fontaine looked back at me and gave another nervous twitter. "You don't know what you are talking about."

"Mr. Stewart and Mr. Archer were worried word would get out that they were culpable for the deaths of the miners in La Linda. They knew the dangers they were putting those men in." I looked over at Mrs. Stewart, whose countenance had clouded over with anger. "You did, too," I said.

Her ice-blue eyes flared. "I sent Ralph to fix the mess Archibald had gotten us into."

"That's right," I said. "Mr. Archer made a mistake in the building of the mine. He wanted to close it down, but your son didn't. He also didn't fix the problem, and because you took away your brother's authority, his hands were tied and he *couldn't* fix it. So, the workers still went into the mines."

Mrs. Stewart's eyes still blazed, but she didn't say anything else.

"Enrique Valdez was blackmailing your son and Mr. Archer. You gave Mr. Stewart the authority to pay him off. That's why he went away after the party in 1882. But he came back about a year ago. Again, around the time of the Winter Festival. As usual, there was another party. And this time—" I turned my attention back to Cherrie Fontaine "—you were successful. You killed Enrique Valdez—to protect Ralph, and perhaps even Mrs. Stewart. You two have grown quite close."

"This is all just wild speculation," Miss Fontaine said, her eyes darting from person to person.

I glanced over at Clayton, who gave me a withering look. His patience with me was running thin, but I soldiered on. "After the party last year, Enrique Valdez came back to the Arabella to play cards, but according to several sources, he wasn't feeling well. The poison was really starting to work by then. He went upstairs to his rooms—" I met Percival's gaze and laughed at the irony "—these very rooms, actually—and he died."

Miss Fontaine scoffed. "Again, you have no proof."

"You're right," I said. "As far as Enrique is concerned, and perhaps even so far as Mr. Blank is concerned, none whatsoever. Only speculation."

She smiled. "Then I suggest you stop wasting everyone's time here."

"Yes," Mrs. Stewart concurred.

I stared at Miss Fontaine and continued. "But then things soured between you and Mr. Stewart. That was because you'd become quite close to Mrs. Stewart, as she has just said. So close, in fact, that she has included you in her will. According to his wife, that made Mr. Stewart quite angry."

Mary Alice nodded and finally spoke up. "He'd been trying to persuade Bertha to keep the money in the family. He didn't want to share. With anyone. Not even me." She looked over at her mother-in-law. Bertha's mouth was set in a hard line, and she didn't look at Mary Alice. But she didn't let go of her hand, either.

Miss Fontaine's shoulders tensed, and her jaw clenched visibly. She glared at me with a hatred that cut right through me, but that wasn't going to stop me. "Perhaps that's why you and Mr. Stewart 'didn't get along,' as you said. You didn't want to be written out of the will. So you stooped to murder because of, what? Greed?"

"This is ridiculous," she said, standing up.

"Have a seat, Miss Fontaine," the sheriff said.

Her jaw flexing and her nostrils flaring, she obeyed. She looked at the sheriff. "It was Dr. Briggs," she said. "You just told us he faked the suicide note, right before they—" she narrowed her eyes at me—"came in here."

"Which brings me to my next point," I said. "Sheriff, do you have the suicide note?"

He pulled it from his pocket.

"May I?" I asked. He handed it to me. "Mrs. Stewart, may I see a piece of correspondence? Perhaps one that Miss Fontaine has penned?"

Mrs. Stewart looked aghast. "Whatever for?"

"Just do it, Bertha," Mr. Archer said.

She rose a little unsteadily and went to the desk. She brought me a letter. I scanned it and found what I was looking for.

"Yes," I said. "Here it is." I gave the suicide note back to Clayton and then handed him the letter. "I noticed something very peculiar about the suicide note when it was first discovered. The *S* in sorry, the last word of both sentences, was capitalized."

I looked over at Clayton, who nodded. "The *S*'s are capitalized here, too."

"Not only were you throwing suspicion on Mary Alice because you knew that she had motive, means, and opportunity to kill Mr. Stewart but you were throwing suspicion on Dr. Briggs. You knew he was embezzling money from the Stewarts. You as much as said so in a letter to Mr. Stewart. You ratted Dr. Briggs out, knowing that Mr. Stewart would confront him. And that worked in your favor. You could kill Mr. Stewart and cast the blame on Mary Alice or the doctor."

My attention was pulled to the doorway where Deputy Fleming stood with his hat in his hand.

"I need a word with the sheriff," he said, an apologetic look on his face. "It, uh, it concerns the case."

The sheriff got to his feet and, using his crutches, hobbled over to the door. They stepped into the hallway and spoke in hushed voices. The rest of us remained quiet. Miss Fontaine was silently seething, Mrs. Stewart's face was registering shock and confusion, Dr. Tate and Mr. Archer were waiting patiently, and Mary Alice was watching her mother-in-law intently.

Clayton stepped back into the room, followed by the deputy. "Deputy Fleming was able to get in touch with Tilly," the sheriff said, "the young girl who helps Mr. Emerson at Archer's Dry Goods from time to time. We had inquired after a religious medal purchased at the store—one that was nearly identical to the medal that Cristoforo Valdez wore. She identified the person who purchased it." His gaze traveled to Miss Fontaine. "You planted this in Ralph's room to make us think Mr. Valdez had been there, that he'd pushed Ralph out the window. But it was you. You were the woman arguing with him in his room that night. Ralph must have been feeling the effects of the poison, opened the window for some air, and you pushed him out."

Her chin quivered, and her eyes filled with moisture. She turned to me, her face full of anger. "I needed the money," she said. "I have . . . I have a family to support—three younger siblings who live with my elderly aunt. Ralph was threatening to tell his mother about what I'd done to Enrique. He knew he wouldn't be blamed. Not the successful, *rich*, businessman. If Mrs. Stewart"—she directed her gaze over to the woman—"knew what I had done, she would have fired me. She would have taken away the money she'd promised me. I couldn't let that happen."

Mrs. Stewart's face had gone as white as the driven snow. She directed her icy gaze at Miss Fontaine. "You killed my boy? How could you?" Mrs. Stewart croaked. "I've provided for you. I secured a future for you."

Miss Fontaine glared at her. "And he was going to take it away from me. He was your golden boy. I didn't stand a chance."

I set the bottle of Coca Wine on the entry table. "But why now? Why didn't you kill him earlier?"

She pulled in a breath through her nose, and her lips pressed downward in a frown. "I wanted to do it when the family was all gathered together."

"So you could throw suspicion onto someone else," I said.

She raised her chin. "I'd had enough of his threats. And when we got here, I saw him with that woman—Victoria Clement. I asked him about her, and he got angry with me. He told me that he was in love with her, that he had been in love with her, even when we were together. He was a liar, a scoundrel! He told me to pack my bags, that he'd bought me a coach ticket and I was leaving the next day."

"The day after the party," I clarified. "So, you went into the woods to find the hemlock. It didn't make sense to me at the time, but I saw some fall out of your reticule the day after Ralph's death. After speaking with Victoria, I assumed it was yarrow root, which is harmless. But then I remembered I also found some at my doorway. It had come from your shoe. You were listening to my conversation with Andrew, Maggie, and Cordelia. You knew we were making headway in the investigation."

"Like I said, I couldn't afford to lose my job."

"So you figured you'd get rid of me and Cordelia. You were the one who brought us the tea tray, not Kitty. You put the hemlock in the tea. But I didn't have time to drink it because I was called away. So, now my companion, my dearest friend, is upstairs suffering because of you."

"What about Cristoforo Valdez?" the sheriff asked.

"What about him?" she shot back.

"You've just confessed to killing Ralph. You'll probably hang for that, so what about Cristoforo Valdez. Did you kill him, too?"

Her lip quivered, and her eyes took on the look of someone facing a firing squad. She shook more violently now. "He was just in the wrong place at the wrong time," she said in a weak voice. "He happened to be passing by my room when I was putting the hemlock in Ralph's Coca Wine that afternoon. He followed me up to Ralph's room when I returned it. When I came out, he confronted me. He knew what I was doing. He threatened to go to you with the information unless I gave him money. He was a blackmailer like his brother!" she spat. "He hung around just long enough for me to get the funds from my bank in California. I gave him every penny I had."

"And then you poisoned the whisky we found in his room. You wanted your money back and Mr. Valdez silenced for good. But you couldn't find the money because it was hidden in a secret compartment of his bag," I said.

A look of horror passed over her face, and then closing her eyes, she shook her head.

"When he succumbed to the water hemlock," I continued, "I suppose that is when he hit his head on the corner of the desk? But I'm confused about something . . . How did you manage to get him to the livery? And precisely at the time Mr. Parkhurst had gone to the bank? You must have had help."

Her eyes opened and then flared with indignation. "He was stealing from Mrs. Stewart," she said, pointing to the woman whose face had gone gray with shock.

"Dr. Briggs? Did he know you knew he was embezzling from the family?" I asked.

"Not until . . . recently."

"Why didn't you say anything to Mrs. Stewart?" the sheriff asked.

"Dr. Briggs was keeping her alive," she said. "And I needed her alive, so I kept quiet."

"But you were in her will. Surely, it would have benefited you if she was dead," I said.

"She has a *very* large estate," Miss Fontaine added, avoiding Mrs. Stewart's gaze. "And I wanted to continue my employment."

"You wanted more money." Mary Alice's nostrils flared with disgust. "You thought you'd get a larger portion of her assets the longer she stayed alive. You'd replace not only her deceased daughter, but her son as well."

"I trusted you!" Mrs. Stewart cried, starting to rise from the sofa. Mary Alice took hold of her arm and gently coaxed her back down.

"You blackmailed Dr. Briggs into helping you," I went on. "That's when you told him you knew of the embezzlement."

"But you had just killed Valdez," the sheriff said. "Didn't he have that to use against you?"

She smiled. "Men are so stupid. I told him that Mr. Valdez tried to take advantage of me and I retaliated. I said it was an accident, but because Cornelius couldn't bear the thought of another man—"

"He was in love with you," I realized.

She gave me a smug smile. "I told him I was frightened that people wouldn't believe me because—"

"—because of your past?" Clayton asked.

I shot Clayton a look. *What past?*

"Excuse me?" I said, confused at this declaration.

"Deputy Fleming?" the sheriff held out his hand, encouraging the deputy to speak.

"Cherrie Fontaine, also known as Melinda Mayfair, was a prostitute in San Francisco where she met Ralph Stewart," he said.

"What?!" Both Mrs. Stewart and Mary Alice exclaimed in unison.

"Why didn't you mention this before?" I asked Clayton.

"I didn't think it had any bearing on the murders. Until now. But, it's all starting to make sense. Was it Ralph who introduced you to his mother?" Clayton asked Miss Fontaine.

She stiffened her jaw, but didn't answer.

"It was," said Mary Alice.

Clayton continued with his thought. "You knew that if it

came out that you killed Valdez, your past might be revealed and you would lose your job," the sheriff continued. "But, because you knew Dr. Briggs was in love with you, you confided in him. He'd do anything for you, and—"

"You also knew his secret," I reiterated.

She scoffed.

"How did you get Valdez's body to the livery?" I asked her again.

She sighed with resignation. "Cornelius rented a flatbed wagon from some farmer. We were able to sneak Valdez out of the hotel. When we saw the blacksmith leaving the livery, it seemed the perfect place to plant the body. Make it look like Valdez was leaving town."

Mary Alice stood and stepped forward, staring into Miss Fontaine's face. "Your cunning is despicable."

I raised a hand to stop her from doing something she'd regret. "She'll pay for what she's done, Mary Alice."

"She will," Clayton said. "Deputy Fleming, take Miss Fontaine to the jail."

"Yes, sir." He approached Miss Fontaine's chair and took her by the arm. Utterly defeated, she stood and let him lead her from the room without protest.

Clayton turned to me with a heaviness in his oceanic eyes. "I'll speak with you later." From the tone of his voice, I didn't think it would be a friendly conversation.

Chapter Twenty-Nine

DECEMBER 12, 1885

As I walked out of the hotel and down the steps onto the street, I smoothed down the front of my new coat. It was made from emerald-green silk velvet plush and trimmed at the cuffs, collar, and hem with ivory lambswool. Miss Mayes had truly outdone herself. Not only was it wonderfully warm but it was beautiful, and I felt beautiful wearing it.

I took in a lungful of the crisp cold air and surveyed the town. Sunlight bathed the freshly fallen snow, making it sparkle like glitter confetti. Shops were decorated in holiday finery and swags of colorful pennants were draped from building to building. The townsfolk were milling through the street, dressed in their Sunday best. At the north end of Main Street stood the massive Douglas fir tree, resplendent with shining decorations. Eager, pink-faced children scurried to the tree to find the presents with their names on them.

Mr. Parkhurst's forge was bustling with activity, as he

was hosting a marshmallow roast. Constance Chatterley had supplied him with her favorite cinnamon apple cider, and Cynthia Mayes was walking through town with a tray of her beloved holiday fruitcake, encouraging any and all to partake. Betty and Mr. Gilroy were also giving out a variety of pastries and baked goods from the warmth of their bakery.

Mr. Archer, in a fine suit and beaver-skinned top hat, stood in front of the General, beaming at the spectacle. The thorough planning the festival committee had done prior to the event made the final preparations go fairly smoothly over the last two days. I was further behind in getting the hotel ready than the other shopkeepers because I had been, well, preoccupied.

Cordelia, still weak from the water hemlock poisoning, took a more managerial and less physical role in enlisting the help of several of the miners' families to decorate the hotel. Some of the wives helped Lottie with the cooking and baking, and Kitty's girls were responsible for making the popcorn and cranberry swags and the other decorations for the grand tree that towered at the foot of the town.

Victoria Clement stood in a patch of sunshine at the corner of the hotel.

"Hello," I greeted her. She turned to me and gave me a hesitant smile. "Are you all right?"

She nodded. "Just nervous. And excited. I can't wait to see Charlie. It's been so long, I wonder if he'll recognize me."

"When are the coaches due to arrive?" I asked.

Mr. Parkhurst had sent two coaches to pick up the nuns and their charges. I had sent the third with Mr. Ellis.

She pulled a watch out of her coat pocket. "It should be

anytime now. I'm so happy the weather cleared. It will make the journey easier for them."

"Yes. Hopefully the storms will stay away until they can return to St. Anne's as well."

Her chin quivered, and a tear rolled down her cheek.

"My dear, what is it?"

"I just hope that Mrs. Stewart receives Charlie well."

I laid a hand on her shoulder. "Andrew has prepared her, and she has agreed to stay, so you might have nothing to worry about."

"Yes, but what I am asking is a tall order," she said. "She might be willing to help Charlie, but I worry that she will try to separate us. What if she wants Charlie all to herself? I have no recourse . . ."

I sighed. "Let's not get ahead of ourselves."

She pressed her lips together in a tight smile. "Right. I have to keep telling myself that Charlie's welfare is what is important. Even if it means that I—" She choked on the last few words.

I wrapped my arm around her shoulder. "Let's head over to the livery and get warm by the fire while we wait."

We made our way slowly down the street, stopping now and then to watch the people drifting in and out of the shops with goodies in hand.

My eyes traveled to the sheriff's office and jail. Clayton and Deputy Fleming stood on the front porch taking in the sunshine. As we passed by, Clayton grabbed his crutches and made his way down the porch steps.

"Arabella, Miss Clement," he said, pausing to tip his hat to us. He directed his indigo gaze at me. "Meet me at the footbridge in about an hour?"

A spike of adrenaline stabbed at my chest. Had he

made his decision in regard to what he was going to do about my forgery?

"Sure," I said. We walked on, and I shoved the feeling of anxiety away for now.

At the livery, Mr. Parkhurst greeted us with a wide smile. I noted that he paid particular attention to Victoria, but she didn't seem to notice. She was biting at her fingernails.

I pulled her hand from her mouth and squeezed it. "It's going to be all right," I said.

"Here they come," Mr. Parkhurst said, pointing down the barren road. Three teams of two horses pulling the coaches came into view. Victoria nervously bounced on her toes.

Soon they pulled up to the livery, and Mr. Parkhurst and the drivers assisted the children and three nuns out of the coaches. I scanned the group, wondering which child was Charlie. Suddenly, Victoria gasped and pointed at one of them. He was indeed a miniature version of Ralph, with wild curls and large dark eyes. She ran to him, and I followed behind. One of the nuns saw her approach and went protectively to Charlie's side.

The boy's eyes were riveted on his mother, but there was confusion in his face. The four of us stood there silently, and then finally, Charlie stepped toward Victoria.

"Mother?" he asked in a small voice.

She let out a gasp and gathered him into her arms. "Yes, Charlie. Yes."

After I had accompanied Victoria, Charlie, and Sister Mary Evangeline to the hotel and up to Mrs. Stewart's room, I left them, hoping for the best. I had done what I could to bring them together, but the rest, it seemed, was up to Mrs. Stewart.

I looked at the watch pendant I wore on a chain around my neck. The sheriff had wanted me to meet him by the footbridge in twenty minutes. I made my way down to the lobby.

The hotel looked beautiful with all the holiday decorations. Swags of holly were hung everywhere, even the reception desk. Bright-red and white bows dotted a large tree Mr. Johns had brought in and placed in front of the grand bay window at the front.

The lobby was bustling with activity. People had stepped inside from the street to get warm and also to have some of the fresh ginger beer Kitty was handing out. The sounds of lively piano music from the Bella reverberated through the walls, as Mick Riley and his traveling band of musicians entertained those within.

I stood for a moment basking in the happiness I felt all around me. This is what the holidays were meant to be like. Joyful and full of the warmth of family and friends. Not the empty ones I had endured in my youth.

Someone tapped on my shoulder, and I turned around to see Constance beaming up at me. Today, she was clad in an ensemble of clashing bright tones. Her dress was predominantly tan but contained accents in a striking fabric of orange, purple, and white that seemed to belong on a sofa instead of a dress.

"Constance! Don't you look . . . festive!"

"Hello, Arabella. What a lovely day, isn't it?"

"It is," I agreed.

"I just love the holidays." She pulled a small notebook and a pencil from her dress pocket. "I'm writing my annual story about the festival, so I'd better get busy taking notes."

"I'm glad to see you are back to yourself." It was the most settled I'd seen her since she'd gotten an eyeful of Percival.

The cheeriness in her face faded ever so slightly, and her eyes scanned the lobby with a wary cautiousness. Instantly, I regretted my words, as they seemed to have brought back her anxieties at possibly having another ghostly encounter.

"Yes," she said, still surveying the room. A tic started in her upper cheek. "I'm . . . I'm right as rain."

I held back a sigh of concern. Clearly, she was not.

"Well," she said, gathering herself, "I must dash! Good day, Mrs. Pryce. The hotel looks lovely." She hurried toward the beveled glass doors.

I shook my head. I feared there may be more to come with this situation, but there was nothing I could do about it now.

The sound of laughter drew me back to the festivities, and I put my concerns about Constance aside. I had other things to worry about at the moment.

I wished I could join the merrymakers in their carefree revelry, but my preoccupation with what Clayton Marshall had in store for me resurfaced, vying for my attention. Would I be sent to prison for forgery? I shook my head at my short-sightedness. How could I have done something so stupid?

I stepped into the Bella to check on Sally. She was overseeing the saloon while Kitty bounced back and forth between the lobby and the kitchen. As I expected, things looked to be running smoothly. Sally was standing behind the bar, helping Mr. Greer serve drinks.

"How's it going in here, Sally?" I raised my voice above the din.

She gave me a broad smile. "It's certainly busy! But everything is fine. People are in a festive mood."

My gaze traveled to my favorite booth, which was occupied by Mr. Archer and none other than my nemesis, Atticus Brooks. My shoulders stiffened. Was Mr. Brooks still intent on writing about the murders at the Arabella Hotel? I let out a snort. I could just imagine how much fun he'd have if Sheriff Marshall decided to punish me for my crime. A sickening feeling swept through me at the prospect. And what about Mr. Archer? Would he be happy to see me behind bars? Was he behind all the strange misfortunes of the hotel?

To my chagrin, he waved me over. I wished I could pretend I hadn't seen him, but as I was looking right at them, that wouldn't work. I made my way over.

"Mrs. Pryce!" Mr. Archer sang out, his face red with gaiety. Or was it whisky?

"Mr. Archer, Mr. Brooks. I take it you are enjoying yourselves?"

"Sit down! Sit down, Mrs. Pryce," Mr. Archer said.

I clenched my fists at my sides but then complied, sliding into the booth beside Mr. Brooks. "I really can't stay long."

"Of course, of course," Mr. Archer said. "You're a busy woman, Mrs. Pryce. And might I say, you did not disappoint with the festival! The town is positively bursting. This is going to be so good for business, Mrs. Pryce, so good. And the hotel looks marvelous. You've done some excellent work here."

I gave him a tight smile. "Yes, despite the recurrent issues we seem to be having and the lack of workers to hire for the job. It seems most of the tradesmen are busy at the General. Or at your home." I wanted to blast him with accusations of sabotaging my hotel, but it wouldn't be prudent. I had absolutely no proof, and I was already in hot water with the sheriff. Best keep my powder dry in regard to the matter.

"Oh, well, you know" —he pressed his eyebrows down —"it's a tough time of year to find laborers, with the weather and all. Come spring it will be much easier, and men will be hungry for work."

I turned to Mr. Brooks. "And how is *your* story about the festival coming along? I hope you'll put the Arabella in the best light," I said, trying to hide my wariness. Constance's story would only reach the nearby areas. Mr. Brooks, on the other hand, had a national platform.

"Of course he will, won't you, Atticus?" Mr. Archer gave him a pointed look from beneath his bushy white brows. "If the Arabella looks good, the town looks good, and that is our goal, isn't it, Mrs. Pryce? I was just telling Atticus that he should write another story about your marvelous detective skills. I don't know what Sheriff Marshall would have done without you, my dear."

From the pinched expression on Mr. Brooks's face, I could tell writing favorably about me or the Arabella pained him. But now that I'd found Mr. Stewart's murderer, Mrs. Stewart was ever so grateful and Mary Alice assured me she did not hold the hotel responsible for his death. Hopefully, I'd dodged that particular bullet.

"Oh, I am no detective, Mr. Archer. Just a hotelier and an actress. Besides, the sheriff now has Deputy Fleming. He is staying on, is he not?"

His smile faded. "It's not decided yet. I have to see if we have the budget."

"Well, maybe at least until the sheriff's leg heals," I suggested.

"We'll see," he said and took another swig of his drink.

I turned my gaze to Mr. Brooks. "How long do you plan to stay?"

"I haven't decided yet. Archie is putting me up at his mansion after the festival. It's a lovely spot. Perfect for writing my stories."

I stifled a groan. I had hoped he'd be leaving soon.

"How lovely," I managed. "Well, if you'll excuse me, gentlemen. Please let Sally know if there is anything else you need."

I left them both, hoping that I had not given them a reason to celebrate.

Chapter Thirty

I found Clayton sitting on a boulder at the snowy edge of the water next to the footbridge. He wore a heavy leather coat, scarf, and his cowboy hat. He looked dashing as always. Bijou scampered up to him and set her front paws on his leg. He gave her a scratch behind the ears and turned to see me standing there.

"Thanks for coming." He reached for his crutches to stand up.

"Don't," I said. I sat on a boulder next to the one he was seated on. Bijou jumped up onto my lap. Her little paws were wet and cold against my skirt, but I didn't mind. I was sufficiently warm in my new coat.

We sat in silence for a few moments. I wanted to get this over with. If I was going to prison, I wanted to know as soon as possible. I would have so many things to take care of before my incarceration. I thought about apologizing again, but he'd heard it before and he'd seemed unmoved by it.

"What do you—"

"I wanted you to know—"

We both started at the same time and then laughed.

"You first," he said.

I pressed my lips together, and avoiding his startling blue gaze, I focused on Bijou as I ran her silky ears through my fingers. "I was going to ask you what you planned to do. About me . . ."

He sighed. "You've put me in a tough spot, Arabella."

I nodded. "I know. It was stupid."

"It was."

"And the worst thing about it is that I've broken your trust, and I'm—"

"You've already apologized."

"Yes." Bijou looked up at me with her sweet button eyes, and I stroked her head. "And don't worry, I won't be a problem for too much longer—" As I said the words, the reality of them struck me like a blow. When I'd first arrived in town, I thought my impending tenure to be excruciatingly lengthy, but now it seemed as if it was to be too short.

"What do you mean?" Clayton asked with concern in his voice.

I snuck a glance up at him. He was intently studying my face with those beautiful eyes, and my throat suddenly went dry. I couldn't force out the words that La Plata Springs was not going to be my permanent home. "Oh . . . I . . . I just meant, I'll try to be good."

The slow smile spreading across his face signaled he was satisfied with my answer. "Look, Arabella. I like you. You're smart, you're funny—"

"Funny?"

"Yeah, you know, how clumsy you are sometimes?"

"Oh. Right."

"And—" he hesitated, looking away from me "—you've actually been a big help to me with this case."

"Ah. Yes. And the last," I reminded him.

He rolled his eyes. "And the last."

"Not to mention I saved your life. You even said—"

"Yes," he cut me off. "And, again, thank you."

He turned his gaze back to me and we stared at each other in silence again.

"Sooooo?" I finally ventured.

"I'm not pressing charges against you for forgery," he said.

I closed my eyes and released a breath of air. *Thank goodness.*

"But no more stunts like that," he added.

I reached out and put my hand on his. I could feel his warmth radiating through the kidskin leather of my glove. "No. No more. I promise. You have my word."

He looked down at our hands and then turned that knee-weakening gaze up to mine again. His lips turned up a fraction, causing my heart to slam against my ribs. I really had to do something about this silly fancy I had for the man. It would serve neither one of us, as it would just complicate things. And I had just gotten back into his good graces. I didn't want anything to get in the way of that again.

Unable to swallow, I cleared my throat. "So, what's going to happen to Cherrie Fontaine? And the doctor? Is he still in the jail?"

He nodded. "Yep. Deputy Fleming is taking them to Denver in the morning. The doctor will serve time for accessory after the fact, theft, and embezzlement, but I'm afraid Miss Fontaine—"

"She'll hang?"

"Probably," he said.

"That's awful. I wonder what will happen to her siblings and her elderly aunt."

"I don't know. She should have thought of that before committing murder."

Suddenly, Bijou sprang from my lap and started to run toward two people coming toward us. It was Victoria and Charlie. It warmed my heart to see them both smiling and holding hands. When they reached us, I could see that aside from the radiant expression on her face, Victoria was pale and winded.

"Hey, Mrs. Pryce," Charlie said.

"Hello, Charlie." I tilted my head toward Clayton. "This is Sheriff Marshall."

The boy's large brown eyes widened. "You're a real lawman?"

Clayton chuckled. "Yes, I am, son."

"Wow! Do you catch bad guys?"

Clayton slid a glance in my direction. "Sometimes."

Noting that Victoria looked as if she was going to buckle, I stood up. "Please, Victoria. Sit here."

Still smiling, she thanked me and sat down. Charlie was preoccupied with Bijou. He picked up a stick and threw it in the snow. Bijou looked back at me as if asking what she was supposed to do. She didn't go after the stick but simply stared at Charlie. He went to get the stick again, and she followed him.

"How wonderful that you and Charlie are together at last," I said.

"Yes. I'm so grateful to Mrs. Stewart. She has agreed to help us." Her gaze trailed after her son and Bijou.

"How are things going with Mrs. Stewart . . . and you?"

She pulled her attention away from Charlie. "Fine. Better. She was so shocked about Charlie at first, but even she couldn't deny that he is Ralph's son."

"He does look exactly like him," Clayton said.

"And Mary Alice?" I ventured, a little more cautiously.

"Surprisingly understanding." She shook her head with amazement. "I knew that she and Ralph hadn't been intimate in quite some time. They didn't really have that kind of relationship. Theirs was a marriage of convenience. I think because of that, Mary Alice always worried about losing her place in the family, but now that Miss Fontaine and Dr. Briggs are . . . well, you know . . . Mrs. Stewart is more reliant on Mary Alice than ever, and I believe they have a genuine fondness for each other."

Victoria's gaze followed Charlie again, as if she couldn't get enough of seeing him. "Mrs. Stewart asked us to go to Denver with them. For the burial. We leave tomorrow."

"Well, that's something," I said.

"Yes. I'm so thankful. I just worry about . . . Charlie's future." I knew she was speaking about her illness and that she might not always be around to see him looked after.

"One day at a time," I said.

"You're right."

"Mama!" Charlie called. "Can we go see the horses again?"

Victoria laughed. "He loves all those horses at the livery."

"Who knows, he might just become a cowboy," Clayton said.

She sighed contentedly. "Whatever he chooses to do with his life, I hope he loves it." She rose and squeezed my arm with her hand. "Thank you. Thank you so much."

Whatever he chooses to do with his life . . .

Her words brought up a surprising feeling of melancholy within me. I had grown to love my profession, but I hadn't been given a choice of what I wanted to do with my life. That decision had been made for me. I hoped Charlie would appreciate the freedom his mother was willing to grant him, even if she wasn't there to see it through.

"You're quite welcome," I said quietly. I watched her go after Charlie. Bijou, having lost her playmate, came back to me.

"You do surprise me," Clayton said, pulling me from my melancholic thoughts.

"What do you mean?"

"I mean, you came to this town with your fancy clothes, your high ideals, and a stick in your craw—"

"I beg your pardon!" I slapped him on the arm.

"You know what I mean," he said with a chuckle. "But underneath all that shiny pomp and circumstance, you're a pretty nice gal."

"*A gal?* I'm sorry, *no one,* and I mean *no one,* has ever referred to me as *a gal.*"

"See what I mean?" He gave me that wicked grin of his.

"Oh! You're impossible," I said, unable to hold back a chuckle of my own.

"Let's get back to town. This boulder's getting cold." He pushed himself to standing. I bent down and got his crutches and handed them to him.

We set off at a slow pace. I breathed in the cool, sweet-smelling mountain air and gazed at the beauty around me. Bijou tagged along behind. After a few more minutes of silence, I decided to break it, feeling pretty good about my mended friendship with Clayton.

"So, you like me do you?" I asked, playfully swatting his arm.

He smiled. "That's what I said."

"How much?"

He stopped walking and looked over at me with that grin again. "Don't push it, Arabella. Just don't push it."

Still reeling from relief that I would not trade in my beautiful silks, satins, and laces for prison garb, and elated Clayton didn't hate me—in fact, he *liked me*—I entered the hotel to find the number of people gathered there had not diminished in the least. Merrymakers were still enjoying the drinks and treats provided by my staff. I stopped by the reception desk to check in with Mr. Pettyjohn, who actually smiled at me. This was the second time I'd seen the man smile, and I didn't quite know what to make of it.

"Mr. Pettyjohn, you look in fine fettle."

"I don't know what you mean, madam," he said, his face all seriousness again.

My gaze slid over to the half-drunk glass of Kitty's cider, and I wondered how many he'd had. "Never mind, Mr. Pettyjohn. Never mind. Tell me, have you seen Cordelia?"

"She's retired upstairs, madam." He gave me the usual glance-above-the-spectacles look I had grown so fond of.

"Thank you." A sudden wave of worry struck me. "She was all right, wasn't she?"

"I believe so, Mrs. Pryce. She said she was tired."

I nodded. "Of course."

She'd nearly died from poison the other day—no wonder she was tired. I'd tried to talk her out of helping with the festival, but she would not be deterred.

I made my way up the stairs. On the third-floor landing I stopped in my tracks, Bijou crashing into the back of my heels, when I saw a young couple "canoodling," as Betty Gilroy liked to say, near the storage closet. They flew apart at seeing me, and with red faces, giggles, and a quick nod of greeting, they dashed past me down the stairs.

I chuckled. *Oh, to be young again.*

We ascended the final flight of stairs, and I opened the door to our rooms. Bijou scurried past me and went immediately to her water dish. I closed the door, and my attention was drawn to the love seat.

My hand flying to my chest, I gasped. Cordelia was sitting on one end of the love seat and Percival on the other. They both turned to look at me.

My mouth dropped open, but I couldn't make any noise come out, couldn't think of anything to say even if my vocal cords worked.

"Hello, Arabella," Cordelia said.

I looked over at the transparent form of Percival, who sat there staring at me, his legs crossed at the knees. A tendril of smoke from his pipe spiraled toward the ceiling.

"How . . . how are you feeling, Cordelia?" I asked, still not sure of what I was seeing. Had they been chatting? Or was Percival just pushing me to the very limit with his insistence on meeting Cordelia. Did he expect me to introduce them? At this very moment?

"Much better, thank you," she said. "But are you all right?" A look of concern crossed her features.

"I'm . . . I'm . . . well." I looked over at Percival, who then looked at Cordelia, who looked back at him!

Staring at Cordelia, I pointed at the ghostly figure. "Can you actually . . . see him?"

She smiled. "Yes, Arabella. I can see him."

"Percival!" I shouted, angry that he'd directly gone against my wishes.

Cordelia rose from the love seat and came over to me. She took me by the arms. "It's okay, Arabella. I'm fine with it. Really."

"But . . . but how?"

She guided me to the chair and urged me to sit down. She again took her place on the love seat. "As you know, I nearly died," she said.

"Yes, but—"

"Percival was there with me. He encouraged me to come back. That's why I got sick. Well, the first time anyway."

My mouth fell open again, and a trembling overtook my body. Percival had saved her life.

"Darling, don't gape so. You're far too pretty for that," he said and blew a ring of smoke in my direction.

"I . . . I d-don't know what to say," I stammered, still in a state of disbelief at what he'd done. "Except . . . thank you."

He nodded. "It seems it is I who should thank you. You solved the mystery of my death. As soon as you said the words to all gathered in Mrs. Stewart's rooms, it came back to me. I remembered drinking the wine, but then I'd fallen sick at the party. The headache was excruciating and the searing pain in my stomach—"

"Don't remind me," Cordelia said.

"Anyway, I vaguely remember young Andrew bringing me back to the hotel, but then nothing after that. And then I became—" He opened his arms wide and looked down on his transparent form, showcasing his otherworldly body— "as I am now. I knew I was different from before—I was better, in more ways than one—but I couldn't put the pieces together of how I became this way." He shook his head with a look of marvel on his face. "It's extraordinary. Now that I know how I died, I feel so—" he stopped short, searching for the word "—liberated!" he finally said with a grin, and then he laughed. A full, joyous belly laugh.

Even though I was still in a state of shock at this surreal turn of events, his elation made me smile.

Cordelia reached out and took my hand in hers. "I wish you had been able to tell me about Percival. That you two were friends. Why didn't you?"

I turned to face her. "Tell me honestly. You don't think it's . . . mad?"

She chuckled. "Mad? No. You're not mad, and I'm certainly not mad. So, why didn't you feel like you could tell me? You know I adore you, Arabella. Nothing would change that."

I blinked at her smiling face, and despite the temperature drop caused by Percival, my heart—my whole body— warmed with her words. I squeezed her hand. "It's— Well . . . it's a long story," I said.

"And you'll tell me about it—" she squeezed my hand back "—when you're ready."

"Yes," I said. "I will."

A knock at the door made me jump.

Cordelia gave a little laugh. "It's all right, Arabella. I'll get it."

My gaze traveled over to Percival who, with his eyebrows jumping up and down at me, blew another smoke ring in the air.

Cheeky ghost.

"Thank you, Clarence." Cordelia closed the door. "It's a telegram. For you." She handed it to me.

"Oh," I said. My fingers still trembling, I fumbled with

the envelope. Finally, I pried the telegram free and read it. The words sent spasms through my body all over again.

"What?" I whispered, staring at the message.

"My goodness, darling," Percival said. "Bad news?"

I looked up at them both. "The worst news. My mother is coming to La Plata Springs."

vinci-books.com/pryceofambition

A deadly performance. A mother accused. Can a quick-witted actress rewrite the ending before the final bow?

Arabella Pryce is settling into her new life—until her estranged mother arrives with a theater troupe and a murder in tow. With ghostly clues and a cunning killer at large, she must unravel the truth before the curtain falls on another victim.

Turn the page for a free preview…

The Pryce of Ambition: Chapter One

LA PLATA SPRINGS, COLORADO

Spring, 1886

I stared into the flames of the blazing fire, sipping my Earl Grey, my mood pensive and overcast with a heavy cloud of apprehension. Bijou, my gold and white Havanese dog, lay at my feet—well, actually *on them* rather, keeping them warm. Darkness bathed the parlor room of my three-room suite, except for the glow coming from the fireplace.

It was early spring, but the morning and evening temperatures in La Plata Springs remained frigid, book ending the warmth of mid-morning to mid-afternoon, hinting at more mild weather to come.

The little mining town, nestled in the La Plata Valley of the Colorado Rockies, had been my home for the last eight months. I could scarcely believe how fast the time had flown.

When I first arrived, I resented the year-long stay mandated by my late husband's will. He required that I leave my New York City life to run the hotel for a year to inherit his substantial fortune. Unforeseen expenses extended my stay to a year and five months, as I had to exchange time for funds borrowed against my inheritance, adhering to the will's terms.

My late husband had written in his will that I leave my celebrity, my theater, and my privileged and lavish lifestyle in New York City, and come to this tiny burg in the mountains to run my namesake hotel, which he had bequeathed to me, for a full year in order to gain my full inheritance. A sum which was, in no uncertain terms, immense.

But, for now, I had to work within the confines of a modest stipend. Because of expenses out of my control, I'd had to borrow money from the estate. In order to keep with the terms of the will, I'd had to use more time spent here as collateral, to make up the difference.

Much to my surprise, I had settled into the provincial community quite comfortably. Once my name had been cleared of murder, that is. An act that had necessitated that I become an amateur sleuth of sorts to get to the truth of the matter. I found that I actually had a talent for investigation, and along with my puritan work-ethic and desire to succeed, I had become known for my Sherlockian prowess in solving several crimes. The notoriety fueled my need for a sense of worthiness and gave me the feeling that I belonged.

But today, those feelings of warmth and accomplishment vanished, replaced by a surge of impending dread. My mother, with whom I'd been estranged, gave word she was coming to town.

I took another sip of my tea and heaved a great sigh as I set the cup back down on the saucer. A wave of coolness enveloped me and with my free hand, I pulled my shawl tighter around my shoulders. In seconds, the smell of pipe tobacco filled the air.

"Good morning, Percival," I said. A bitter chill, and the juxtaposing warm, spicy fragrance always accompanied my ghostly friend.

"Hello, my dear. You're up early."

I glanced out the window at the grayness of impending dawn and then returned my gaze to the flames. "I couldn't sleep."

In my periphery, his transparent form settled into the chair next to me. I turned to look at him. As usual, his luminous eyes regarded me with some intensity. He was classically handsome with a head of dark wavy hair and bore the Byronic quality of masculine broodiness that I somehow found attractive.

"Care to share?" He set his pipe between his lips and inhaled, making the bowl of it glow red.

"It's my mother. She sent word she is coming to town, but gave no mention of when. Her inconsiderateness is beyond the pale. It's in poor taste to tell someone you plan to visit—uninvited, no less—but then to not tell them when is just plain rude. I suppose she expects that when she makes her grand entrance, I will drop everything to entertain her."

"Goodness. You really don't want to see her."

I shot him a look. "What do you mean by that?"

With his pipe firmly between his teeth, he held up his hands in surrender. "I haven't any earthly idea. Don't be so defensive, dear. I didn't mean any harm."

I swallowed, embarrassed at my sharpness. "I'm sorry. It's just that—my relationship with my mother is—complicated."

"What's this about Millicent?" Cordelia emerged from her bedroom, which was next to the parlor, in her dressing gown, her hair disheveled from sleep. She stretched and yawned. "Hello, Percival."

I flinched, still not used to the idea that Cordelia now knew my deepest, darkest secret, that I could see and communicate with otherworldly spirits. A capability that she now shared, because of her near-death experience some months ago. In fact, it was Percival who had brought her back from the brink.

I had held this secret close since my childhood, for fear of ending up like two of my relatives with the same capacity, who'd ended up in an asylum, one accused of insanity and the other witchcraft.

Percival nodded a greeting to her. "Arabella is out of sorts."

"If you are talking about Millicent, I don't blame her."

"Is she really that bad?"

Cordelia and I shared a glance.

"Yes," we said in unison.

Percival raised his brows. "My, my. I know you've shared some of your childhood with me, Arabella, and I realize you feel she was a little over ambitious and controlling. But, with your father abandoning the two of you—"

"Don't!" I held a finger up at him. It was true, my father had abandoned us when I was young, but my love and longing for him was still strong, even after all these years. He was the one person whom I felt truly understood me in this world, and loved me completely, flaws and all. I honestly didn't understand how he could leave me, but had put it up to not being able to live with my mother anymore. In my heart and mind, it was her fault that he'd gone. I couldn't abide anyone—especially someone who never knew him—disparage him.

Percival pulled his chin back in surprise at my admonishment. "I—I'm sorry, my dear—I didn't mean to . . . "

I stood up and set my teacup and saucer on the mantle above the fireplace. "I'm going to get dressed. I have a riding lesson with Clayton in an hour. If you'll excuse me."

"Would you like some help?" Cordelia offered.

"No. Enjoy your tea."

I swept past them, leaving an icy chill in my wake, for which I felt terrible but couldn't seem to help. I wanted to be alone for a few moments. The threat of tears pricked at the back of my eyes, stinging my nose, and an ache rose in my throat. I swallowed it down, determined to resume control over my emotions.

I would carry on as normal. It could be days, perhaps weeks, before my mother arrived. And with any luck, she might just change her mind entirely.

I walked to Archer's Livery, at the far edge of town, unsuccessful in putting thoughts of my mother's upcoming visit out of my mind. If I knew when she was to arrive, I might mentally prepare, but this looming uncertainty was like a dark cloud hanging over my head.

I would have to distract myself, and my riding lessons with the handsome sheriff were indeed a welcomed diversion. Many occasions and various circumstances have tested my friendship with Clayton. One of which was our growing attraction to one another that seemed to go absolutely nowhere. It was both frustrating and yet a relief. Knowing that I was not to remain in La Plata Springs for long, it seemed silly, and even unkind, to embark on a relationship I knew would abruptly end. I had not shared with Clayton that I was to leave at the end of my stipulated tenure—for reasons that confused me. Was it because I secretly wanted to stay and pursue the friendship, or was it because I feared that very thing?

Pushing my uncomfortable feelings aside, which was my habit as I had more important things to do, I put it up to the fact that it really was none of the sheriff's business what I intended to do with my life. In the meantime, I would enjoy his company and his instruction in horsemanship.

"Hello, Mrs. Pryce." A voice shook me out of my reverie. It was Mr. Parkhurst, the blacksmith who ran Archer's Livery, and the forge connected with it. It appeared he was fashioning horseshoes ...I had been so lost in my thoughts of my mother and Clayton, I scarcely knew how I got there.

"Mr. Parkhurst. Nice to see you." I dredged up a smile, still preoccupied with my musings.

He returned the greeting with a wide smile, his teeth glowing white against his dark skin, and his coal-black eyes dancing with merriment. He was a strapping man of approaching middle-age, charming and friendly, and I often wondered why he wasn't spoken for.

"You must be here for another riding lesson," he said. "Do you want me to get Monty tacked up for you?"

"No thank you, I think I should do it myself. I enjoy spending a little quiet time with Monty before our ride."

I enjoyed grooming the snowy white gelding, and he seemed to like it, too. I hated to admit it, but I was becoming attached to my equine friend. He was owned by Mr. Archer, but there was no love lost there. Mr. Archer had several horses at his livery, for the purposes of renting them out or selling them. Clayton had kindly entered into a long-term lease of the horse for my lessons.

"All right then, I'll let you get to it." Mr. Parkhurst bowed gallantly.

"Thank you," I said, and walked toward the livery barn.

Once I had Monty groomed to gleaming and dressed in his saddle, rope halter and bridle, I led him out toward the open area near the river where my lessons took place.

It was a deliciously serene spot, set away from the bustling crowd and surrounded by leafing cottonwoods. The sound of the water rushing against scattered boulders in the riverbed, and the heat of the sun melting the chill from the morning air, soothed my senses. I stood facing Monty, running my hand down his face. He uttered a low nicker, returning my affections.

"Either you're early or I'm late."

I turned to see Clayton, perched upon his beloved Queenie, a beautiful chestnut mare. He looked dashing, as always, in his rugged leather coat and Stetson cowboy hat.

"I'm early," I said.

"Good." He swung his right leg over Queenie's rump and hopped down from the saddle. Settling his hands in his pants pockets, he strode up to me, Queenie following behind. His sapphire gaze settled on mine and I quickly glanced away, afraid of getting lost in it.

"You all right?" he asked, his voice low and with an intimacy that both thrilled and terrified me.

"Of course," I said, shaking my head like his concern was preposterous. "I just have a lot to do today, so want to get started as soon as possible."

"Okay, then. Why don't we start with some ground work?" He handed me his rope lariat.

I nodded and unclipped Monty's reins, handing them to

Clayton. I then attached the lariat to Monty's halter, which I had placed on him before I put the bridle on.

I attempted a variety of quick exercises with Monty, as Clayton showed me, to ensure he remained focused on me. Clayton had explained that once I developed a connection with the horse on the ground at each session, our ride would be much more pleasant and productive. So far, he'd been correct. I had always assumed that when riding, the horse did all the work and the rider was merely a passenger. But Clayton taught me it was a dual effort, like a dance, and both partners needed their attention focused on one another and the task at hand. It was far from a passive endeavor.

Soon, it was time for me to climb on board. I led Monty over to a fallen cottonwood, lined him up next to it, placed my foot in the stirrup and gently got on astride, thankful for the new riding skirt I'd had Cynthia Mayes, the dressmaker, fashion for me.

Clayton instructed me through each of the gaits, stops, turns on the forehand, and turns on the haunches. My heart swelled with pride at how well Monty was responding to my cues. After a circle at the canter, I brought him to a halt with my seat and beamed at Clayton.

"That was impressive, Arabella," he said with a slow smile as he approached us. "You are a quick learner."

My cheeks flared with heat at the praise. "Thank you. Monty is a good boy."

"He's only as good as his rider." Clayton sidled up to us, his chest mere centimeters from my thigh. He looked up at me with those dreamy eyes and a devilish grin. "What would you think about jumping that fallen down tree?" He pointed to the tree I'd used to mount. My heart picked up a staccato at the suggestion.

"Jumping? Oh, I-I don't think — "

"You never know when you might need to jump something when riding in these mountains. There can be all kinds of obstacles in the wild. It's a good thing to learn, and I think you are ready. We'll start small, with that tree. If you go for that bend," he pointed to a curve near the top of it. "I reckon it's only about three feet tall. A piece of cake for Monty."

Apprehensive, I bit my lip, hesitating to answer. I was still flying high from my accomplishments in the lesson thus far, but a niggle of anxiety flared at the idea of soaring through the air on a thousand-pound animal. Would I be able to stay on?

"As you approach at the trot, put your weight in the stirrups and tilt forward to get off his back, let him have his head and he'll do the rest. If you keep your heels down, you'll stay put."

It sounded simple enough. A flutter of excitement welled up in my chest. "All right, I'll try it."

"Okay, then," Clayton said with a wide grin. "I want you to take up the trot and make a circle. Once you've got a steady rhythm, turn him face on to the jump. Keep your eyes and energy forward."

"Right," I murmured, envisioning the plan.

I turned Monty away from him, brought him to a trot and headed for the open space in front of the fallen down tree. I made three large circles, just to be sure the horse and I were in perfect sync. Turning him toward the lowest point of the fallen down tree, I kept my focus forward. As we neared it, I took in a deep breath, waiting for the launch, when something in the distance distracted me from my mission. It was a caravan of several brightly decorated carriages, and colorful enclosed wagons.

Before I knew it, Monty and I arrived at the jump, but I had lost my focus. Right as I thought we were about to take flight, Monty set his feet and ground to an abrupt halt, but I kept going, catapulting right over his head.

Time slowed as I flew through the air and then suddenly, with deafening swiftness, the ground rushed up at me, meeting my body with a bone-crushing concussion of hardness, and then everything went blank.

The Pryce of Ambition: Chapter Two

"Arabella!" A deep, muffled, faraway voice echoed in my ears. A dense heaviness slowly filled my chest, and I couldn't move. The pressure of something warm pressed in on each side of my face.

"Come on, Arabella. Don't do this to me. Wake up." The voice was becoming clearer, and with it a ringing in my ears and deep resonating pain in my upper body. "God, if I've hurt you, I'll never forgive myself. Arabella, please. Come on."

The weight in my chest and the ringing in my ears persisted.

"Don't leave me, I—" the voice said.

My body tensed and I suddenly, desperately, needed air. I sucked in a lungful, electric shock shooting through my chest.

I opened my fluttering eyelids and found Clayton's beautiful face inches from mine, his blue eyes a stormy sea of anguish. His palms cupped the side of my face.

"Oh, thank goodness," he breathed and sent his eyes heavenward.

I pulled in another deep breath, and this time it didn't hurt as much. The pain in my chest was slowly subsiding. His hands gripped my shoulders, and I let out a yelp. My left shoulder screamed with pain.

"That's where you landed. May I continue?"

Biting my lip, I agreed. His hands did their probing, causing a measure of discomfort.

"Doesn't feel broken," he said. He then tenderly, but firmly, ran his hands down my arms. "Does anything here hurt?" I rolled my head back and forth slowly, telling him 'no.' I squinted my eyes against the pain in my shoulder. He then palpated my legs. "What about here?"

"No," I gasped.

"How about your back?"

My breathing was becoming easier, and the heaviness in my chest had subsided, along with the ache.

"It feels okay," I said, my voice almost a whisper.

"Your head?"

"I'm a little cloudy, but there's no pain."

"Do you think you can sit up?"

I nodded.

He gently pulled me to sitting and then settled in next to me, on my right side. He wrapped his arm around my waist to keep me steady. I leaned heavily against his chest, my head clearing.

"You just got the wind knocked out of you, but I'm worried about that shoulder. I'll have to get you to Doc Tate's."

"No," I shook my head. "I'll be fine."

"Sorry, I'm taking you in."

The clattering of wagon wheels caught my attention, and I looked up to see one of the caravans, painted bright red, approaching us. The horse pulling it was brilliant white, with a gray mane and tail. A red plume of feathers between its ears fluttered with each bob of its head.

"I say." The man driving the carriage, a wiry figure dressed in a dark suit with a waistcoat of the same crimson as the wagon, pulled the horse to a stop. "Everything all right here?" He had an air of sophistication about him. His thick, shoulder-length, heavily pomaded dark hair was parted on the side and shot through with a single streak of gray that looped over his left ear. His face was handsomely chiseled in long lines, and his gray eyes carried a look of intelligence.

"She came off her horse," Clayton said.

"How unfortunate. May I be of assistance?"

The other two caravans pulled up behind the first, followed at a little distance away by three more.

"I need to get her to the doctor in town. I'm just letting her catch her breath." Clayton explained to the man.

"I'm fine," I said flatly, a little irritated that the two were talking about me while I was sitting right there.

"Victor!" a female voice rang out. "Why have we stopped?"

Suddenly, a young woman emerged from the caravan. She wore a simple dress of pink and green pastel. A matching pink ribbon held a cascade of rich chestnut curls off her face. Even from a distance, I could see that she had a classical elegance reminiscent of the heroines found in old paintings.

"Just a moment, Celine." The man climbed down from his perch and the young woman came to stand beside him.

"Is she hurt?" the young woman asked.

"No," I said a bit tersely. Being an accomplished and celebrated actress, I was used to being the center of attention. In fact, I quite liked it, but when I was on stage giving a performance. Not when I was to be pitied and fussed over. I attempted to get to my feet. Clayton swiftly rose and, taking my right arm, helped me up. He held me steady while I got my bearings. The ache in my left shoulder deepened with the change of position.

"Are you heading into town?" Clayton asked.

"We are indeed," the man said.

"Could I bother you to take her there?"

"Don't be silly," I said, with a weak wave of my hand. "I can walk."

"It would be my pleasure," the gentleman said with a bow. "Victor Langston, at your service."

"No, really," I pleaded.

"Thank you," Clayton said, ignoring me. "I'll follow behind with the horses."

I shot him a look, which he also ignored, as he led me toward the caravan.

"She can ride in back with me," the young woman gave me a captivating smile. "I'm Celine Dubois."

At the mention of her name, I stopped short. Now that she was closer to me, I suddenly recognized the large, expressive mismatched eyes, one hazel, shimmering with specks of green and gold, and the other, deep blue, the pair of them capturing the light in a way that always added an almost mystical quality to her gaze.

Staring at her, I muttered, "I haven't seen you since you were a little girl."

She smiled at me. "Hello, Arabella."

"Victor, what is going on?" Another female voice rang out from behind the caravan.

I turned to see the woman, and the blood froze in my veins.

"Mother?"

Grab your copy…

vinci-books.com/pryceofambition

About the Author

Kari Bovée is an award-winning author of historical mysteries, weaving suspense and unforgettable characters into captivating tales. Her enthusiasm for storytelling began in early childhood, as illustrated by a note sent to her parents from her third-grade teacher praising her talent for writing. This passion flourished during her pursuit of a Bachelor of Arts in English Literature at the University of San Diego. There, she customized her studies to include independent projects in short story writing, playwriting, novel writing, and even a debut as a theater director.

Her acclaimed Annie Oakley Mystery Series, Grace Michelle Mysteries, and The Pryce of Murder Series have earned recognition in national and international writing competitions. Her awards include the Chanticleer International Goethe Grand Prize for *Peccadillo at the Palace* (2020) and the New Mexico/Arizona Hillerman Award for *Girl with a Gun* (2019).

Before turning to fiction, Kari worked as a technical writer, educator, and consultant, but storytelling has always been her true passion. She and her husband, Kevin, spend their time between their horse property in the beautiful Land of Enchantment, New Mexico, their home on the sunny shores of Hawaii, and their travels to inspiring destinations.